Casey Hill is the pseudonym of husband and wife Melissa and Kevin Hill. Melissa is already a Number 1 bestseller in her native Ireland with her novels about contemporary women's lives. A desire to delve into darker aspects of fiction led her to team up with Kevin and create the Reilly Steel series. The couple live in Dublin.

Also by Casey Hill

Taboo
Torn
Hidden

THE WATCHED

CASEY HILL

SIMON &
SCHUSTER

London · New York · Sydney · Toronto · New Delhi

A CBS COMPANY

First published in Great Britain by Simon & Schuster UK Ltd, 2014
A CBS COMPANY

1 3 5 7 9 10 8 6 4 2

Simon & Schuster UK Ltd
1st Floor
222 Gray's Inn Road
London WC1X 8HB

www.simonandschuster.co.uk

Simon & Schuster Australia, Sydney
Simon & Schuster India, New Delhi

A CIP catalogue record for this book is
available from the British Library

Paperback B ISBN 978-0-85720-988-7
Trade Paperback ISBN 978-0-85720-987-0
eBook ISBN 978-0-85720-989-4

Typeset by Hewer Text UK Ltd, Edinburgh
Printed and bound in Great Britain by CPI (UK) Ltd, Croydon CR0 4YY

To our wonderful agent, Sheila Crowley.
Thank you.

Prologue

It wasn't supposed to happen this way. It always worked like a charm in the movies – put some chloroform on a rag, hold it over the person's mouth and out they went.

Too bad this wasn't the movies.

First of all the fat bastard remained conscious and fought back, almost landing a punch before being silenced with a rock. Then the skinny bitch made some weird snoring sounds before she stopped breathing altogether.

Apparently, the quantity of chloroform in relation to the weight of the person it was being used on was an important factor. Too little didn't work and too much could kill. Again, not something discussed in the movies. Lesson learned.

He had always been a quick study. Dragging the mismatched couple behind some rocks, he waited for another couple to pass along the narrow stretch of secluded beach. He wasn't picky; all that mattered was that he got one male and one female. He preferred they both be in their twenties but they could be a little older, just as long as they could pass for younger in the right conditions.

He sat on a large rock staring at the sea for half an hour, just another tourist relaxing in the spring sunshine. To add to the image of an easy-going beach bum, he'd even draped a damp beach towel beside him on the rock – though it wasn't damp with seawater.

This part of the beach was too rough for sunbathing, but a well-worn path cut through the rocks, making it perfect for couples looking for some privacy. A salty breeze blew in off of the gulf, cooling the sweat on his skin. He didn't mind waiting; thrived on it actually, felt his mind sharpen when the wits of those around him became muddled and foggy.

He heard them first and turned as they came around the bend, their arrival interrupting his musing. He was pleasantly surprised; two perfectly chiseled blonds: Surfer Ken and Big Boobs Barbie looking so cosy with their arms around each other, with golden tans and matching black swim gear. With the way the rocks hemmed in the sandy path, they had no choice but to walk within inches of where he sat, and he greeted them with a lazy, deceptively uninterested nod of his head.

Then, the moment their backs were to him, he sprang. He'd doused the ends of the towel in the right amount of chloroform this time, and quick as a flash he grabbed it and shoved it into their faces.

It still didn't work instantly like in the movies, but between the narrow confines of the path, the shock of the unexpected attack and the way the victims were wrapped so closely together, they barely had time to struggle before the solvent completed its work.

As soon as their bodies stopped twitching, he pulled back the towel and checked their pulses. Still alive. Perfect.

He couldn't help but smile. He'd got it right on the second take, and after that was even able to get them into the bed of his truck with relative ease. Not that it was actually his truck.

The vehicle rumbled to life with a quick twist and then he was on his way. As he drove, he wondered if he should find himself a theme song, something to play in the background while he worked.

Turning on his radio, he selected a classic rock station, and turned the volume up as loud as it would go. He grimaced at the music; he wasn't a fan. Rock had no finesse.

Then, distracted by flashing lights in his rearview mirror, he turned off the radio, the wail of a siren filling the cab of the truck. Damn. The pickup truck he'd 'borrowed' was twenty years old and in no shape to outrun a police car. He had no choice but to pull over.

Damn it again. For all of his carefully laid plans, he'd gone and got himself pulled over for speeding. He chastised himself for the rookie mistake, but some of his frustration faded as he realized only one police officer seemed to be in the car. Maybe the situation was still salvageable.

He watched in his side mirror as the beefy cop exited his car and immediately reacted to muffled sounds coming from the truck bed. OK, so maybe he hadn't got the dosage down as well as he'd thought.

The officer put his hand on his sidearm and cautiously approached the rear of the vehicle. 'Hello,' he called out, 'this is the police. Is there anyone under the tarp?'

Not pausing to check underneath, the officer drew his gun and pointed it at the driver's side window. 'Sir, I'm going to ask you to please step out with your hands over your head.'

He wished he had a gun of his own, but it had never crossed his mind to bring one. He wasn't a killer, after all; he was an artist. That first attempt at the beach had been an accident. But he also wasn't a quitter, and wouldn't back down from an obstacle, no matter how tricky the solution.

Tenacity, drive, ambition – weren't those qualities what separated the mundane from the great?

The one thing the pickup truck's cab did have going for it was a wide, sliding rear window. It'd been open when he'd nabbed the vehicle and had since tried to close it with no success. Now he was thankful for the malfunction.

He started to open his door, then with the cop's full attention on that he grabbed the bottle of chloroform from his bag and, with just the quickest of glances to aim, tossed the remaining contents of the bottle at the officer's face.

The cop screamed and gurgled as the chemical burned his eyes and throat, but the man didn't pay any attention. He had more important things to worry about.

He dropped the empty bottle into the truck bed, turned back around and put the truck into gear. The tires spun as he reversed and swung around toward the officer, knocking him to the ground. He didn't hesitate as he drove forward over the cop's head, grinding it into the asphalt with a vicious turn of the wheel and a bit of extra gas. He knew that the area would soon be swarming with police officers and briefly considered finding a new location for the rest of his project. One glance toward the descending sun eliminated that possibility.

No time for any more mistakes.

Thanks to that son of a bitch, now he was going to have to rush. And everyone knew what they said about rushing perfection.

The blond cried and pleaded for her life as he yanked her off the truck bed.

He frowned, wishing he'd thought of gagging her when he'd hogtied her. Not that her screams weren't perfect; they really were. He was just afraid she'd wear out her voice.

He dragged her a half-dozen feet to a large tree he'd selected a few hours ago, leaving her there for a moment before returning with some heavy chain. He bound her feet to the tree, then removed the rope that connected her wrists to her ankles. She wriggled, trying to move her body, but the effects of the chloroform made her movements sluggish. He wrapped a second length of chain around her still-bound wrists and secured the other end to the hitch of his pickup truck. Taking a moment to eye up the length, he then climbed back into the driver's seat. He inched forward, just enough to tighten the slack in the chain, and then stopped.

She was screaming uncontrollably now, justifiably terrified and no doubt guessing what was going to happen. He really needed to put a stop to that noise though – she should conserve her energy. He'd be pissed at going to all of this trouble to make things just right only to have the main attraction screw it up by passing out from exhaustion before the real fun began.

The man walked over to Blondie and crouched next to her. He leaned down and whispered in her ear, 'If you care about that guy you came with, you'll shut the hell up.'

'Please don't hurt us,' she pleaded, eyes wide and full of fear. He saw a bit of a spark in them too; a rebellion that meant she was a fighter, even when begging for her life. That was good. He needed someone who wasn't going to just give up and go along with what was about to happen. 'I'll do anything you want.'

'I just want you to stop screaming.'

She quieted, the occasional whimper escaping, but he didn't care about that. It didn't take much energy to whimper.

Satisfied, he returned to his male victim. This one didn't need to be gagged. The first thing he'd done after knocking them out was to stitch the guy's lips together with heavy black thread. He didn't get to scream at all.

He was heavier than he looked though, certainly heavier than Blondie, in any case, and fought like a crazed pig while being pulled out of the truck. All that flailing had sent the empty chloroform bottle bouncing around the truck bed. There were only a few drops left.

It took some shaking, but he got every last drop onto the victim's shirt and then pulled it up over the struggling man's nose. Moments later, the guy passed out again, much to his relief. This was turning out to be much more physically demanding than he'd anticipated.

Dragging the guy up to the cab of the truck, he wrestled his deadweight body into the driver's seat. In the back of his mind, he was very aware of time passing, knowing that any moment the mess he'd left back on the main road could lead to his discovery.

But again, art can't be rushed.

Using the always-useful duct tape, he bound his victim's hands to the steering wheel and his feet to the accelerator. The remote-controlled wireless webcam went on the dashboard. He turned the radio back on and frowned, wishing he had more time to find the right music to underscore the scene. But as so often happened to even the greatest, he was out of time.

He grabbed two wooden wedges from behind the seat and shoved them in front of both front tires. After making sure they were secure enough to prevent an accident, he put the truck in drive. As long as the guy didn't move, Blondie would be just fine.

Then, closing the driver's door, he took out a cellphone, leisurely dialing 911. When the operator answered, he spoke, his tone as frenzied as his expression was serene. 'Oh, man, I think he's going to kill her. You have to send a squad car out here. Hell, send frickin' SWAT. The guy's beating the crap out of some girl – oh, shit, he just pulled a gun on her. And he's making her – just hurry!'

He dropped the cellphone on the ground and walked away, imagining what it would be like for the main players to realize what was going on and what was about to happen. They'd be so excited to know they were going to be such an indelible part of history.

He knew he was.

The man hurried on, wanting a front-row seat for the big reveal.

Chapter 1

Eight Days Earlier

Reilly Steel parked the Garda Forensic Unit van alongside the curb near an apartment complex in West Dublin.

Another day, another crime scene. She looked out the window to see that there were several emergency services vehicles parked outside the main doorway of the complex, and the area immediately around the entryway was cordoned off with crime-scene tape. The building seemed to be part of a multi-use development of commercial units on the ground floor below residential apartments rising five or six stories high.

Getting out of the van, Reilly grabbed the kitbag containing her dust suit and forensic toolbox from the back seat and headed in the direction of the doorway.

A growing crowd of onlookers stood behind the tape, waiting for something to happen so they could post it up on Twitter or YouTube, she thought darkly, wondering why everything – including (and perhaps especially?) people's misfortunes – needed to be recorded and shared around the world for entertainment purposes.

The entrance to the building was understated: a large gray-framed door with frosted glass and a wall-mounted intercom on the right-hand side. The door had been propped open by a Garda traffic cone. Reilly hurried through the entryway and was struck by the pungent aroma of some kind of herb or spice – tamarind, she decided – likely coming from the Indian restaurant that had taken up residence in one of the commercial units.

'Reilly Steel, GFU.' She offered her ID to the officer standing sentry at the lift.

'Morning, Miss Steel,' he replied with a smile, not bothering to check her identification badge. Reilly was used to getting appreciative looks; the California-blond thing just seemed to do it for most men. But notwithstanding appearances, she knew that she'd long since proved herself to the Irish force since taking up her role at the GFU three years ago. Not that she'd ever felt she needed to prove herself to anyone – her investigative record spoke for itself, but boys will be boys. Cops especially.

Her track record at the San Francisco FBI field office and Quantico-trained background was the reason she'd been offered the job in the first place, but lately she was beginning to question whether the move away from the US had been the right one.

It had been at first, when her dad was going through such a dark phase in his life, and the Dublin position meant that Reilly would be able to keep an eye on him firsthand when he moved to the city to be closer to his roots. But in the ensuing years, Mike Steel had banished his demons, given up the bottle and completely turned his life around, so much so that he was currently vacationing in the US with his current lady-friend. Reilly had received a postcard from him only yesterday, its sun-filled, carefree imagery completely incongruous with the damp, gray and bitterly cold Dublin weather.

She had returned home after work, struggling against strong biting winds as she tried to open the heavy old Victorian door serving as the entryway to her building in Ranelagh, while trying to keep her shopping bag from being snatched out of her hands by the stormy gusts. In the three years she'd been in the city, she'd slowly come to realize that springtime in Ireland was pretty much the same as any other time of year: bleak and miserable.

Among some white and brown official-looking mail that all looked like payment demands, was a brief flash of color. Reaching down, she'd scooped up the envelopes and sought out the postcard upon which 'Greetings from Santa Barbara' was emblazoned diagonally across four cloudless images. The scenery was instantly (and painfully) recognizable: a golden Pacific sunset, an old-fashioned wooden pier, a sandy beach and the old town area. Keenly aware of the dark skies and worsening storm battering the windows around her, Reilly had felt more than a little tortured as she turned the card over to read the message inscribed.

Hey honey, just a note to let you know we're alive. The party went great – really nice to see all the boys again. We're on our way down the 101 at the moment in a soft-top, no less! Weather's getting warmer as we head south. Maura really loves Cali and it's been great to revisit some old haunts. Hope all's good with you. Call you soon for a catch up, OK?

Lots of love, Dad and Maura

A retired firefighter, Mike had gone back to the States to attend the retirement bash of a colleague from his old job and, while Reilly was pleased to hear that her dad was having fun, what she wouldn't give for a snazzy convertible, some warm sunshine, blue skies and the open road . . .

Turning her attentions back to the job at hand, she waited for the uniform to point her in the right direction. 'Third floor. Stairwell is the last door on the right.' He gestured down the well-lit corridor lined with post boxes. 'Do you need somebody to give you a hand with that?' he asked then, indicating her heavy-looking kitbag.

She hid a smile. 'Thanks, but I'll manage. The rest of my team will be here shortly and we'll be processing that lift first, so we can get it up and running again. Make sure no one goes near it in the meantime.'

'Of course.' The officer nodded as Reilly made for the timber door that led to the stairwell.

She began to move quickly up the stairs, before suddenly starting to feel out of breath, acutely aware of how her carb-filled Irish diet and declining opportunities for exercise were starting to creep up on her. She cursed herself for the ready-meal mac 'n cheese she'd 'cooked' for dinner the night before. At the time, she'd considered it a little taster of home, when in reality back in the US she'd never touched the stuff.

Reilly felt a long way from the person she'd been upon first crossing the Atlantic to take up this job. Back then she'd enjoyed picking up in-season fruit and veg at farmers' markets or the local organic shops close to where she lived in Ranelagh, and had relished trying out different recipes with unfamiliar ingredients. When had it all changed? she wondered now. When had she gone from embracing the gastronomic (and indeed cultural) differences to feeling alienated by them?

By the time Reilly got to the doorway that led to the third floor she felt like she'd just run a marathon. Pathetic for someone who used to pound out fifteen miles straight and barely break a sweat. The inevitable guilt descended as she was reminded of more leisurely pursuits, but lately there hadn't been much time for non-work activities of any kind.

Not only was she getting old, she admitted dourly, thinking about the recent non-existent celebrations for her thirty-third birthday, but she was getting soft with it and lately in particular could feel herself starting to lose her edge. Not good for a CSI investigator and certainly not for one who was responsible for the smooth running of the forensic operational center on behalf of the Irish police force.

As she pushed through the door with her shoulder she swore to herself that she'd head out for a proper run when she got home later, regardless of the weather.

'Speak of the devil . . .' Detective Chris Delaney said with a grin as she emerged through the heavily sprung fire door.

'Hey,' she greeted, trying her best to conceal the effects of her exertion. 'Should my ears be burning?'

'You just lost me twenty quid,' Kennedy, Delaney's middle-aged overweight partner commented.

'How so?'

'I reckoned you'd arrive up already suited and booted,' the older detective explained.

'What he actually said, *again*, was that you probably slept in them,' Chris elaborated, rolling his eyes as this was a very old joke of Kennedy's and it was by now long past wearing thin.

'Full marks for originality, detective,' Reilly said, shaking her head. 'And too bad neither of you will ever get to collect on *that* bet,' she added archly, enjoying their familiar banter.

In truth, Chris Delaney and Pete Kennedy were probably the closest thing she had to friends in Dublin, which spoke volumes. Not so much about the quality of any friendship, but more about the time they'd spent working on challenging, all-consuming investigations. The three had worked side by side since Reilly's arrival at the GFU and knew each other well. They'd been through a lot over the course of their investigations together – not all of it good – but Reilly knew she could trust these two men with her life, and was secure in the knowledge that the feeling was mutual.

And while there might once perhaps have been something stronger brewing between her and Chris, she was now pretty sure that ship had sailed. Which, Reilly supposed, might also be contributing toward her increased sense of isolation lately. While nothing was ever said out loud, the relaxed, easygoing nature of her and Chris's relationship in the early days had since become somewhat more reserved. Probably for the best, Reilly thought. Everyone knew it was never a good idea to mix work and personal stuff.

Especially in this business. 'So do you mind if I get to work?' she said, moving on. 'What's the lie of the land? Has the ME been called? And how many . . .?'

'Don't worry, nobody's been in or out since the ambulance crew,' Chris assured her, instinctively realizing that she wasn't in the mood for joviality. 'And yes, Karen Thompson's on her way.'

He quickly brought her up to date: 'Dead girl in the bedroom, looks like an OD. Her mother and four-year-old son called it in, they'd just come back after a weekend away . . . poor kid.' Chris shook his head in dismay, and Reilly grimaced at the thought; she knew all too well how that felt.

'OK, let me get started. Gary and Julius will be here shortly.'

Reilly pulled her dust suit from the kitbag and began to pull it on, retying her blond hair back in a tight ponytail, before pulling the hood up over her head. Perching a face mask on her forehead, she slipped blue plastic covers over her shoes, before picking up her toolbox and heading for the doorway the detectives had pointed out.

This led into a short hallway with doors left and right. Straight ahead was the bathroom, a cramped windowless space with long shelving above a bath partly obscured by a shower curtain. Vying for space on the shelf were numerous colorful bath toys and toiletries. A kid's toilet seat and footstool were tucked in between the toilet and the wall.

As Reilly approached the bedroom she made a quick reconnaissance of the full layout of the flat. To the right was a kitchen/living room with a large sliding door that led out to a balcony. In the opposite direction was the first of two bedrooms; the door for the second bedroom was now visible.

Inside, she immediately saw the double bed and the lifeless figure of a young woman draped across it. The bed was covered in vomit as was the bound and naked body, the pungent stench almost making Reilly recoil. But there were other scents vying for attention too: cheap perfume and alcohol but also cooking – fried onions, garlic and some kind of red meat . . . veal, she decided quickly. The contents of the kitchen would confirm or deny whether

her famously sensitive nose and odd knack for cataloguing scents – for the most part a major plus in this particular line of work – had got it right.

Making her way to the bedside, Reilly took out the camera and began taking pictures. She looked again at the lifeless form on the bed, but there was no indecision or hesitation – she knew exactly what to do and where to start. She moved around the bed, checking the floor and bedside table, but saw nothing visibly out of the ordinary. Then she gave the victim's body a brief once-over – keenly aware that her hands were tied, so to speak, until Karen Thompson, the medical examiner, arrived to carry out an initial appraisal of the corpse. Afterward, she moved on to the kitchen to look for evidence and try to get a full mental picture of the scene, before the other GFU field techs arrived.

On the small kitchen table were two bowls, with spoon lines of what looked like cream and red syrup streaked across the bottom. Dessert had been served and devoured.

One look at the stack of crockery by the sink told Reilly that a meal of at least two if not three courses had been shared by two people. She took several shots of the table and the contents of the kitchen from a few different angles.

Then, temporarily finished with the camera, she set it down on a nearby countertop. Earlier, when zooming in on the table surface for a shot, a thin layer of fine whitish dust had caught her attention. She guessed it was icing sugar (possibly the non-bleached organic kind) or something related to dessert, but would be taking samples in any case. Finding out exactly what was on the menu before the murder occurred could be crucial.

Taking a pack of sample dishes from her kitbag, Reilly used a cotton bud to pick up some of the fine powder. She also procured a few scraps of the leftover food, before assigning a number to each dish, attaching a sticker and then number to the corresponding sample, before placing each dish into individual evidence bags.

Feeling suddenly warm in her dust suit, she wiped her forehead with a latex-clad hand. She guessed the heating in the flat must be set on high, and knew this was something the ME would have to take into account, given how it would affect her time-of-death assessment.

It was the last thought Reilly had before she collapsed to the ground, and her head crashed against the tiled floor with a sickening thud.

Chapter 2

Tampa, Florida

Holly's little Russian doll, Todd Forrest of the Tampa PD forensic unit decided.

That was what this crime scene reminded him of: one of those Russian nesting dolls that opened up to reveal another one inside. Babushka dolls, he thought, recalling what they were called. His childhood friend had carried that damn thing with her everywhere until she was eleven years old. Todd shook his head. He didn't want to think about such memories now, not while he was standing at the scene of a vicious murder. It seemed like bad luck, somehow. Besides, he had a case that needed his focus.

The south city apartment complex was laid out in four two-story blocks, forming a square surrounding a fountain. Inside the square was a section blocked off by yellow crime-scene tape, an area filled with a group of police officers. The top of the fountain was just visible over the heads of the tallest officers, but no one was looking up. All eyes were on the base of it, upon which their victim, a brown-haired, green-eyed Russian girl, was splayed.

She didn't look older than seventeen and she'd never be older than that now. She'd also been just as cute as the little babushka doll Todd remembered. And like that doll, it looked like someone had been expecting to find a smaller one inside. The girl had been sliced from ribcage to groin, leaving her stomach a gaping mess.

Todd felt the sudden desire to try to put her back together, good as new, the way you could with a toy, and he had to swallow around a lump in his throat. No one could ever put this poor girl back together. But he set his jaw; what he could do was piece together any clues he found to find the monster who did this, and help nail the son of a bitch to the wall.

He raked his thick dark hair back from his face and thought, not for the first time, that he needed a haircut. Between that and the clear blue eyes and fine features he'd inherited from his mother, he'd earned the nickname 'Pretty' almost immediately. One of the reasons he got on with his partner, senior forensic investigator Bradley Ford, was that the 42-year-old never used the moniker. Part of it could've been that Bradley's Italian heritage had given him fairly exotic looks that attracted quite a bit of attention too.

Todd raised the camera and started snapping photographs from every angle. He'd learned to detach himself from what he saw through the lens. If every time he had to document a crime scene he saw the body as a person, he would've quit long ago. But too detached was just as dangerous, he knew. His father – esteemed ex-FBI criminal profiler Daniel Forrest – had taught him that.

So Todd had learned over time to try to balance emotion and professionalism, yet now at thirty-six years old and ten years working with Tampa CSI, he still wasn't sure he'd gotten that particular equilibrium right.

He always took a few minutes when he was first on a scene to allow himself to absorb the shock and horror, and grieve for the victim. Then he shut down those emotions and studied the area like he was trained: as a scene with separate components – the dead person was no longer the body of a human being, but remains to be studied and analyzed.

Once he finished photographing, he retrieved a small glass vial from his forensic kit and dipped it into the bloody fountain water. He wiped the glass clean with a sterilizing wipe and stripped off his gloves, carefully depositing the wipe and gloves into a hazard bag. As he pulled a second pair of gloves from the toolbox, he idly wondered how many gloves his team went through in any given month. It depended on how many crime scenes they were called to and how many of the team were on site. So far this month, things had been busy.

While his colleague went over the body with tweezers, vials and bags of his own, Todd scoured the immediate area around the fountain for anything forensically interesting or important. He ignored the chatter of the local cops as he sought out and collected seemingly mundane items in the hope they would lead the chief investigators to the killer.

He and Bradley took their time, doing everything by the book. They were meticulous and good at their jobs, and by the time all of the samples had been packed up in the CSI van and the corpse released to the coroner for autopsy, the pair had been at the scene for over two hours.

Most of the cops had drifted away, the monotony of what the forensics team was doing boring them. Neither Bradley nor Todd paid them any mind. While Todd scoured further out in the hope of finding the murder weapon, Bradley sent their intern back to the lab with the samples to begin analysis. He then joined his partner in the hunt, Bradley's dark eyes intense as they each studied every inch of the courtyard.

When Bradley's phone rang, the senior investigator paused to answer it. He was good enough to talk and search at the same time, but Todd knew that his partner was too professional to take the risk – no matter how minute – that he might miss something.

Some people, it was said, wore their hearts on their sleeve but Bradley wore his feelings on his face. And now, judging by the shift of expressions on that face, Todd knew the call was nothing good.

'OK, we'll be right there,' Bradley said into his phone, before ending the call.

'Be right where?' Todd asked, straightening. 'We're not done here yet.'

'We are now.' His partner was already moving. 'Let the cops finish the canvass for the murder weapon.'

Todd had no choice but to follow, still arguing as they made their way through the complex's entryway toward Bradley's SUV.

'Don't worry, this is already looking like an open-and-shut case,' Todd's colleague continued. 'Detective has an eye-witness who places two known members of the Russian mob at the scene, arguing with the victim. She was pregnant and seems the father wanted her to have an abortion. The witness heard one of the men say that if she didn't, he'd give her one.'

Todd stopped short. 'Are you serious? That's just . . .'

'Despicable? Heinous? Sickening?' When Todd gave him an exasperated look, Bradley said, 'I could go on. I own a thesaurus. Monstrous? Deplor—'

'How can you be so flippant?'

Bradley's eyes darkened even further. 'Department shrink says it helps us keep our sanity. Didn't you get the memo?'

'Look, I just want to bury this bastard in forensic evidence so deep he'll never see the light of day again.'

'Todd,' Bradley's voice softened and he put a hand on the younger man's shoulder. 'All joking aside, I know how you feel, but from what I've heard, I think you'll have a much harder time finding a word to describe the scene we're headed to now. Pure evil is what comes to my mind.' He got into the SUV.

Todd stood for a moment, dumbstruck. Truth was, he usually made more wisecracks than Bradley about the things they encountered day to day. His partner was right: it was a coping mechanism and, the way he saw it, a damn sight healthier than some of the other vices available to people in their line of work. But while Todd could find the dark humor in a dentist killed by his own drill, or a pimp beaten to death by a hooker, he paled at the thought of what his been-around-the-block colleague might consider 'pure evil'.

When he and Bradley arrived at their second crime scene of the day – this one just off a roadside close to the holiday town (and Todd's old childhood haunt) of Clearwater Beach – at first, he thought there were three corpses: one in the truck, one behind the truck and one by a tree. Two appeared small and he immediately felt his gut clench. He hated working cases involving kids.

As he climbed out of the SUV, he was trying to figure out what had happened. At first, it looked like the truck had crashed into the tree and the children had been thrown backward. Maybe they'd been in the truck bed? A parent driving recklessly with kids in the bed of a pickup was certainly idiotic, heinous even – but evil?

Maybe it had been intentional – one of those tragic murder-suicides. If so, it was a lot more creative than using a gun.

Todd took a deep breath, before he and Bradley got any closer to the carnage. Wouldn't do to look weak in front of the uniforms. In addition to being the partner of one of the best forensic investigators in his field, he had the added pressure of the Forrest name and reputation to contend with. Somehow, it made people automatically expect Todd to be smarter, tougher and more capable, as if his dad had discussed cases in detail with him since childhood.

When they were still a few yards away, Detective Julie Sampson stepped in front of them, her pretty face full of warning. 'Watch out.'

'What . . . ?' Todd started to ask, then noticed what the crabgrass had partially obscured. Someone had lost their lunch. 'Who's the rookie?'

Julie scowled. For a petite brunette with a baby face, she could look fierce when she wanted to. 'The officer who shot the man in the driver's seat actually, Mr Insensitive.'

It didn't take a genius to figure out who she was defending. 'Not my fault your boyfriend has a sensitive stomach,' he shot back.

Julie looked at him warily. 'How'd you know I was talking about Ralph?'

'Word around the station is he's a fast shooter . . .'

It took a second for the insulting innuendo to register, and when it did, Julie's cheeks turned bright red and her temper flared.

Bradley had already moved on, leaving Julie's partner, Mark Reed, to handle the situation. 'Enough flirting, we have a serious situation on our hands here.'

'Flirting?' Julie sputtered. 'With him? I'd never . . .'

Todd let that slide since, in fact, she had. *They* had. It was the oldest story in the book. Their eyes met, the attraction was instantaneous and they'd tumbled into bed just a few hours later. And that, of course, had led to 'You never called. You said you'd call.' Todd had tried explaining that he'd been in quarantine after being exposed to a toxic virus from a corpse he'd examined. It sounded like an excuse and she'd never forgiven him for it.

'Fact is, I wouldn't lose my cool about shooting some moron driving like a maniac with his kids in the back of his truck.' Todd didn't bother to mention that he wouldn't have been stupid enough to draw on an unarmed man in any case. There was a whole other department that would take care of that.

Julie's indignant expression was quickly replaced by confusion. 'What are you talking about?'

'Those two kids.' Todd gestured toward the remains.

'I think you'd better have a closer look,' Mark said softly.

Todd squinted and saw the chains that Bradley was currently examining. Then the pieces clicked into place and he realized what had disturbed Bradley so much upon taking the call.

The remains weren't in fact a couple of kids, but pieces of a single body torn asunder.

His jaw tightened. 'Well then, Ralph should've cheered, not puked, after shooting the sicko who did that.'

'You don't get it, Todd.' Julie's eyes flicked toward the

crime scene and then away. She'd seen quite a bit since joining homicide, so the look spoke volumes. 'The guy in the driver's seat didn't do this, but we didn't know that at the time. The girl was still alive when we arrived. The truck started to move and Ralph did what he thought was right. He shot the driver.'

'The way the driver was tied up, his foot was propped on the accelerator.' Mark picked up the story. 'When his body went limp, the accelerator depressed and . . . well, you can imagine the rest.' He swallowed hard.

'Shit . . .'

As Todd tried to visualize how it had all gone down, he followed Bradley to where the arms of the girl's body – which had come apart from the torso – lay. But all thoughts vanished from his head as his gaze rested on the face of the victim. Her pretty visage was contorted, jaw still open in a silent scream.

And he immediately thought again about the little Russian doll.

'Holly,' he whispered, feeling the strength go out of his legs. He staggered, struggling to stay on his feet, then swallowed, fighting down the bile in his throat.

That caught Bradley's attention. His head came up, pale eyes widening when he saw his face. 'Todd?'

Todd didn't answer. He couldn't take his eyes off the body, the familiar blond hair matted with blood and dirt, mischievous sparkling eyes now horribly glassed over.

He turned and ran a few steps away, barely making it back to where the other cop had vomited before contributing his own lunch to the mess. He looked up to see Julie Sampson staring at him, scorn evident on her face. He didn't care.

Todd put his hands on his knees and closed his eyes, before immediately opening them again, the image of that face seared into the back of his eyelids. All of the horror he'd felt at the other scene earlier, the anger that someone could do that to another human being, all of that paled in comparison to the myriad emotions racing through his body just now.

This wasn't just some faceless, nameless corpse. It wasn't even someone he felt sympathy for. This was Holly. The chubby little girl with pigtails who'd begged him to push her on the swings on summer visits. The scabby-kneed, gawky eleven-year-old who always wanted to hang out with the closest thing she had to a big brother and was overjoyed when he'd taken up a permanent job in Tampa. The beautiful young woman who'd called only a few months ago to tell him that she'd met the man of her dreams. The little girl who used to adore playing with that babushka doll.

Todd's knees finally buckled and he didn't try to stop himself this time. A part of him wanted to pass out, to not have to deal with this a second longer. But he didn't faint, and he ignored the urge to curl up and let his grief over-take him. Summoning up a reserve of strength he didn't know he had, Todd shakily pushed himself to his feet.

'Come on, man,' Bradley said as he strode across the sandy ground, his face unusually serious. 'Not more than two minutes after you rag on a cop for losing his lunch, you nearly pass out yourself? I know this is bad, but what's with the rubber chicken-routine? We've seen more disturbing things in the drain of the locker-room showers.'

At first, Todd just stared at Bradley, struggling to process his colleague's words, the attempt at levity not registering on a conscious level. Finally, he managed to utter a few words: 'I need to call my father.'

Chapter 3

Reilly cried out as she bolted upright, her naked body bathed in sweat.

She pressed her hands against her chest, feeling her heart pounding against her palms. Despite the darkness, she didn't want to turn on the bedside lamp. It was irrational, she knew, but even a child sensed that the fear experienced through nightmares didn't ever fully burn away until touched by the light of day.

Her pale blue eyes were wide, straining against the curtain-drawn darkness, and she fought the automatic urge to reach for a sidearm. Even a weapon-free three years in Dublin hadn't quelled that instinct.

She felt wooly and disorientated, much like she had when waking up in a hospital bed barely a week before. The last thing she'd been able to remember was running that scene in the apartment block, and packing away the evidence bags before starting to dust the table for prints.

After that, nothing, until she'd come to, alone and frightened, in Tallaght hospital.

Scrambling at the time to try to figure out what had happened, Reilly thought back to what she'd been doing at the crime scene. The dust . . . the table surface had been covered in a fine powder – icing sugar, she'd presumed, when taking samples. It was then that the horrible realization struck her. The mask . . . she'd neglected to pull the mask down over her mouth. Which meant that she must have inhaled some of the dust, and it clearly wasn't organic icing sugar. A rare situation in which her typically reliable nose had worked against her, she thought, remonstrating with herself for being so careless.

Reilly had spent three full days in the hospital under observation, until the doctors were confident that whatever substance she'd consumed was no longer a threat to her. The GFU lab were still working on analysis of the powdered substance and Reilly still had no idea what had upended her in such a way.

Once she'd finished berating herself for her stupidity, the following two days flat on her back in the hospital were the worst she could remember. First off, she was lonely – Mike was on vacation in California, so there was no one to visit or sit by her bedside.

Chris, arguably her only friend in Dublin close enough to visit, was deeply engaged in the associated murder investigation, and her colleagues at the GFU were heavily backed up, especially now they were one member down.

Chris had offered to call her father and update him but

Reilly didn't see the point as there was nothing he could do but worry, and she certainly didn't want Mike to cut short the first vacation he'd had in decades.

But the situation illustrated for Reilly just how few relationships she'd made in the city since her arrival, and highlighted the sense of disconnection she'd been feeling lately. Save for flowers from her team at the GFU, and a couple of quick phone calls from base to check on her progress, she'd spent most of the hospital stay on her own, feeling as low as she could ever remember.

Until the call from Inspector O'Brien, on day three. After a brief exchange of niceties and polite enquiries about her health, the chief got straight to the point.

'The incident is currently with GIA,' he told Reilly in his typical no-nonsense tone. 'Standard procedure in such a case where somebody gets injured on the job, you know the drill.'

Reilly knew all about Garda Internal Affairs.

'Well they have been kicking up a bit of a stink about the fact you weren't wearing a mask,' he continued, and her heart sank. 'Of course, I've pointed out your exemplary record and advised them not to create issues where there doesn't need to be any, but we just have to go along with it for now.'

Hundreds of thoughts rushed through her head. She'd fucked up, hadn't she? Was she being suspended? It was her own fault; she'd been so distracted lately she wasn't thinking straight – forgetting the mask was a greenhorn mistake.

'It's really an ass-covering exercise,' O'Brien continued, 'and I don't want you stressing about it. In the meantime, you'll need to take leave – time off to fully recover
till things settle down. Fully paid, of course. And I've
arranged to pull in some cover to make sure GFU runs
smoothly in your absence,' he continued, leaving Reilly
under no illusions that the matter wasn't up for
discussion.

'How much time?' she enquired tentatively, trying to
gauge what the response would be, or indeed what this
'enforced leave' would mean for her future.

'Just while we await the GIA findings,' O'Brien replied
crisply. 'It'll be a few weeks; six at the most. After that we
can review accordingly.'

She understood how slowly the wheels of bureaucracy
moved, but still six weeks felt like an enormous length of
time. It was now close to the end of April, which meant it
would be at least mid-June by the time she was back. Six
long weeks without work to occupy her? Reilly didn't
really know how to feel about it, and guessed she should
feel angry or upset. But instead, a strange sense of accept-
ance washed over her – relief almost. With the way she'd
been moping about lately, maybe some time off could
turn out to be a blessing in disguise?

Shortly afterward, a GIA representative contacted her
to arrange an interview, and once Reilly had recounted to
him every aspect of the crime scene search in painful
detail, a sustained period away from work and its associated responsibilities awaited her.

For the first time in her professional life she had absolutely nothing to do and all the time in the world to do it. The question was, what *was* she going to do with it?

The answer came to her as she checked out of the hospital on yet another dull and damp Irish spring day.

Now, the sight of her surroundings – however unfamiliar – was comforting. She ran her fingers through her hair, yanking hard when she hit a tangle. The pain was sharp, immediate, and drove the last of the sleep from her mind.

Reilly reached for her cellphone, and swore when she read the time. She'd just wanted a short nap to help with the jet lag and now she realized that she'd been sleeping almost all afternoon. She scrambled off the bed and looked in the mirror above the dresser. Scowling at her reflection, she headed for the bathroom. A shower was definitely in order.

As the hot water pounded into her travel-stiff muscles, Reilly still tried to tell herself that what had happened over the last week or so wasn't just a dream, and that she really was here.

Standing in the shower, she squirted generic-brand shampoo into her hands and made a face at the astringent smell. Seemed they didn't keep the guest bathroom stocked with the good stuff.

Then her stomach growled in protest and she realized it had been hours since she'd last eaten, and she still needed to unpack.

But not until she got something to eat, and right then Reilly could eat a horse. She just hoped the fridge was better stocked than the guest room.

Going downstairs, she was distracted by a warm breeze coming through the open doorway and the sound of waves washing gently against the shore. She wandered out onto the ocean-front deck and inhaled the warm, salty air. She'd always loved being by the beach, loved the way the ocean waves rolled in, smoothing the sand and wiping away traces of everything.

And she'd been unprepared for how much she'd missed that.

Dublin had a beauty of its own, but there were times when Reilly longed for the heat of summer, real summer. The gentle breeze that came off the Gulf of Mexico this evening was warm, salty and comforting, and the knot that had been in her stomach since she'd flown out of Dublin airport the day before gradually started to ease.

Reilly knew he was there before he spoke, but she waited for him to break the silence. 'Sleep OK?' Daniel Forrest was sitting in one of the deck chairs beneath the lanai covering.

'Longer than I'd planned, but good, thanks.'

'Beer?' He held a long-neck bottle out to her.

'Thanks.' Reilly had never been much of a drinker, but this evening she welcomed something to take the edge off, as well as something to cool her down. She took a sip of the chilled alcohol. It was a few hours before sunset and the Florida heat was still enough that the cool liquid soothed as it slid down her throat. 'And yes, everything is wonderful. I'm glad to be here. Thank you for inviting me.'

'No problem. I'm just glad you finally took up the invitation. Even if – and this is just a guess – the decision was slightly forced on you . . .' Persistence was Daniel Forrest's middle name, but she wasn't yet willing to discuss the reasons for her out-of-the-blue call last week, asking if she could come and stay at his beach house.

After hanging up his FBI boots, Reilly's former Quantico tutor had semi-retired to his holiday home in Clearwater Beach almost eighteen months before. His four-bed wooden colonial house was situated in a quiet, residential part of the popular Florida beach town, and located right on the white sandy beach of the Gulf of Mexico. It was an idyllic location and even better than Daniel had described during his many phone calls entreating her to visit since he'd moved there from Virginia. A behavioral psychologist by profession, he was now freelance, occasionally working for the local law-enforcement agencies on a consultation basis, as well as running investigations on behalf of private individuals and companies.

Their relationship ran deep: somewhere between father and older brother. Daniel had been in his mid-forties when they'd first met a little over a decade ago, when Reilly was a wide-eyed rookie at the FBI's training academy.

She'd had a crush on him at first, but so had most of the females in her class. Ruggedly handsome with salt-and-pepper hair, warm brown eyes and lots of charisma, Agent Forrest had never lacked for attention. Though it hadn't taken long for the crush to turn into legitimate admiration absent of romantic notions. Daniel was brilliant and engaging, treating his students with respect and challenging them to excel. But they both knew that his relationship with Reilly ran deeper than student/ teacher. He knew all about her family difficulties and troubled past, and had been there for Reilly at the very worst times of her life – on one occasion even travelling as far as Dublin to help her out and show his support.

Now, Reilly took a seat beside him and closed her eyes, letting her head rest on the back of the aquamarine-painted wooden deck chair. She knew she should go into the kitchen and get something to eat, but right then she was almost mesmerized by the sound of the waves crashing into the shore.

As usual, it was almost as if Daniel could read her mind. 'I made fish tacos,' he said, standing up. 'Local grouper is great here, especially blackened.'

Reilly's mouth watered at the very notion. She hadn't eaten fresh fish tacos in years. Oddly for an island country, the Irish weren't much of a fish-eating nation. And Cajun-blacked grouper with guac and salsa, all washed down with a cold beer . . . it sounded like a feast for kings.

Easing back into the chair while Daniel bustled around in the kitchen, she realized how much she'd yearned for home comforts as well as good weather. And the light . . . it was hard to describe how different the world seemed when bathed in sunlight, and it seemed so long since she'd seen a sky as blue as this one.

When he returned with the tacos, along with a fresh round of Coronas, Reilly launched on the food as if she hadn't eaten a morsel in years. Afterward, she took up Daniel's offer of a tour of the property. They skirted the small dipping pool just below the deck, and took the wooden steps leading down to the beach.

The fine white powdery sand was still warm on her bare feet, and she was again struck by how much she'd missed the joys of living in a hot ocean-side environment. The Irish coastline had its own wild beauty, but there was something to be said for the feel of sun-warmed sand between the toes.

'So, anyone new in your life?' Reilly decided that Daniel's earlier inquisitiveness deserved a response. After all, turnabout was fair play.

'Let's see.' He gave her a mischievous glance. 'Since we last spoke, there's been Maria, Danielle, Grace, Stephanie, then another Maria . . .'

'Seriously?' She rolled her eyes. 'You really haven't changed. I'd hoped the slower pace of life would mean you'd finally start getting serious with someone.'

'Not a chance,' Daniel said, shaking his head. 'I'm not looking to get married again. Once was enough for me.'

'At least your son comes by it honestly.' They reached the shore and Reilly let the water splash over her toes. She remembered his son, of course. Good-looking in that 'almost too pretty for a guy' way. They'd both attended

Quantico around the same time; he was only a few years older than her as she recalled, and she remembered him as being amicable, if a little distant. While she would trust Daniel with her life, her relationship with Todd Forrest had never really progressed past basic pleasantries.

'That he does,' Daniel said. 'Just don't tell him I said so.'

She quirked an eyebrow in her old friend's direction.

'Despite a stellar career with Tampa CSI, Todd's still in the "proving myself" stage of life,' Daniel clarified. 'I thought kids were supposed to grow out of that.'

'He will,' Reilly reassured him. She couldn't resist adding with a grin, 'Eventually.'

Daniel smiled benevolently at her. 'You know, the first time I saw you . . .' his voice slowed a little, taking on the familiar cadence he always used when explaining a theory or outlining a suspect's profile. 'You were this skinny twenty-year-old with big blue eyes and blond hair pulled back in a haphazard ponytail.' He gave a fond shake of his head. 'And you were wearing a suit like something off *Law & Order* but didn't look old enough to pull it off. I remember wondering if you'd be tough enough to take being a woman in a mostly male environment, never mind up to the challenges of working in this crazy field of ours. And yet, as you stood there in the doorway, I watched your face change, almost as if you knew what I was thinking. You set your chin and marched right up and introduced yourself to me.'

'And you said,' Reilly continued playfully, taking his arm, '"Steel, if you keep that same stuff in your backbone, you're going to do just fine."'

'And you certainly did. But—'

Suddenly, Daniel's cellphone rang. The Florida sun was now slowly inching its way toward the horizon, casting stunning orange/red rays across the sky and causing blinding reflections in the water.

'Are you sure?' Reilly heard him ask, suddenly alert. Then he swore and she looked at him, perturbed. Daniel rarely ever cursed. She saw that his tanned face had turned pale, and he looked like he was going to be sick.

Concern flooded through her. He wasn't old, but he wasn't exactly young either. Heart attacks for people in their fifties weren't uncommon, even for someone as athletic as Daniel Forrest. Hadn't there been some ice skater who'd collapsed at practice and died when he was only twenty-eight?

Daniel moved away from her and strode off a little way down the beach, still talking to whoever was on the other side. Reilly could only hear snatches of the conversation but whatever it was, she knew it couldn't be good.

Eventually, he started to turn back toward the house. 'No, hold off for as long as you can. I want to be the one to tell her.' His voice shook as he spoke. 'And Todd, keep me in the loop on this. OK?'

Todd? Hadn't he just mentioned that his son worked with the local PD? That plus Daniel's reaction could only equal something bad. Still, she was puzzled. The former

FBI behavioral profiler had experienced countless horrible things in his line of work; same as she had. What made this so different?

Back at the house, Daniel sank down onto one of the deck chairs, setting his phone aside without a glance. Then he buried his face in his hands, and Reilly was shocked afresh to see his shoulders shaking. She crouched in front of him, tentatively reaching for him. When her hand touched his, he looked up, not trying to hide the tears in his eyes.

'What's going on, Daniel?'

The reply came out in a whisper. 'My god-daughter, Holly.' He paused, appearing to struggle with what he had to say next.

Reilly tensed, desperately wanting to know what was upsetting him so much, but at the same time reluctant to hear the details of what was bound to be terrible news. Anything that could reduce Daniel Forrest to tears was not to be taken lightly.

'She's been murdered.' His voice broke on the final word, his fingers curling around hers.

'Oh, Daniel.' Reilly wrapped her arms around her old friend's shoulders, pulling him toward her.

'She was only a kid,' Daniel managed, between gasps.

'I'm so sorry,' Reilly kept repeating, hating herself for the obligatory useless platitude. She knew better than anyone how empty those words sounded, but she also knew that there were no words that wouldn't sound empty. No sentiments or condolences that could possibly soothe away the grief and anguish that came with getting the news that someone you loved was gone forever.

They sat together until twilight began to fall, as Daniel tried to overcome the initial shock of the phone call. When finally he sat forward and wiped his face, Reilly saw the expression on his face change from grieving friend to what she'd always called his 'work mode'.

While maintaining the compassion needed to do what he did, Daniel had always had the uncanny ability to set aside his emotions and view things in a clinical manner when he needed to. She knew that even though he was still hurting, he'd be able to focus. She was somewhat of a pro at that herself.

'I told Todd to try and get the department to hold off. I want to be the one to notify her mother. She lives nearby.' Daniel stood. He held out a hand to help Reilly to her feet, keeping her hand in his for a moment longer, taking a last little bit of comfort before releasing it.

'Will you let me come along? That's if you don't mind the company.'

He shook his head. 'You just got here . . . you're still jet-lagged, to say nothing about the fact that you're supposed to be on vacation . . .'

Reilly shook out her legs. Her muscles were still stiff but the beer had helped. 'Don't be stupid. I've been sitting around on my ass for over a week now. It'll give me something to do. And you'll need moral support.'

'OK, if you really don't mind, I'd appreciate it. Thank you.' He nodded tiredly but then took a deep breath, and she saw his features settle into what Reilly had always thought of as his scary face. She'd seen it a few times with a handful of cases, the ones that really got to him. And she'd once seen that same look reduce a six-foot-four, 250-pound drug dealer to tears. 'I guess I could do with some moral support.'

Reilly stood up with purpose, jet lag already fading into the distance, and wondered why she managed to smack face-first into death and violence everywhere she went. It was almost as if it sought her out.

Throwing one last longing look at the beach, she followed Daniel out to the front of the house to where his Chrysler SUV was parked in the driveway; the cicadas sounded louder than usual in the now eerily still night.

So much for a vacation.

Chapter 4

Back at the CSI lab in Tampa, Todd could feel Bradley watching him. Not directly of course; but his partner was a master of the sideways glance.

From the moment he'd revealed his relationship to the victim, Todd knew he was going to have to tread lightly. With their forensic toxicologist on vacation, and the usual fallback field technician on maternity leave, the unit was short-staffed enough that Bradley had said he wasn't going to take Todd off the case unless it became necessary. Translation: keep it together, professional and by the book, or sit this one out.

At the crime scene itself, that had been harder.

Bradley had directed Todd to concentrate on the vehicle, the 'driver' and the surrounding area, but every once in a while, Todd had caught a glimpse of blood-stained blond hair waving in the breeze and it had hit him like a punch to the stomach.

Holly was gone. He'd fought back the new flood of emotion and continued with his work. In a way, the familiar monotony of cataloging evidence had helped keep him from losing his composure . . . again.

Now in the lab, it was easier to just think of the victims as evidence and not by name. There had been a crime and it was his job to process the evidence, point the detectives in the right direction and give them what they needed to convict the killer.

'We've got an ID on the male vic,' Dr Owen Kase announced as he entered the lab. In his late thirties, he'd been the chief medical examiner in Tampa for six years and was good at his job. He was also a complete ass, but if the good doctor could help figure out who did this, Todd vowed he'd never say another word against him.

Both Bradley and Todd looked up from their workstations and waited. After an unnecessarily dramatic pause, the doctor continued: 'Aaron Overton, age twenty-one. Prints in the system from a drunk and disorderly a couple of years ago.'

Aaron. The new guy Holly had said she was dating. The one she'd gushed over the phone about for twenty minutes the last time they'd spoken. Todd swallowed hard. He'd suspected as much, but to hear that the person Holly had loved had been the one who had – intentionally or not – killed her made him sick.

'You could've just sent Matthew over with that.' Bradley crossed his arms over his chest, uncharacteristic impatience tingeing his voice. Usually, only the doctor could ruffle the normally cool investigator. 'What else?'

Dr Kase grinned and Todd clenched his hands, fighting back the urge to mess up the doctor's chiseled jaw. Though punching the medical examiner wasn't exactly keeping it together. Besides, no one but Bradley knew of Todd's personal connection to the case and it needed to stay that way.

'Toxicology came back. It seems our killer used chloroform to incapacitate both victims.' He handed Bradley a folder. 'I found traces of the compound around both victims' noses and mouths. What's more interesting, however, is what I got inside the mouth and trachea.'

Todd's fists loosened. So he really did find something.

'Cotton.'

'Cotton?' Bradley repeated.

'Specifically, brightly colored cotton fibers soaked with chloroform.' The ME sounded smug. 'My guess is . . .'

'Beach towel,' Todd cut him off and ignored the resulting glare. 'No one would think twice about a guy walking along the beaches with a damp beach towel.'

'Right.' Owen's tone was petulant at having his moment of glory stolen. 'Anyway, both bodies had traces of saltwater in the hair, indicating that they'd both been in the ocean a few hours before their death. The female victim's body was covered with debris and sand, which was to be expected given the manner of her death and being dragged along the ground. What was unusual, seeing as he was inside the car, was that the male was also covered with similar amounts of sand and some of the same debris. I gave the particulates to Emilie to analyze.'

Emilie Ryan was the newest member of the team. At twenty-four, she was actually the youngest lab technician in Tampa's CSI history. She was also the most cheerful person Todd had ever met. Even when she passed by a table full of gruesome crime-scene pictures, her wide smile never faltered. Granted, she never really studied them in close detail, but in this line of work it was still rare to find someone with such a positive outlook on life. Though he guessed that over time, that would change.

She only occasionally went out into the field depending on the workload, and had only been with them a few months; another reason why Todd didn't want to be forced to take a back seat during this investigation.

'Thank you, Dr Kase,' Bradley said, opening the folder and scanning the contents. 'I'll pass this information along to the detectives. Let us know if you find anything else.'

'They must've been moved,' Todd mused, when the ME had left. Bradley looked at him and he explained. 'The victims, I mean, after he overpowered them with the chloroform.' He swallowed the lump in his throat and continued. 'The nearest stretch of beach was way too rough for swimming.'

'Maybe they walked?' Bradley pulled up a map on his laptop and sent the image to the large PowerPoint projector screen at one end of the lab.

'Well, here's where they were found.' Todd pointed at

the map. He trailed his finger down the long stretch of coast before coming to rest at a spot several miles away. 'And here's the closest point they could've gone into the water.'

'With that type of terrain, they wouldn't have walked any further than a dozen yards before giving up,' Bradley said. He reached for his phone, understanding the point Todd was making. 'We've only got a secondary crime scene.'

While Bradley made the call to the investigative team, Todd turned his attention away from the map and back to the duct tape he'd been examining.

As expected, hair and skin trace decorated the inside of the tape, some dotted with blood. He took a couple of samples to type, but only because it was standard proce-dure. The chances of the DNA not matching the victims were nearly non-existent. When they caught the guy, though, they would need to make sure all i's were dotted and t's crossed.

Once he'd processed the tape, he moved on to the next evidence bag.

The keys had been taped into the ignition with the same type of duct tape. There were two keys on a plain metal ring, one for the truck and one so far unidentified. Todd turned both keys over in his gloved hands, eyes narrowed as he searched for anything noteworthy. Nothing. He heard Bradley come up behind him as he slid the keys under his microscope. Maybe there was a partial of some kind to be found . . .

'Anything new?' he asked as he made the necessary adjustments to his equipment.

'Reed said that the truck had been reported stolen from the Westfield Mall parking lot this morning,' Bradley said, referring to the detective.

'And they're sure the owner's not in on this?' Todd cut in. 'Could be lying just to throw us off.'

'Todd.' Bradley's tone made Todd look up. 'The guys know how to do their job.' He gave a half-smile. 'Besides, the owner is a 72-year-old half-deaf widow named Beatrice Cowen, who reportedly fell asleep twice while Reed and Sampson were interviewing her.'

Todd reluctantly conceded that the detectives had called it right and returned to his examination of the keys. 'The widow happen to mention what the other key is for?'

'Her house,' Bradley said as he walked over to the center table where they'd put the remainder of the unprocessed evidence.

'Well, no prints or partials on either the duct tape or the keys,' Todd announced dully. 'The perp was either wearing gloves or wiped everything down.'

'My guess is the wipe down, at least for everything he would've needed at the abduction site.' Bradley picked up a soil sample. 'A guy with a beach towel may not be out of place on a beach, but a guy with gloves definitely would be.' He looked at the vial in his hand. 'Emilie,' he called out to the other side of the lab. 'Dr Kase gave you the samples from the bodies earlier?'

'Yes,' the younger lab tech replied.

'Can you compare the sand found on the bodies to the sand in this vial?' Bradley asked. 'See if it's from the same place.'

Todd found it funny that his superior still asked for things. Bradley had been the senior investigator for six years and still talked to the other team members as if they were all equal. At first, Todd had assumed the habit would fade, especially once people started taking advantage of Bradley's good nature. To his surprise, it hadn't happened and he continued to run the team with a quiet, polite authority that made coming to work, while not enjoyable due to the nature of the work itself, far less stressful.

'Of course.' Emilie took the vial.

'And thank you for agreeing to stay late to work through some of the evidence,' Bradley said as Emilie walked away.

Then she turned, her expression suddenly somber, the expression seeming out of place on her typically cheery face. 'Of course,' she repeated – her catchphrase of choice, Todd noted. 'We need to find the psycho who did this, and soon.'

'Dramatic much?' Bradley smiled at the tiny redhead as she returned to her work area.

'Problem is, I think she could be right,' Todd replied, looking thoughtful. 'Unless we find out that Hol— the victim had some jilted lover or other enemy, something this fucked up *is* looking like the work of some psychopath.'

'Well, we should try not to make any assumptions for the moment,' Bradley warned as the doors to the lab opened and one of the interns entered with another evidence box. 'You know what they say about making assumptions.'

Chapter 5

As Reilly stood with Daniel on the doorstep of a little white Cape Cod-style house in downtown Clearwater, she was starting to regret her decision to tag along.

Not that she didn't want to support him with the unenviable task he had ahead; it was just that one of the reasons she'd chosen to go into forensics rather than profiling was because of the lack of interaction with the victims' families, and confrontation of the damage evil left behind. Daniel had always claimed that she'd had a knack for people, and maybe she did, but it didn't automatically make her want to be around them more. Give her things to test and measure and examine. Leave the feelings and emotions to everyone else.

Which made her think of something.

'Tell you what,' she said to him on the drive across the gorgeously scenic intercoastal waterway bridge, which connected the smaller Clearwater Beach area to downtown Clearwater via a wide waterway teeming with wildlife. As they crossed, pelicans, egrets and seagulls flew all around them, occasionally diving in and out of the water below. 'Why don't I take a look around while you talk to the mother? See if anything stands out.' According to Daniel, Holly had still been living at her mother's house.

Daniel's wry expression betrayed that he'd expected or anticipated this, before Reilly had even thought to suggest it. 'Exactly the reason I let you come along. I got Todd to hold off for the same reason. We need to get a handle on this before the locals come in and mess it up.'

She frowned. 'You don't trust your own son?'

'Of course I do – just not some of the idiots working with him.' But Reilly figured this was less of a reflection of the Tampa PD and more an indication of Daniel's control freak tendencies. She should have guessed that when it came to something this personal, he'd want to get his own angle on it.

'I'm sure the investigative team will do everything they can to—'

'I'm on retainer with the department, Reilly; I know these guys all too well. The detectives are competent, yes, but completely overworked and won't be able to give this their full attention even if they want to.' He pulled up outside a small but well-tended home which Reilly assumed belonged to Holly's mother.

'Daniel . . .' The woman who answered the door was taller than Reilly's own five-foot-five, but just barely. Mrs

Young had big blue eyes that took in the expression on Daniel's face, and instantly revealed that this wasn't the first time she had opened her door to bad news. 'Come in.' Her voice was barely above a whisper and she seemed to shrink back into herself as she led them toward the living room.

The house was tidy and old-fashioned. The same pale blue wallpaper that had lined the hallway continued into the living room, accented by darker curtains. The furniture was old but well cared for. The walls were decorated with pictures, nearly all of a pretty blond girl at various ages. Reilly didn't need a psychological background to tell her that this woman doted on her beloved daughter Holly.

'Would you like something to drink?' Mrs Young asked, after Daniel had made introductions, referring to Reilly as his 'associate'. If the woman was wondering about Reilly's floral-patterned sundress and flip-flops as her choice of professional attire, she didn't show it, but Reilly cursed herself for not changing into something a little more formal beforehand.

Mrs Young's hands fluttered anxiously and she almost seemed to be stalling, as if she could somehow change whatever the news was by delaying it.

Daniel shook his head as he settled on the couch. Reilly sat next to him, unease churning in her stomach. She didn't know this woman. She didn't belong here. This wasn't a place for strangers. But she kept her mouth shut and controlled the urge to bolt. This wasn't about her. This was about helping Daniel find out if there was anything in the house that might provide some answers as to why Holly Young had been murdered.

'Alice . . .' Daniel hesitated, searching for the words.

Mrs Young seemed to make a decision. 'Just tell me,' she said, visibly bracing herself.

'The police found Holly's body a few hours ago.' He said it as gently as possible, but Reilly knew there was no way to soften this sort of blow.

'Oh, my God . . . how?' She seemed to collapse in upon herself and crossed her arms over her chest, as if literally trying to hold herself together. 'What happened?'

'I'm so sorry, Alice.' Daniel reached out and put a hand on the woman's knee. 'I don't know the full details yet, but it seems that she was murdered.'

'Oh, dear God.' The words seemed to break down the last of the woman's defenses and she crumpled.

Daniel moved from his seat to gather the sobbing woman into his arms. He looked over her head at Reilly and motioned toward the hallway. She immediately understood and hurried out, eager to be away from the rawness of a mother's anguish. She glanced in the first two doorways and found a bathroom and the mother's room. The last door on the left had obviously belonged to the victim.

Reilly took a deep breath and then stepped inside, pushing away her misgivings about getting involved in something that was really none of her business. She would do this. For Daniel, and for the grieving mother in his arms, she would do this.

Going straight into work mode, she began to look at it like just another job. First things first – most people are killed by someone they know. Careful not to touch anything she didn't need to, Reilly began her perusal.

She'd seen the bulletin board of pictures across from the door when she'd first entered, but she ignored them for now. If she immediately went there, she might miss something important. Instead, she went to the right and slowly walked the perimeter of the room, taking in everything.

Holly's room was small, neat but not obsessively so. Her dresser was cluttered with what one would expect from a young woman in her mid-twenties. Some make-up, jewelry, a few odds and ends.

The closet floor was a bit more cluttered, about a dozen shoes scattered about haphazardly. The clothes hanging up were fashionable but not expensive. The bed was rumpled, the sheet and blanket tossed back over it but not tucked in. Her pillow was crooked; the smiley face on the pillow case appeared to be watching the rose-printed wallpaper. A pair of cute pale green pajamas lay in a ball at the foot of the bed.

Reilly turned to face the bulletin board she'd first noticed. It was less than a foot square and covered with thumbtacked pictures. She paused, noting the positioning of each one. She didn't need Daniel to remind her that the pictures of most importance were typically placed on the top, overlapping others.

There were three pictures that Reilly figured were the girl's favorites. One was of a pre-teen Holly with her mother and a blond man who Reilly assumed was her father. The second was of Holly, her mother and Daniel at Holly's high school graduation, which she found curious. Where was the father on such a big occasion?

The one in the center – and the most important, Reilly guessed – was of Holly with a smiling blond guy who looked to be about the same age. Their arms were around each other's waist, body language implying they were more than just friends.

As she headed back into the living room, Reilly made a mental list of the items the investigators would want to ask for: the picture of the mystery guy, any new jewelry, and the dress purse that Reilly had seen hanging in the closet.

The CSI team would need to more thoroughly search the room for other evidence of Holly's boyfriend, birth control, a journal, anything like that. With so little information to go on, they needed to start with the basics. Unfortunately, that meant looking into those closest to Holly first.

Reilly paused at the end of the hallway and peeked around the corner. Daniel had returned to his seat on the couch and caught her eye, indicating that she should come back in. As she walked over to the couch, Reilly cast a surreptitious glance in Mrs Young's direction. The woman's eyes were red, an occasional tear making its way down her cheek, but she seemed relatively composed.

Reilly settled back onto the couch and gave Daniel a nod.

'Alice,' Daniel said, his voice gentler than Reilly had ever heard it. 'The police are going to be here a little later to ask you some questions to try to figure out who did this. But, if you're up for it, I'd like to ask you a few things now. Reilly took a look around and may have noticed a couple of things.'

'She's a cop too?' Mrs Young sniffled as she glanced toward Reilly, this time giving a dubious glance at the sundress. She reached for another tissue.

'Reilly's a former student of mine from Quantico. She's a crime-scene investigator now. The best in her field,' Daniel said. 'And she's going to help us.'

Mrs Young nodded. 'All right then, go ahead and ask.'

'Thank you.' Daniel's tone took on a more professional note. 'When was the last time you saw Holly?'

'This morning.' Mrs Young took a shuddering breath. 'She was going to an audition and then spending the afternoon at the beach.'

'An audition? What kind?'

'For a movie, I think. She wants to be an actress.' She looked at Daniel. 'You know how much she loves . . . performing.' The woman's voice broke as she realized she'd been speaking about her daughter in the present tense.

'Did she mention anyone specific she was going with?' Daniel shot Reilly a sideways look and she gave a minute nod. 'Maybe a boyfriend?'

'Um . . .' Mrs Young closed her eyes for a moment. 'She'd been seeing a boy from the community theater. They'd go to auditions together sometimes, I think.'

'His name?' Daniel pressed.

'Aaron. Aaron Overton.' Mrs Young stood abruptly, her eyes brimming with tears. She shook her head and her voice caught. 'I'm sorry . . . this is so hard. If you'll excuse me for a moment.' She hurried away without waiting for a response.

'There's a picture of Holly with a young guy in the bedroom,' Reilly said, pitching her voice low once Mrs Young was out of ear-shot. 'Probably him. There's some jewelry that he might have bought for her. We could test for prints; run them to see if he's in the system.' She shook her head, feeling a little silly for temporarily forgetting where she was. 'I mean, *they* could test for prints. The room looks pretty clean for forensics, but there could be a journal. Maybe get a few leads that way.'

Daniel nodded. 'I'll see if I can get Alice to let us look for a journal.'

'Daniel . . .?' Reilly began, then hesitated. She didn't want to pry, but she knew she needed to know how involved he was in this. Was Alice Young an ex-girlfriend of his, perhaps? She was so timid and nervous she didn't seem the type, but who knew with these things?

He must've read the question in her eyes because he answered it without her having to ask. 'Alice's husband Bruce and I grew up in the same neighborhood back in Virginia. We started hanging out in junior high and stayed in touch even after we graduated. Bruce became an accountant and met Alice, who's from here. I was the best man at their wedding, was at the hospital when Holly was born. Our friendship is partly the reason I bought the vacation home down here. Our families spent every summer together for as long as I can remember until . . .' He trailed off and shook his head, his eyes full of anguish.

'Are you sure this is such a good idea then?' Reilly put her hand on her old mentor's arm. 'I understand that you want to help your friend but—'

Daniel continued as if he hadn't heard her question. 'When Holly was still at school, Bruce was in Tampa on his way home from work when a drunk driver ran a red light. I was in the city at the time, and got to the hospital before Alice. Bruce made me promise to look after his family if he didn't make it through surgery. He died on the table.'

'This wasn't your fault.' Reilly felt a sympathetic stab of guilt. There was always guilt. Should have done more. Should have been me. I could have done something if only. Sometimes, the 'if only's were the worst; Reilly knew that better than most.

'I promised Bruce that I'd take care of his little girl.' A hard light flashed in Daniel's eyes, and Reilly knew there would be no dissuading him. 'And since I didn't do that, I'm sure as hell going to make sure I help nail the son of a bitch who killed her.'

Chapter 6

They rode away from the Young house in silence, Reilly's mind buzzing as feverishly as she knew Daniel's was, though perhaps not about the same things.

'Mind if we head down to Tampa for a bit?' he said, breaking the silence. 'I want to talk to Todd, let him know about this boyfriend, and where Holly was today.'

'Sure,' Reilly said. She pulled her thoughts back to the present. She quite liked the idea of visiting the Tampa police department. Her few years abroad made her curious about the advances made in her native land. Things were bound to be different.

The humid night air was oppressive as, some twenty minutes later, they arrived in the heart of the city and climbed out of the air-conditioned Chrysler. Before she'd taken two steps, Reilly could feel the sheen of sweat on her skin. Even so, the moment she entered the building, she wished again she'd had on one of her work suits.

Designed for use in the much cooler Dublin, they'd be nearly unbearable here, but at least she'd have felt more professional.

In her sundress and sandals and in this setting, she felt more like the wide-eyed girlfriend being taken to see where the big bad investigator worked. She'd seen far too many of her male colleagues – and a couple of female ones – use the profession like their own personal aphrodisiac. The patter usually went something like this: 'I'm not just a doctor, you know. I help catch criminals. Would you like to see where I do my best work?' The worst line she'd ever heard was from a newbie in the medical examiner's office in San Francisco: 'I have to warn you, when we get down there, there'll be two naked bodies; and the corpses, of course.'

'Good evening, Dr Forrest.' The officer at the desk greeted Daniel with respectful familiarity and Reilly had to remind herself that of course he was no longer Agent Forrest, and since leaving the FBI would have defaulted to his doctorate status.

'Evening.' Daniel's smile was tight, forced. 'Do you know if my son is still in the lab?'

'Yes, sir.' The officer nodded. 'Mr Ford's got them all staying late tonight, even the ones not usually on call.' He leaned forward. 'Something bad happened, I guess.'

Daniel nodded. 'Yes, something bad happened.' Quickly introducing Reilly again as an associate, he was buzzed through a nearby doorway and motioned for her to follow him.

As they moved down the corridor toward the crime lab, Reilly felt her mind absorb the new surroundings. The hallway was well lit, the floors clean white tile. So far, so familiar.

To her left, she saw a set of double doors with the lettering: 'Dr Owen Kase, Chief Medical Examiner.' A few feet further on were another set of sliding glass doors, these bearing three letters, and three words in smaller typeface.

Daniel knocked on one of the doors and, a moment later, they slid open. Reilly followed him in, eyes scanning the crime lab in her usual thorough manner.

The girl closest to the doors gave the two of them a dazzling smile and Reilly immediately knew that the redhead wasn't flirting; she was just one of those shiny, happy people who would've been grinning on the *Titanic*, talking about how excited she was for the opportunity to go for a swim.

She sincerely hoped the young woman was good at her job because people with her personality usually didn't do well in these types of circumstances. Then she checked herself, immediately reminded of Lucy, a GFU colleague back in Dublin, who was of a similar cheery disposition – or at least she had been until recently.

So she really should keep an open mind. Judging by the instruments in front of the young technician, the girl was analyzing dirt and other particulates, nothing particularly interesting.

The equipment was good, Reilly noted, some of it more up to date than the lab back in Dublin, some less so. Unlike the GFU one, though, the mass spectrometer looked absolute state of the art and she curled her fingers into fists, suppressing the urge to touch it. Like many women, she did like shiny things.

'Dad?' Todd's surprised voice caught Reilly's attention. 'What are you doing here?'

Whoah . . . Todd had grown up, Reilly thought, and then had to smile at her foolishness. Of course he'd changed. Almost a decade had passed since the last time she'd seen Daniel's son.

It wasn't that he necessarily looked older though, she realized, amending her original impression – more that his eyes looked tired, more world-weary.

The rest of him looked the same. Same face that had always been too pretty for a guy. Same ebony curls that made her want to run her fingers through them. Not because of any type of attraction, but more because they were there. Those curls just had that shiny texture that made everyone want to know if they were as soft as they looked. Kind of like a cat.

'The famous Reilly Steel.' Todd's eyes changed, a grin curving his lips upward. 'Steel by name, steel by nature. Dad mentioned he was having a house guest.'

'Todd,' she said, extending a hand. 'How have you been? I was so sorry to hear about your—'

'So Dad's got his prize pupil running interference already?' he muttered darkly. 'That didn't take long.'

'Reilly,' Daniel interjected before she could reply, and she assumed he hadn't noticed the barb. 'I'd like you to meet Bradley Ford. He's senior investigator here at the CSI unit.'

'Pleased to meet you.' Reilly smiled, eyes trailing over the other man. He had to be in his early forties, but he didn't look much older than her and Todd. And he was handsome, not in a teen-heartthrob kind of way, but with more of an exotic appeal. She wasn't looking for romance – she was a disaster at that kind of thing in any case – but she could definitely appreciate the view.

'Bradley,' Daniel continued, 'this is Reilly Steel.'

A look crossed Bradley's face and Reilly knew that for some reason he'd recognized her name. 'Well, it's an honor to meet you, Ms Steel.'

'Thank you.' She felt heat rising to her cheeks, wondering how and why her reputation had preceded her.

'Todd never mentioned that you were friends.'

'Daniel was my mentor at Quantico,' Reilly explained smoothly, 'and we've stayed close ever since.'

Bradley's expression and tone grew somber and he turned again to Daniel. 'I'm truly sorry for your loss, Dr Forrest, and let me assure you that the team will do everything they can to bring this killer to justice quickly.'

'Thank you.' The words were stiff.

'I hear you requested to be the one to inform the family? Understandable given your personal connection.' Bradley's sympathy was slowly turning into the familiar businesslike tone of an investigator addressing a family member.

'Yes. I thought it best that Holly's mother should hear the bad news from a friend.' Reilly saw Daniel tense and she knew what was coming next: the 'thank you and we'll take it from here' speech. Bradley didn't disappoint, though he said it far more nicely than others Reilly had heard before.

'Thank you for your assistance; as always, I know the detectives will be very grateful for your input.'

'Of course.' Daniel's response was polite but terse, and she noted how he didn't divulge to Bradley the news about the boyfriend, or the audition.

Out of the corner of her eye, she saw Todd's mouth flatten for just a moment and knew that he too had noted the barely-there current of tension beneath his father's voice.

Reilly wasn't fooled either. Daniel wasn't letting anything go. It didn't matter that he'd given the same speech to other cops and agents over the years. Forget protocol . . . nothing mattered to him right then but finding Holly's killer.

'So how was Alice?' Todd put his hand on his father's shoulder, acknowledging their shared grief, and Daniel's expression softened a bit. Father and son moved away to the side to discuss Mrs Young's reaction, and to console one another in the wake of the tragedy.

'So you're the same Reilly Steel who made Neil Pearce cry and brought on a nervous breakdown?' Bradley asked her.

She was surprised to hear him mention a defense attorney from her San Francisco days.

'How do you know Pearce?' she asked.

'I don't. But I'm still in touch with some California guys from the academy. It was the talk of the department at the time, as I recall.'

'Well, for what it's worth I didn't really make the guy cry,' Reilly said, shrugging. 'Though I think the guilty verdict did.' She looked at Bradley. 'He had a nervous breakdown?'

'Last I heard. After the incident with you, he basically stuck with low-profile cases he could plead out. I don't think he saw the inside of a courtroom for anything but arraignments and allocutions until three years ago. He must've decided to give it a try again – or maybe he just needed the money – because he took on a known drug dealer.' Bradley continued the story: 'When he tried cross-examining the arresting officer, the detective took a page from your book and called Pearce a dumbass. It must've hit a nerve because he completely flipped out. He started crying and yelling. Rumor had it, he even tried to take off his clothes, but he couldn't figure out his shoelaces. The judge had to declare a mistrial to let the defendant retain new council.'

'What happened to Pearce after that?' She was fascinated.

Bradley was nonchalant. 'Last I heard, he moved up north. So listen, I'd love to talk to you more about it sometime – maybe pick your brains a bit,' he added with a mischievous grin.

She laughed, suddenly realizing where the conversation had been leading. 'Really? That's the best line you've got? I was expecting something slick and original.'

His grin widened. 'I'll try harder next time.'

The smile was proving hard to resist. 'Sounds good.' What the hell. Just because she didn't want any romantic entanglements at the moment didn't mean she couldn't make new friends. And she was on vacation, remember?

'Could we have a few minutes, Bradley?' Todd spoke up then, his voice tight.

'Of course.' The somber expression on the senior investigator's face revealed he'd just realized how inappropriate his timing must've appeared. He hurried to make amends. 'I was actually going to go on a food run to the taco bus, clear my head, since we're going to be here for a while longer. Do you want anything?'

On her way in, Reilly had spotted a bright yellow taco truck just down the street from the station, and guessed it would be a huge favorite with the department. Todd shook his head; his pallid complexion and tired eyes suggested that he'd lost his appetite for the day.

Once Bradley left, Daniel glanced at the redhead across the lab and raised an eyebrow in an unspoken question. Todd lifted up a finger and called out to his colleague.

'Emilie, we need to talk in private. Do you mind?'

'No problem.' She pulled out a pair of earbuds from a drawer, stuck the end in her phone and the buds in her ears. She gave Todd a thumbs-up and, a moment later, was bobbing her head in time with something high energy. Reilly had her money on bubblegum pop.

'All of Emilie's clearances haven't come through yet,' he explained. 'Something about time spent in South America – so when we have anything she's not cleared for, she gets to wear headphones.' Todd's tone was brisk, businesslike, but Reilly sensed something deeper behind it. 'So, I assume you asked Alice some questions while you were there, probably had a sneak around the house too I'm guessing.' He glanced directly at Reilly, correctly deducing that this was the reason for her sudden appearance as Daniel's sidekick. 'Anything interesting?'

She looked at Daniel, who nodded for her to continue. 'Holly's room didn't indicate any trouble. It was fairly neat with a small amount of clutter. She had a picture of a young man that Mrs Young identified as . . .'

'Aaron Overton,' Todd supplied the name. 'He was victim number two.' He hesitated, before adding, 'Technically.'

'What do you mean, "technically"?' Daniel asked.

Reilly's heart sank, anticipating what was coming next. She'd been afraid of this. Holly's death wasn't a crime of passion by an ex-lover, and Reilly had a bad feeling it wasn't a mugging gone wrong either. Nothing quite that simple.

'Overton was shot by a police officer. One of ours.'

'But he couldn't have been the perp.' Daniel was shaking his head. 'Otherwise, there wouldn't be a murder investigation.'

'Dad, you know I can't . . .' Todd began, but he looked pained at having to keep any knowledge about the circumstances from his father.

'Tell us how Holly died,' Reilly surprised herself by asking. 'How they both died.'

Todd's face paled and she immediately wished she could take the request back. When, with a halting voice, he started to describe the scene he'd arrived at earlier that day, the desire to do so grew even stronger, but, of course, there was nothing she could do now, no way to un-hear the gruesome details.

And, as bad as it was for her to hear, it had to be so much worse for Daniel, who'd been like a father to Holly. And Todd . . . despite his apparent stoicism, Reilly's heart ached for him. No one should ever have to see a loved one mutilated like that.

By the time Todd fell silent, Reilly knew that her face was probably as white as his and she had the sudden need to sit down. She swallowed hard and clenched her teeth. She'd heard worse and she'd certainly seen worse.

Maybe.

'My God . . .' Daniel was equally horrified. He closed his eyes.

Todd looked at Reilly. 'Was there anything Mrs Young gave you that could tell us maybe where the two of them were in the hours leading up to their deaths?' Todd struggled to find his professional voice again.

Reilly answered so Daniel wouldn't have to. 'She said that they had gone to an audition that morning.'

'Do the detectives have any other leads?' Daniel asked after a beat, his voice hoarse.

'Dad.' Todd's eyes dropped, unable to meet his father's gaze. 'You know I can't. Bradley's barely letting me stay on the case, and unless the department want to bring you in . . .'

'Don't give me "can't".' Daniel's voice hardened and Reilly looked up at the rancor in his tone. 'This is Holly we're talking about. You've known her since she was a kid.'

'Which is exactly why I can't say anything.' Todd looked to Reilly for help, his expression beseeching. 'And even if we both weren't too close to this case, you know I couldn't. I've already said too much. If Bradley found out I gave information . . .'

Daniel took a step toward Todd, his hands clenching into fists. 'I worked for the FBI for nearly three decades and I'm on retainer with this department. My security clearance is so far above yours—'

'Was, Dad, it was.' Todd held his ground, his inherited temper flaring. 'You're not with the Bureau anymore and this isn't your case.'

Daniel took another step forward and Reilly knew she had to act before his frustration made him do something he couldn't take back. She slipped between the two men, facing Daniel, and put her hand on her friend's chest.

'Daniel.' She gave him a gentle push. 'Can I talk to you for a moment?' When he didn't answer, she pressed. 'Now.'

Still glaring at his son, he allowed Reilly to lead him away. As soon as they were out of earshot, he opened his mouth to speak, but she shook her head, effectively cutting him off.

'You know better.'

'But—' Daniel started to protest.

'How many times have you said "no" to a grief-stricken relative or friend?' Reilly interrupted. 'How many perps have you seen get off on a technicality or the implication of impropriety? Do you want to see the same thing happen to Holly's killer? Todd needs to do this by the book. At least until they ask for your help.'

'But I don't trust them on this,' Daniel confessed, keeping his voice low. 'The department's understaffed and overworked. I know of at least four other ongoing cases the detectives already have. This is going to get pushed back and the longer the trail's cold, the harder it's going to be to find this guy. They *need* my help.'

'Daniel.' Reilly's voice was soft. 'Bradley has everyone in the lab working late. That tells me they are making this a priority. And didn't you tell me yourself how good Todd is at his job? Do you honestly think he's going to miss something?'

Daniel sighed, his shoulders slumping in defeat. 'They're all good at their job, Reilly. But we don't need just good on this. We need great.'

Chapter 7

This one had been much easier than the last. He was rather impressed by his own learning curve. His hands shook with excitement. It was time to stop being passive and get right into the thick of it.

Now that he'd made his first big splash, it was time to show the world just what he could do.

His eyes narrowed as he examined the angle. Not quite right. He looked around the bathroom with distaste. What a dump. Granted, it was clean, but that was about the only positive thing he could say about it.

'How can you live here?'

A groan was his only answer and the only one he'd expected. The chloroform had worked wonderfully since he'd gotten the hang of it. He hadn't even needed it to get in the door. All he'd had to do was tell the stupid bitch who he was, and she'd all but tripped over herself inviting him in. Worked every time, as he knew it would.

Girls in this business were all the same.

This one appeared to be in her mid-twenties, dark hair though not precisely the right shade, and pretty enough. She was also fairly tall which was going to make this much easier. He smiled with satisfaction, pleased with his choice.

When he'd told her that there was something she had to do for him before he could consider her, she'd readily agreed. Although, judging by the tiny shorts and 'Damn Right I'm Sexy' T-shirt she'd been wearing when she opened the door, she'd had something else entirely in mind as a trade.

It didn't matter. Whatever she'd been thinking let him get close enough to do what he needed to do.

He stepped back and looked over the area with a critical eye. The bathroom was small, but had what he needed: a tub.

He crossed to the tub, gloved hands moving expertly over the wires, though he stopped short of touching the steaming water, the heat bringing a sheen of sweat to his face. Then he took a step back.

It was time.

Over the rubber gloves, he pulled on a new pair of ordinary black ones.

Then came the newest addition – a mask. He had too much work to do to risk his actual face being seen. The last thing he needed right now was the inconvenience of a police investigation.

He checked himself in the mirror, just to make sure he couldn't be identified. Pleased with his reflection, he moved on. After making sure everything was set up to his satisfaction, he squatted next to the girl and ran his hand over her hair.

'Time to wake up, Sleeping Beauty,' he whispered, keeping his voice low. The girl moaned; eyelids fluttering as she struggled to open them. Perfect timing.

He grabbed a handful of her hair and stood. As he dragged her from the corner to the tub, she began to move, body responding to the pain in her head. Noises fell from her lips, but nothing loud or intelligible enough to cause a problem. The walls in the apartment might have been paper-thin, but the pounding music from the party down the hall was laying a rather loud soundtrack to proceedings.

He manhandled the young woman into position, easily brushing aside her attempts to push him away as she slowly returned to consciousness. His fingers tightened in her hair and he took a deep breath, excitement coiling hot and hard in his stomach. He was going to have to do this again.

'What . . . ?'

That was his cue. He shoved the girl's face into the now bubbling water. Her limbs flailed, fingers scrabbling against the wet porcelain. Her screams were muffled and the smell of boiling flesh filled his nostrils. He forced her head further under the water, wincing as the hot liquid soaked into his gloves, but not letting up. There was always a price to pay for art.

Besides, the thrill of the moment was more than making up for the pain.

All too soon, the girl's struggles weakened and the only bubbles in the tub were from the heat. He released her, letting her face stay under, dark hair fanning out in the water.

He stood, panting, every cell in his body humming as adrenaline raced through him. Logically, he knew his fingers were scalded, but his brain wasn't processing anything negative at the moment. This had been the most exhilarating experience of his life. The girl's muscles were twitching, one involuntary spasm sending her arm over the edge of the tub. Her hand splashed down into the water, the sound drawing him from his reverie.

He reached down and grabbed a handful of wet hair. Balancing himself carefully, he pulled her from the water, her body somehow heavier in death.

The skin was red and blistered, swollen to the point of making the girl unrecognizable. Beautiful . . .

He carefully lowered her to the floor, not wanting to damage his prize.

He took a step backward and, for a moment, he just stood there, admiring his work. Then reluctantly, he slipped off his gloves and placed them on the floor next to the doorway. They'd never touched his skin so there'd be no trace of him on the fabric, and were common enough that they could be found at any one of a hundred stores.

No, it would be much riskier to take them with him. The gloves couldn't be linked to him unless he took them, but they were easily linked to the crime scene, most likely covered with the young woman's hair and maybe even skin cells.

Much safer to leave them.

He slipped his mask into the pocket of his jacket and exited the apartment, all the time keeping his stride even, looking for all the world like someone who belonged.

Even if anyone had been looking into the grubby hallway at three in the morning, all they would see was an average-looking man leaving a girl's apartment so as to avoid risking an awkward morning-after conversation. He doubted a single person would have even been able to describe him.

Soon, though, everyone in the world would know who he was.

Chapter 8

'Everything all right?' Bradley handed a bag of takeout food to Emilie, though he was speaking to Todd.

'Fine.' Todd knew his reply was clipped, but he really didn't feel like talking about it. He'd already got close to the line by letting his dad notify Mrs Young, but knew he'd overstepped it by explaining to him and Reilly how the victims had died – though Bradley didn't know the last part.

He knew that he couldn't push his luck by sharing any other information about the investigation. Not that they had much to share.

'I see you decided to look over the camera equipment,' Bradley said, ignoring the tension in the room as he pulled out a thickly rolled burrito from the bag. 'Find anything?'

Todd carefully set down one of the cameras found at the crime scene and stripped off his gloves. 'This is an expensive piece of equipment, but nothing that can't be bought at a local Radio Shack. The serial numbers have all been burned off with some form of acid, which is tricky without damaging the equipment.'

'So it's not his first rodeo.' Bradley spoke through a mouthful of chili beef. At Todd's look, he said, 'Sorry, been watching too many Westerns lately. Go on.'

Todd continued, 'All of the equipment's clean. No trace of the acid used, though I'd guess it'd be nitric. Easy to obtain, hard to track. No prints, no partials or trace. Nothing we can use. He probably wiped everything down, and used gloves when handling.'

'Did you check for a memory card?'

He nodded. 'Clean as well. And empty.'

Bradley took another bite of food before replying, 'If the memory card was empty, then there's a good chance the recording was transmitted somewhere else.'

Todd swore as the penny dropped. 'The bastard was watching.'

'Let's get a tech in here and see if we can get something that way.' Bradley tossed his chopsticks back into the box.

'Is anyone even working tonight?' Todd asked.

'Actually, I've got someone better who owes me.' Bradley grabbed his cell. A few seconds later, he spoke. 'Peni? I'm cashing in that favor.'

Twenty minutes later, a young woman who looked more like a model than a computer tech entered the lab. Nearly six feet tall, with short black hair and obsidian eyes, she was exactly the type of woman Todd would've been hitting on under different circumstances. Not, he had to admit, that he limited himself to a specific type. It was more about the intelligent fire he saw in the eyes, no matter the color. At the moment, he had a pair of light gray ones sneaking into his thoughts; light gray framed by blond hair, sparkling as perfectly shaped lips curved upward in a smile.

Bradley's words cut through the reverie. 'Peni Westmore from the Cyber Crimes Unit, meet Todd Forrest.'

'Daniel Forrest's son, impressive. Though no doubt there are some latent daddy issues.' She winked at Todd. 'Another time maybe. Now, where's this stuff I'm supposed to take a look at?'

Todd motioned to the table, amused despite himself. He liked the way she handled herself even if he didn't care for the mention of his father. Still, he guessed he should have been used to that by now. It had been hard enough trying to overcome the specter of the respected criminologist when Daniel was still at Quantico. But when he'd moved down to the beach house permanently last year and started working with the department, all bets were off.

'Am I looking for something specific?' she asked, her tone becoming more professional.

'Pretty much anything you can give us is good.' Todd stood and stretched. His joints were stiff from sitting so long.

'This makes us even now, Bradley.' Peni pulled on a pair of gloves.

'I don't know about that . . .' he said.

'I do. I'm missing Ivy's poetry reading. Do you know how pissed she's going to be?'

'Sleeping on the couch tonight, then?' he grinned and Todd turned to look, intrigued by this revelation about her sexuality. He never would have guessed.

'Thanks to you.'

Bradley chuckled. 'Just yell if you find something interesting.'

'Erm, sir?' Emilie cleared her throat across the room. 'I finished the analysis comparison you asked for. Only some of the sand and debris from the bodies matches the soil sample you took from the scene.'

'And the rest?' Bradley asked, all playfulness gone now.

'Dr Kase found dried leaves and wood slivers not consistent with the crime scene photos,' Emilie continued. 'In fact, it's not consistent with any beach.'

'Could all of that have come from being transported in the back of the truck?' Todd asked.

'Get me a sample to match and I can tell you for certain,' Emilie said. 'But that's as good a theory as any. What I can tell you is that the extra sand that doesn't match with the crime scene has a higher concentration of quartz, which is consistent with a stretch of beach approximately fifteen miles from where the bodies were found.'

'Good work,' Bradley said.

'The trace came back on the 911 call too,' she went on.

Todd sighed. 'Let me guess, burner cell, no way to track who made it.'

Emilie nodded. 'And it hasn't been used since that call was made.'

'Do you think we can get a hold of the call?'

'I'll see what I can do,' Emilie said as she returned to her desk.

'Damn.' Peni sounded impressed.

'What?' Bradley and Todd turned their attention to the cyber expert.

She looked up from the laptop. 'This guy's good.'

'So he was watching then?' Bradley said, crossing to his friend.

'He wasn't just watching.' Peni pointed to a set of specs. 'See this here? Your unsub sent the footage to an email address. This is some serious encryption.' She shook her head. 'I can't crack it tonight though, not with this laptop.'

'What do you need?' Bradley asked.

'My own equipment.' Her expression was serious. 'Whoever this guy is, he knows what he's doing.'

The phone rang and, as Bradley reached for it, Todd mulled over the new information. The killer had come prepared with chloroform, and had stolen a truck that could transport the victims. He'd set up cameras to not only watch the kill he'd staged, but to keep a record of it, for what purpose Todd wasn't sure he wanted to know. Then there was the murder itself. This wasn't just a garden-variety killing. No knives, no guns, no suffocation.

This was . . . Todd searched for the word he wanted. Dramatic, he decided. Holly's killer was creative and intelligent.

Never a good combination.

The following morning at the beach house, Reilly swung her legs over the edge of the bed, rubbing her temples. The jet lag was still affecting her as it was hours later than she usually woke in Dublin, and still way too early in Clearwater, but since she was up she might as well get something out of it and go for a run.

A shower and food could wait for the moment. There was something about sunnier climes that made her crave physical exercise and outdoor activity, and it had been years since she'd run on the beach. At least the temperature should be cooler first thing in the morning than it had been yesterday.

She thought about what time it was in Ireland now and what they were getting up to back there. It reminded her of her last conversation with Chris before she'd left. He'd been taken aback by her decision to head to the States, albeit with clearance from Inspector O'Brien.

'A little sudden, isn't it? How long will you be gone?' he'd asked, frowning.

Reilly didn't want to admit to him that she'd been feeling homesick for months. 'A couple of weeks at the most. I'm long overdue a vacation as it is, and it beats sitting around here waiting for O'Brien to give the nod for me to come back. The chief says six weeks is typical but you and

I both know it could be more than that depending on how InternalAffairs want to play it.'

'A couple of weeks at a beach house sounds like heaven – any room in your suitcase for me? Though I'm not sure Agent Forrest would be too thrilled,' he joked wryly. He'd met Daniel that time the American had travelled to Dublin and the two men hadn't exactly bonded.

She and Chris had become quite close throughout that particular investigation – their first – and Reilly wondered if he'd viewed Daniel as some kind of rival. It was always so hard to tell with Chris. Open and straightforward in so many ways, he was like a closed book when it came to emotions.

As was she, of course, Reilly admitted. Which was possibly the main reason the two of them had been dancing around their attraction to one another for the last three years. Or was she seeing something that wasn't actually there? Reilly had no idea. All she knew was that she'd miss being around Chris Delaney when she was gone.

'You're as bad as I am; I know you couldn't survive more than a few days away from the job,' she'd teased him.

'Don't be so sure. This murder investigation is a complete mess. Until we find out what that powder was, we've got little else to go on.'

'What about the victim, did she die from this stuff then?'

'No, ME listed cause of death as respiratory failure.'

'Seems strange.' Then Reilly shook the thoughts away, reminding herself that through her own actions, she was out of this particular investigation and any other GFU-related cases for the next month at least.

She was of course anxious to find out what the powder had been, but for different reasons, although she guessed that if the substance had been dangerously toxic, she wouldn't have been back on her feet so quickly. Still, she asked Chris to let her know when the lab results came back.

Now, running along the beach, she could barely breathe in the muggy air as her feet sought out the harder packed sand, but she forced herself to keep going. She was stopped in her tracks a little way down the beach by the sight of a small pod of dolphins frolicking in the glassy gulf waters only a few feet away. Surprised at the unexpected but delightful sight, it put a spring in her step and gave her the impetus to keep going a little longer. And despite the insane temperature and humidity, as well as her lack of fitness, she managed to take in five miles.

By the time Reilly ran back down the beach toward the house, she was drenched with sweat but her mind was finally empty. Stripping off her running gear and down to her underwear, she launched herself into the small pool, relishing the immediate refreshment, though in truth the water wasn't much cooler than the outside temperature. She remained in the water for a few more minutes, watching the pelicans and egrets gliding across the gulf waters, occasionally swooping down for breakfast as the sun gradually rose higher in the sky. Man, there was so much to be said for a warmer climate.

But speaking of breakfast . . .

Getting out of the pool, Reilly tiptoed back upstairs to her room, hoping not to wake Daniel at this early hour. No doubt the horrible events of yesterday evening would have given him a troubled sleep and she hoped he'd managed to grab a few hours' rest.

A little while later, her still-wet hair was twisted up behind her head and the perfume of mango shower wash – newly bought from the local CVS on the way home last night – lingered on her skin.

There was also a lot to be said for the therapeutic value of sweet-scented cosmetics, and Reilly's sensitive nose appreciated them more than most.

To her surprise, Daniel was already in the kitchen making coffee when she entered. He poured her a cup and she took a sip of the dark, aromatic liquid and sighed, wrapping her hands around the mug. Boy, had she missed American coffee.

'How are you feeling today?' she asked.

'Better, now that I know I can officially do something.' When she looked enquiringly at him, he elaborated. 'Alice called this morning. She wants me to investigate Holly's case.'

'Are you sure that's a good idea?'

But she knew it was a stupid question. Daniel was already knee-deep in his god-daughter's investigation, her mother's request notwithstanding. And she had to admit that if she were in his shoes, she would do the very same.

'So I was wondering . . . did you have any plans for today?' he asked, in a tone Reilly knew only too well.

She eyed him suspiciously, playing along. 'Well, I was actually thinking about working on my tan. I've got so pale it's embarrassing. Why?'

He handed her a bagel slathered in fat-free cream cheese. 'I thought you might like to come and see the office – *my* office.'

'Nice try, but it won't work, you know.'

'What?' He was all innocence.

'The not so subtle recruitment drive. I'm on vacation, remember?'

'Exactly. And last I checked, sight-seeing was a major part of that.' He grinned. 'So let me give you the grand tour . . .'

Chapter 9

Todd had heard his phone buzzing, the annoying ringtone he'd set for his boss repeating for the fourth time, dragging him from sleep. Swearing, he'd fumbled with the phone. Bradley wasn't the type to call in the early hours and especially after such a late night, unless there was an emergency. That didn't really make Todd feel any less annoyed. He swore again as he saw the time.

'Sorry to wake you but we've got something.' Bradley's voice sounded just as weary as Todd felt, though his partner's words were enough to drive the last of the sleep from his mind. He swung his legs over the side of his bed and switched his phone to speaker.

'Go ahead.' Todd crossed to his bathroom. He splashed cold water on his face. His sleep had been restless enough that he wasn't sure that being woken was a bad thing. Images of bloody Russian dolls and little girls with pigtails had danced behind his eyelids and haunted his dreams.

'A call came in about a couple of dead bodies found a few miles up at a quiet non-residential area along Belleair Beach, not far from Clearwater,' Bradley told him. 'And a cop by the side of a road. The officer was halfway between Belleair and yesterday's crime scene. Apparently, he called in a traffic stop, not too long before that 911 call reporting a man beating his girlfriend.'

That was the call that had tipped them off about Holly's murder and ostensibly from the killer, seeing as there had been nothing of the sort.

Bradley and Todd decided to split up, with the senior investigator taking the murdered police officer. A dead cop was always difficult and required diplomacy and delicacy, and Todd wasn't sure if he could provide that after an almost all-nighter at work and the couple of hours' sleep he'd grabbed.

He was also still smarting from his father's behavior at the lab yesterday evening, insinuating that the department wasn't good enough, that they needed help.

His father had always been meddlesome. He just couldn't leave things alone, couldn't let Todd be an adult. Pretty much everyone assumed that Daniel was the reason Todd had made it this far. Sometimes he suspected his dad believed that too. He just wanted to prove that he could do this on his own; it was one of the reasons he'd taken the job in Tampa, far enough away from Daniel's stomping ground, but familiar to Todd, who'd spent so many childhood summers here. But then, of course, Daniel had to up and retire to

Clearwater, where once again his shadow loomed large.

Todd didn't need his dad's help to be a good investigator: he'd proved himself capable of that all by himself.

Then again, reason countered, Daniel Forrest was the best criminalist in the business. Or had been. It couldn't hurt to get his take on things, Todd reasoned, not if they wanted to catch Holly's killer as soon as possible.

Still, his father had had no business trying to get information from Alice Young before the detectives could get a handle on it. And it didn't matter if someone close to him had been one of the victims. To insinuate that Todd and the department didn't know how to do their job was just insulting. He'd cared about Holly too.

Now, he forced himself to think about this new crime scene and if it was indeed connected.

The couple didn't look like Holly and Aaron, Todd decided as he carefully circled the bodies. Also mid-twenties but the similarities stopped there. The man was huge. Six-foot-two, easily 240 pounds. It was impossible to say what color his hair was, what with all the caked blood from the head wound.

The woman was much smaller. Barely over five feet and if she'd been a hundred pounds soaking wet, Todd would've been shocked. Her body showed no visible signs of trauma.

He set aside his camera and picked up his kitbag. The first thing to go to was the bloody rock next to the man's body. It wasn't going to take the medical examiners long to confirm it as the murder weapon. Aside from the blood and brain matter on the rock, its edge was the same size and shape as the concave wound in the side of the man's skull.

Todd leaned closer to the female victim. Her mouth was slightly open and he could see something caught between her front teeth. Taking out his tweezers, he carefully extracted the fiber.

'What is that?' Detective Mark Reed spoke up from behind him.

'Looks like a fiber.' Todd slipped it into the bag.

'A fiber?' Reed echoed as he crouched down next to Todd. His eyes narrowed as he studied it.

'I'm willing to bet that it came from a towel soaked in chloroform.' Todd's knees popped as he stood.

'Why's that?'

'Towel fibers soaked with chloroform were found in the mouths of the other couple from before.' Todd crossed to the male victim and bent over him. A moment later, he held up another fiber.

The detective turned, studying the scene, a thoughtful expression on his face.

'What are you thinking?' Todd asked.

'The path,' Mark said, motioning to it, 'leads down to a public beach. Maybe the couple comes up here to get a little alone time, and the killer jumps them.'

Todd nodded slowly, seeing where the detective was headed. 'He kills these two; the woman with chloroform, the man with a rock. Drags the bodies out of sight and then waits for the other two. But why kill them? Case of mistaken identity, maybe?'

'Which begs the question,' Mark mused, 'did he know the other two victims from yesterday and waited here specifically for them, or was it random?'

Daniel's office suite was located in downtown Clearwater, and looked like the private doctors' offices Reilly had seen up north: small, brick and more or less nondescript. Letters on a plaque out front spelled out 'Forrest Consultations' in plain white block print.

Inside, the lobby was tastefully decorated in various shades of beige and brown. A couch sat along one wall, two chairs against the other, and a table between them. A few of the usual fake-but-looks-real plants sat in the corners. A receptionist's desk faced the door, its style simple but elegant. The whole thing was clean and professional, nothing less than what Reilly expected. The friendly woman at the front desk also met her expectations.

'Daniel speaks very highly of you.' The Cuban accent was faint, but there. 'It is nice to finally put a face to the name.'

Reilly gave an embarrassed smile. She hated compliments; never knew quite how to take them.

Daniel stepped in to save her. 'Teresa's little brother Tomas works as a part-time investigator for me,' he said. 'He's finishing up a Fine Arts degree and I'm hoping I'll be able to hire him full-time after he graduates.'

'Our mother would like that as well.' Teresa gave Reilly a warm smile. 'Tomas is the baby in the family and Mama doesn't want him going anywhere.'

Reilly's smile faltered as a familiar ghost waved from the shadows of her mind. She pushed it away and forced a return smile. It felt weak, but was enough. Then the phone rang and Daniel motioned for Reilly to follow him. Giving Teresa a half-wave goodbye, Reilly followed her friend down the hallway.

'That's my office.' He motioned to a door nearby, but kept walking past it toward a set of double doors at the end of the corridor. 'And this is the lab.'

Reilly let out a low whistle as she stepped into the room. It wasn't as large as the CSI lab in Tampa had been, but the toys were definitely nicer. Expensive comparison microscopes, six different computers, a centrifuge near a stainless steel refrigerator, and . . .

'Is that an EDD?' Reilly couldn't help but sound impressed. She'd wanted an electrostatic detection device back in Dublin but it had been deemed an unnecessary extravagance.

'Daniel does like pretty things,' said a voice from the far corner of the room, pulling Reilly's attention from the equipment.

'Reilly, meet Shawn Meyers, my forensics expert,' Daniel said. 'Shawn, this is Reilly Steel.'

'Hey there.' The slight widening of Shawn's hazel eyes as Reilly nodded a greeting told her that he too had recognized her name. Did Daniel really talk about her that much?

'At any given time, we can have up to five cases that we're working on,' Daniel explained, gesturing around the room. 'Generally, we're called in by the local PD or, occasionally, the nearest FBI field office when there's a backlog. Sometimes they bring me in for behavioral expertise if one of their profiling people is out.'

'But why the lab?' Reilly asked.

'Most of our work is on behalf of private companies – for insurance fraud, mostly. We're also used when a lawyer requests that an outside source runs tests or looks over results. Most of the time, if we're called into court, we're expert witnesses for the prosecution, but we can also testify for the defense. And one of the reasons we have a good reputation is because I've testified for both sides. I stand by my findings, no matter which side likes them.' Daniel's cellphone rang then, interrupting. As he reached for it, he gestured for Reilly to take a look around.

He didn't have to tell her twice. She walked the perimeter, pausing to admire each piece of equipment, lingering near the EDD.

She'd love to see it in action.

'Christ . . . !' Daniel slammed his hand against the wall nearby, and Reilly jumped, spinning around.

One look at Daniel's face and she knew. Holly's murderer had already struck again.

Chapter 10

'About five-thirty this morning, a building super called 911 after responding to an anonymous tip that one of his tenants had drugs on the premises,' Bradley informed Todd, who was on his way back from the beach. They were both making their way to the newest crime scene. 'When no one responded to the super's knocks, he let himself in, which is when he saw water from the bathroom soaking into the carpet. Tenant was DOA.'

'Drowned?' Todd asked, into the phone.

'From what I was told, looks like drowning may be a secondary cause of death.' Bradley paused a moment before continuing. 'The water was apparently hot.'

'How hot?' Bile rose in Todd's throat.

'Detective Sampson said it looked like it had been boiling.'

The police had already blocked off the scene by the time Todd arrived, their yellow and black caution tape fluttering in the wind.

As he flashed his badge at the rookie holding the line, Bradley's SUV parked nearby, Todd waited for the senior investigator, scanning the crowd that had inevitably gathered.

Some criminals liked to see the results of their handiwork. He might not have been a profiler like his dad, but Todd knew a trick or two. Unfortunately, it looked like just the usual reporters, unemployed lurkers and morbid teenagers.

Bradley pinched the bridge of his nose, a sure sign of fatigue.

Todd had come to recognize his friend's gestures over the years, particularly that one. He took a small bottle from his pocket as they stepped onto the elevator. 'I think I may need to pick up some more energy drinks.' He took a swig, grimaced, and said, 'Maybe we should invest in the company that makes this. Shoot for early retirement?'

'Give me coffee any day.' Bradley raised his Styrofoam cup. 'That stuff tastes like goat piss.'

Todd quirked an eyebrow. 'I've always wondered why people say that. How do you know what goat piss tastes like?'

Bradley gave him a grin, a tired one, but a grin nonetheless. 'You weren't you in a fraternity then?'

'That's just wrong.' Todd shook his head. 'Seriously, where do you come up with this stuff?'

Bradley shrugged. 'A gift, I guess.'

When the elevator doors opened on the third floor, Detective Sampson was waiting, her expression more grim than usual. Any good humor they'd managed to muster up immediately disappeared.

'Daphne Angelo, twenty-four, lived alone. Neighbors say she was a wannabe actress.' She led Todd and Bradley down the hall to the tiny apartment where half a dozen uniforms milled just outside the door, then left them standing by the entrance to the apartment.

'Well, that was illuminating; she's obviously still pissed at you over Ralph,' Bradley muttered as he tossed his now-empty cup into a nearby trashcan. He pulled on a pair of gloves and turned to Todd. 'Ready?'

Todd took a moment to mentally steel himself for what he was about to see. 'As ever.'

By the time they emerged from the building, it was after lunchtime, but both Bradley and Todd had lost whatever appetite they'd had when they awakened that morning.

The ride back to the lab was silent, completely devoid of the normal dark, morbid jokes or witty banter that usually accompanied a ride from a crime scene. Todd didn't think even a good sense of humor would be able to keep them all sane by the time this was done.

They'd both seen their fair share of violent, gruesome deaths. The difference was, the motive was usually fairly clear, especially in the extreme cases. Battered wife takes pickaxe to abusive husband. Jealous spouse runs over wife fourteen times. Todd's mind immediately went to the one they'd been working when they'd gotten the call about Holly. Gangs and drug dealers sending messages via executions and dismemberments. Rape victims killed so they couldn't identify their attackers. Robberies gone bad. There'd even been a man who'd claimed an alien overlord had commanded him to stab three prostitutes to death and mutilate their corpses.

All of these cases had some obvious motive. Money, sex, anger, insanity. The victims had some sort of connection either to their killer or to each other. Todd couldn't see the motive or the pattern in their current case.

Six dead in the last two days. The two couples at the beach, the police officer and the girl from the apartment just now. Three men, three women. All of varying ages. One in her own home; three left where they'd been murdered; two moved to a secondary site.

Todd was still mulling it over when they arrived back at the lab.

Emilie was at her computer when he and Bradley entered. The smile she flashed their way was less brilliant than usual, and Todd knew it had to do with the fact that she, like them, had left late and been called in early.

He'd been wondering how long it would take for the horror of what they saw to break through the redhead's bubbly persona. It always made him a little sad when the newbies hit reality, but it was necessary. Most of them didn't last long afterward, but he hoped that Emilie would be the exception. She was a sweet girl and good at her job. If she could get through this case, she'd make it all the way.

Also already in the lab was cyber-crimes expert, Peni. This morning, she was looking decidedly comfy in a pair of gray cut-off sweats and a red tank top. With her running shoes, she looked more like she was preparing for a work-out rather than examining equipment for the next few hours. She snapped on a pair of gloves and grabbed a bag from one of the new bins – the cameras they'd just taken from the latest crime scene.

'Hmm . . . new toys,' she commented, examining them.

'So they're not the same as the other ones?' Bradley's tone was more serious than normal.

Todd wasn't surprised. There was something about seeing a young woman boiled like a lobster and set out on display that tended to take the humor out of the situation. This girl's death had been much more drawn out than Holly's. And while there was always the off chance that she'd already been dead when her head was put in the water, he seriously doubted it. The autopsy would show for sure.

'No.' Peni turned the bag over in her hands a few times before passing it to Todd.

He took it, half-listening as she explained the visible differences between the equipment. Then he carefully dusted the outside for prints.

'All have the capability of sending the video footage to a receiver.' Peni tucked her long legs up underneath her. 'So I feel pretty safe in assuming that he did the same with this video that he did with the other, and sent the data to an email address. The larger of the two cameras from the first crime scene is specifically designed for long shots, which explains why there had been a tripod set up. The camera from the interior of the truck is smaller, cheaper. The further away it is, the more the quality of the picture deteriorates. The one you have here, my guess, is about halfway between the two. But, if I'm not mistaken, it's going to be a bit more expensive than either of the other two.'

'Why's that?' Todd carefully removed the casing to check inside for any trace evidence.

'Because that casing is designed to withstand some water exposure,' Peni explained.

Bradley swore, raking his hand through his hair. 'He wanted to make sure it wasn't ruined when he drowned her.'

Chapter 11

Reilly and Daniel sat in silence in the upstairs Tampa PD reception area as they waited for Todd, both lost in their own thoughts.

Reilly felt sick, the coffee and bagel from earlier now roiling in her stomach. She'd dealt with countless murderous nut-jobs in the near-decade she'd been in the job. None of them had ever torn a victim in half and then boiled another one. Vacation or not, she would offer whatever help she could to get this bastard.

Daniel had claimed one of the two nearby chairs while Reilly had chosen to sit on the far end of the waiting area couch. They sat in silence, watching the news story break in a special report on the TV close by.

The handsome, dark-haired, on-the-ground reporter wore a plastic expression as he relayed information from the street across from an apartment building. In the background, a half-dozen or so uniforms could be seen milling about outside.

'At this point, we're still trying to separate fact from fiction, but what we do know is that a young woman from this apartment complex was found dead early this morning and, judging by the seemingly excessive presence of local law enforcement, it's safe to say that the police suspect foul play. This raises the question, are the streets of Tampa safe?'

When Todd entered the lobby, he frowned at the television for a moment before diving right in. 'Six bodies, and enough forensics to keep twenty people busy for a year.' He looked from Reilly to Daniel. 'So whatever this is about, I really don't have time—'

'Sit down, son, please.' Daniel's anger from the night before had since melted away. He turned away from the TV. On screen, the reporter was attempting to question an annoyed-looking Detective Julie Sampson as she climbed into her car. 'And you know what it's about.'

'Dad, I get it. I want to find Holly's killer as much as you do – it's why I kept you in the loop about this new find. But you know I can't break protocol.' Todd sat on the open end of the couch. 'Not if I want to stay on the case. Bradley's watching me like a hawk as it is.'

'Just talk to us.' Daniel leaned forward, elbows on his knees, palms pressed together. 'I spoke to Alice earlier. She wants me on the case.'

'Dad . . .' Todd shook his head as if wrestling with his conscience, but then, with a sudden efficiency that surprised Reilly, he quietly ran through what had happened since the day before: the cop and couple found this morning, then the poor girl from earlier, drowned in boiling water, and the cameras found at two of the crime scenes. As he spoke, Reilly found herself watching him, surprised by the maturity with which he was handling himself. She could see a lot of his father in him.

'Bradley has a computer whiz from cyber crimes tracking down where the footage was sent. She's found an email address registered to Thailand, but is still running the IP addresses to see if she can get a point of origin.' Todd stared at his hands. 'What I can't figure out is why the cameras? I understand the cop. That was unplanned, bad luck, probably. But why kill two at the beach, then snatch two more and kill them somewhere else in a completely different manner?'

'How were the two at the beach killed?' Reilly asked.

Todd looked up, appearing startled to see her, almost as if he'd forgotten she was there. 'The medical examiner hasn't started on the autopsies yet, but unless there's a complete shock in store for us, I'd say the woman died from a chloroform OD, the man from blunt force trauma to the head. I bagged a pretty blood rock. I also pulled a couple of fibers from their mouths that I think are going to match ones Dr Kase found in Hol. Kase said they were likely from a towel soaked in chloroform.'

'Maybe you're looking at three unintentional murders while in the process of committing the first one . . .' Reilly mused.

'You think the couple at the beach might have been an accident?' Daniel asked.

'Having not seen the evidence, I can't be sure, but . . .' She turned to Todd. 'The killer goes to the beach to find his victims and happens upon the first couple. He tries to knock them out, but there's a problem, something goes wrong. Maybe he uses too much chloroform on the woman, maybe not enough on the man and has to hit him with something. But he needs live ones for what he wants, so he waits for another couple.'

Todd shrugged. 'Could explain why there was no camera at the beach site. He never intended to commit a murder there.'

'Which also means he could've made mistakes there.'

'She's right,' Daniel said. 'As detailed as two of the crime scenes have been, the murders he didn't intend to commit would probably be where the perp would slip up. You need a profile on this guy,' he said to his son, leaving Todd in no illusion that he was already working on it. Once a profiler, always a profiler. 'It will at least help you figure out what evidence is the most important, prioritize what you look at.'

He looked again at Reilly. 'Knowing what we know, anything else hit you off the bat?'

She thought again for a moment about what Todd had told them. 'If the police officer and the couple on the beach were unintentional, the murder weapons – especially the rock – will be the most likely to hold any clues to his identity because usage would have been impulsive, unplanned.'

'So while he's organized and detail oriented, he doesn't plan for contingencies,' Daniel added, his mind fully focused on the killer's probable motives and intentions. 'While most likely not his first crime, he's still relatively new to the game.'

'Not his first rodeo . . .' Todd whispered absently, then shook himself out it. 'Sorry, just something Bradley said before.'

'The locations with the cameras, the planned ones, those are going to tell us what he's really about,' Reilly theorized. 'And why what he's doing is important enough for him to make a record of it.'

'Staged,' Todd said. 'Both locations, the bodies, everything looked like he'd put it all into place. Like he was setting up a scene for maximum dramatic effect.'

Daniel stood up and put his hands on his hips as he paced, a look of intense concentration on his face. 'I don't think there's going to be any connection between the victims other than the two couples' relationship to each other.'

'Why so?' Todd asked.

But even as Daniel said it, Reilly figured it out. 'If the killer had originally tried to take a couple before Holly and Aaron, then they had been a crime of opportunity.'

Daniel nodded. 'Agreed. With Holly and her boyfriend' – a muscle in his jaw twitched when he mentioned his goddaughter's name – '*how* they died seems to be more important than who they were. He would've had to take the time to set everything up before finding his victims. And with the other, the boiling victim, if already he knew she lived alone, he could take more time to set things up after he got into the apartment.'

Reilly nodded this time, adding to Daniel's budding profile. 'If he's taken this much time and care to set up those deaths, he might not be keeping them just for himself. Maybe he's hoping for an audience?'

'It would take quite an ego to do that,' Daniel said. 'Someone who's sharing isn't going to stay quiet very long.'

'You think he's going to start bragging?' Todd asked.

'Wouldn't surprise me.' Daniel stopped and faced the pair on the couch. 'You've got the usual white male, late twenties to late thirties. Highly creative with a flair for the dramatic. He's not trying to hide or be subtle. Arrogant. High IQ with an eye for detail, but acts impulsively when something unexpected happens. After that mistake with the couple at the beach, he took a chance waiting for another more suitable possibility. Same applies with killing the cop. So he's willing to take risks to get what he wants.'

'A dangerous combination.' Reilly ran her hand through her hair.

'Doesn't matter.' Todd's voice had taken on an unfamiliar hard note. 'He killed Holly. Alice won't need your help, Dad. *I'm* going to find him.'

Despite herself, Reilly was impressed. She'd heard it said that a man's true character was found in adversity and, if that was the case, then Todd Forrest was turning out to be something more than she'd originally thought.

'I think I've got something.'

Much later, at the lab, Todd turned to look at Emilie as she spoke, his eyes bleary. It was late in the evening after a very long day and spirits were flagging.

'The gloves found at the apartment earlier, I found some skin flakes.'

'We have DNA?' Todd felt a wild hope rise in his chest but Emilie's forehead wrinkled and his heart sank. Of course not. It couldn't be that easy.

'Not necessarily. The inside of the gloves had a fine dusting of powder consistent with latex gloves, so anything inside the black gloves was most likely deposited there from the outside of the latex ones. The skin flakes were on the outside of the black gloves.'

'It's the victim's skin then,' Bradley cut in.

'Again, not necessarily.' Emilie nervously twisted a strand of hair around her finger. 'The skin appears to be old. Also, while the gloves themselves are damp, the flakes show no exposure to moisture.'

'So where did they come from?' Todd asked.

'That's just it.' Emilie shook her head. 'I'm not sure. I'm running the DNA now, but even if we do get a hit, I won't know how that person connects to the case. Killer, accomplice, victim . . . unless I find something else, I don't know how much help it's going to be.'

'Great,' Todd muttered.

'And there's something else.' Emilie frowned. 'The amount of moisture still present in the fabric of the right-handed glove indicates that the fingers and at least part of the hand itself were in the water.'

Bradley's mouth flattened into a thin line. 'He held her head under.'

'You're telling me that while drowning the victim, our perp stuck his hand into boiling water and held it there?' Bradley stared at Emilie.

'It's the only way to explain why the fabric was still wet,' Emilie said. 'Common sense says he would've yanked his hand out, but the fibers show thorough saturation. The glove was held in the water for a considerable amount of time before it was removed.'

Silence fell after Emilie finished. It was Todd who finally said what all of them were thinking: 'Who the hell is this guy?'

As darkness fell, Reilly sat alone on the deck at the beach house, listening to the waves lap the shore. After their return from Tampa, and following the information from Todd, Daniel had retired to his study to work on a basic profile for the investigative team.

Her cellphone buzzed and she bit her lip as she looked at the display. Taking a deep breath, she answered the call.

'Hey, Dad . . .'

'I've been trying to get a hold of you for days now.' Mike Steel's voice held no accusation, but that didn't stop her from feeling a stab of guilt. 'And when I couldn't reach you on the mobile phone or the one at your flat, I tried your office. Imagine my surprise when they told me that you were on leave and in Florida! What's going on, honey?'

Wincing, she quickly filled her father in on the work incident back in Dublin and her subsequent enforced leave. 'I didn't want to ruin your holiday by worrying about me when there was nothing to worry about. So after a few days lazing around, I got bored and I decided to get some sunshine.'

'OK, but why didn't you call me anyway? You could have hooked up with me and Maura here.'

'Well, it's just that there are direct flights from Dublin to Orlando, and none to Cali. Not to mention I wasn't sure where you'd be . . .'

She knew it was a lame excuse. The truth was that the idea of tagging along on Mike and his girlfriend's West Coast road trip held little appeal.

'And in any case, the doctors told me I needed peace and quiet, so Daniel's beach house sounded perfect.'

'Forrest? The FBI fella who was your lecturer?'

'Yes, he's a friend. And he's going through a tough time at the moment.'

'And divorced too, as I recall?' There was obvious disapproval behind his tone and Reilly's eyes widened as she realized what he was getting at.

'What? Dad, no, don't be stupid, Daniel's old enough to be my father. It's nothing like that. We've always kept in touch and, like I said, it was an easy option. How's life cruising down the 101?' she asked then, hoping to change the subject. 'Did you visit Hearst Castle?'

'We didn't get that far actually,' he told her. 'Went down as far as Monterey and then decided to come back and stay local for a while.'

'Oh? Back home in Marin County, you mean?' It was where the family had lived when Reilly was growing up.

'Yeah. Maura loves San Francisco, and she hit it off with Mack's wife at the retirement party. So we thought we'd rent a place here for a while. One of the boys said they might be able to fix me up with a couple of small jobs – handyman stuff, you know.'

'I see.' Reilly's eyes widened. She wasn't sure what to think. How long was 'a while'? Was her father considering a return to the States for good? It certainly sounded like it.

'So seeing as you've got time to spare, you should pop over this direction when you're bored of sunbathing.' He chuckled. 'Knowing you that won't take long.'

'Well, actually I'm kind of helping Daniel out with something here,' she informed him quietly.

'Helping out with something . . . you mean an investigation?' She could picture him frowning. 'I thought you said you needed peace and quiet.'

'Well, yes, that was the idea but . . .' She went on to give him a quick rundown of recent events, and how she'd offered to help Daniel with the investigation.

'Sweetie, this is not good. You're addicted to work . . . a bit like myself and the bottle, I suppose,' he added, and she smarted a little at the words. 'Why spend so much of your time – free or otherwise – caught up in all this tragic business? I would've thought this family would have had enough of that by now . . .'

He was right, Reilly admitted. It *was* an addiction of sorts.

But Daniel had asked for her help and she wasn't going to refuse. Not when there was a sadistic killer out there.

The question was, Reilly wondered, as she said good-bye to her father, how many such killers did she need to chase before it was enough?

Chapter 12

It was amazing how much goodwill a couple of bags of donuts and a few hot coffees could buy. Reilly had come up with the idea for her and Daniel to bring breakfast to the CSI team the following morning, and it hadn't taken much to convince him to go along with it.

He'd since completed his unofficial 'official' profile the night before and emailed a copy to the detectives investigating Holly's death, but hadn't yet received a reply.

She knew he was frustrated, especially when his son was only able (or indeed willing) to fill in very few of the informational gaps.

'Thought you guys might not have had time to get breakfast,' Daniel smiled as Bradley appeared in the corridor outside the lab to take the goodies.

'Bless you.' He grinned as he reached for one of the cups of coffee. 'We're going to be pulling sixteen- to eighteen-hour days from now on. Sugar and caffeine are now officially my best friends.'

'So, nothing yet?' Daniel tried to keep the question casual, but the look on Bradley's face said he wasn't fooled.

'You know I can't share details of an ongoing investigation, Dr Forrest,' the investigator said, his voice gentle but firm. 'On the other hand, if the department decides to bring you in then I'd be only too happy to get your take on what little evidence we have so far.'

Daniel nodded, his lips pressed tightly together.

Then Bradley smiled at Reilly. 'Speaking of evidence, how did you figure out that Otto Wright was innocent that time? All the news said was forensics cleared him.'

She found herself pleasantly surprised by another reference to her previous career, another blast from the past from her San Francisco days, and she wondered if it was another attempt at flirtation on Bradley's part. If so, she was happy to humor him.

'Toxicology revealed that Mrs Wright had been poisoned by a certain brand of insecticide,' she told him. 'When the crime scene techs brought in the bottles they'd found in the Wrights' garage, I noticed that both bottles were still sealed and appeared to have the same amount of liquid inside. Everyone assumed that Wright had just thrown away the bottle he'd used to poison his wife. I took a closer look at the two bottles we had and noticed that the seal in both had a tiny hole, just big enough for a syringe.'

Bradley made a face. 'Still don't understand how that proved his innocence.'

'Wright had passed out when I showed him the needle I was going to use to draw his blood. He couldn't even look at a syringe, much less use one,' Reilly told him. 'That meant the killer had to have access to both a syringe and the Wrights' garage.'

'His paramedic nephew.' Bradley nodded.

'That one was just luck,' Reilly admitted. 'If you want complex forensics, you should've been on the case I had in Dublin my first year there . . .'

Just then, a twenty-something young man poked his head out of the lab. 'Bradley? Detective Reed just called, said you weren't answering your phone. He wants to know when you're going to get those prints done for the Sheldon case.'

'Tell him we're working on it, Miguel,' Bradley called back. 'And that would be why I wasn't answering my phone,' he added with no small measure of irritation.

'The Sheldon case?' Daniel repeated, and Reilly's gaze darted toward Todd, who'd just come up behind his partner. A frustrated shake of his head answered the question. 'You're working another case?' Daniel's voice had gone dangerously hard and Reilly tensed.

Bradley instantly went on the defensive. 'We're working on lots of cases just now, Dr Forrest,' he continued, his tone once again formal and professional. 'Thank you again for breakfast.' With that he retreated inside the lab.

Todd remained in the hallway. 'Some hotshot Hollywood screenwriter in town for the Tampa Film Festival hasn't been seen for two days,' he informed them quietly. 'His daughter reported it yesterday and the department's taking it seriously. There are only so many of us—'

'So Holly's murderer walks free while you waste your time trying to find some coke-head who's probably sleeping it off somewhere?'

Reilly put her hand on Daniel's arm, giving it a gentle squeeze. For a moment, she thought he was going to shake her off. Then the muscles relaxed beneath her fingers and he was in control again.

'I'm just trying to help.'

'No, you're trying to take over.' Todd's face was pale, this time with anger, his entire body radiating tension. 'I think you should go.'

'Fine,' Daniel snapped. He thrust a finger in Todd's direction. 'But if you fuck this up, you get to be the one to tell Alice Young.'

Afterward, as Daniel and Reilly walked back to the car, he tried to explain the reasons behind his determination.

'For a while after Bruce died, I was worried that Todd was going to be jealous of all of the time I spent with Holly whenever we came down here to the beach house. It never happened. She used to follow him around and he loved it. About a year after it happened, he asked me if I thought I'd ever date Alice. He wanted Holly to be his little sister.'

Reilly didn't say anything. She couldn't. Better than anyone, she understood the need to talk about someone lost in a vicious and cruel manner, but she also knew that there wasn't really anything she could say. She hadn't known Holly, had no memories to share. The only thing she could do was listen. The ride back to Clearwater was quiet, punctuated by other snippets of Holly's life, anecdotes that Daniel needed to share.

Reilly stared out the window, her mind filled with the images Daniel was drawing. Images of a cute little girl with blond pigtails.

'Every year after Bruce died, Holly would give me a card on Father's Day that said, "To my Number Two Dad". As the years passed without Alice dating anyone, I became the closest thing Holly had to a father. I was there for volleyball matches and school plays. I taught her to drive, sat next to her mother at graduation.'

As they travelled along Gulf To Bay Boulevard, the sun warmed Reilly's face as it peeked out from behind the clouds and she closed her eyes for a moment. The little girl that appeared in her mind had blond pigtails, but it wasn't Holly. No, this face was familiar.

Daniel looked across at her. 'You need to be on this, Reilly.'

'I wish I could help but—'

'You heard what Bradley said, this case is only one of many for the department.' Daniel's voice took on a pleading note Reilly had never heard before. 'I know I've offered you a job with my firm before, but this isn't a job offer this time. This is a friend asking for help.'

He put his hand on her arm, his expression grave. 'You have a knack for reading people as well as their surroundings. Most crime scene investigators don't have that. You don't just understand the science, Reilly; you get the whole picture. I need you to help me get the whole picture.'

Chapter 13

He was pleased with his next location. He'd checked it out weeks before, confirming that the boarded-up housing estate was virtually abandoned after dark.

It was risky, he knew, doing this outside at night. If he'd just been a mere killer, it would've made more sense as the shadows and dark would have hidden the crime.

But he was an artist. He needed people to see his work.

And to do that on film, especially a night scene, he needed good lighting. After all, what would the point be of going to such lengths to create his masterpieces if the lighting was poor? Especially when filming in black and white.

Once satisfied that he'd eliminated any interfering shadows, he stepped out of the line of sight and turned on the cameras. Donning his mask, he returned to his car. He'd parked nearby, trusting in the dirt he'd allowed accumulate to obscure the color. He'd also liberally applied dirt to the license plate earlier that evening. Most of the time, he parked far enough away from his locations that no possible witnesses would see it.

Tonight, that hadn't been an option.

He opened the trunk of the car. Eyes as black as pitch glared up at him.

The young man's skin was dark brown, his face still holding on to a bit of baby fat that made him look even younger than the twenty years his license claimed. Again, easy pickings, another desperate wannabe hoping to see his name in lights.

Well, that would be a certainty now, though possibly not in the way the kid had anticipated.

Wiry muscles indicated that this one might have put up a fight if he'd tried to use chloroform. Fortunately, he'd found a better way to get what he needed.

He picked up a bottle of water from the truck and spritzed the liquid over the bound and gagged youth, ignoring the young man's thrashing. He then took his new toy from his jacket.

He may have been overly warm, but it was worth not having scratches from fighting victims. It also allowed him to carry things such as the electric cattle prod he'd found online.

He was unable to contain a gleeful smile as he jabbed the end into his captive, chuckling as the young man's body twitched and jerked as electricity ran through him.

Then he pocketed the prod and grabbed the young man's shoulder, dragging his prize from the trunk, and ignoring the sound of pain when the young man's head hit the ground.

The soon-to-be-famous wannabe could barely walk, stumbling as he was dragged toward the cameras. He shoved the young man to the ground and grabbed the prod.

One more jolt and those black eyes glazed over.

He manipulated the limp body into a kneeling position and bent over his victim. The young man's eyes were fluttering, but he was still awake enough to do what was needed. Ripping the tape from the young man's mouth with one hand, he used his other to shove the weakly protesting face toward the curb.

'Bite it,' he hissed into the young man's ear.

It didn't matter if the cameras picked up his words. He'd learned enough to mask his voice. Only a true sound expert had any hope of matching those two words to his regular voice and he doubted it would ever come to that. He considered it well worth the risk.

The young man had tears rolling down his cheeks as he did as he was told. He rested his teeth gingerly against the concrete. With his hands bound behind his back, he had no way to defend himself and the man watched the realization come over the youthful face.

He recognized the scenario, understood what he was supposed to do. And more to the point, what would happen when he did.

Beautiful. It was time.

He straightened, took a step back and, before the young

man could react, lifted one heavy boot and slammed it into the back of his star's head.

A satisfying crunch. Limbs twitched as the blood pooled.

Another perfect death scene.

It was Saturday evening and Daniel had called Todd to invite him over to the beach house for dinner in the guise of wanting to discuss Holly Young's memorial service, which Reilly guessed was more of an attempt to try to break bread, and smooth the waters after their bust-up at the station the day before.

When Todd arrived around seven, she could tell that he was trying to remain respectful to his father, but there was an edge to him that made her nervous. She could only imagine how pressurized things must be at the lab.

They dined outside on the deck beneath the lanai, and Reilly and Todd did their best to make small talk over drinks while Daniel finished preparing creole jambalaya in the kitchen.

'So how long are you in town, Reilly?' Todd asked, popping the cork on a bottle of Corona. She could hear the tiredness in his voice.

'I'm not sure, to be honest – as long as your dad will put up with me, I guess.' She sipped a glass of chilled sauvignon blanc and explained about her enforced leave from the GFU and the reason behind it.

'And the lab still doesn't know what the stuff was? Jeez, I thought we were slow.'

'They're a good group, just backed-up and busy – same as you guys.'

But she too was wondering exactly when the team in Dublin would complete their analysis and come back with an answer about the mysterious off-white powder.

'Can't think of anything off the top of my head that would cause you to black out,' Todd was saying. 'Arsenic wouldn't do anything fast . . . ricin is easy to identify – not to mention that if it was that, you'd already be dead – and white heroin would have you bouncing off the walls. Are you sure it wasn't just a rogue batch of cocaine?'

Leave it to a pair of crime scene investigators to turn small talk into a discussion about the side effects of chemical compounds, Reilly thought, raising a smile.

She shook her head. 'I really can't say. I didn't get to see, taste or have anything to do with it once I got out of the hospital.'

The peppery creole scent wafting out from the kitchen filled her nostrils, and her stomach growled, threatening rebellion if she didn't feed it. She closed her eyes and savored the aroma. She'd missed the way her home country's ethnic cuisine borrowed flavors from so many other cultures. She'd never really taken to the Dublin versions of Mexican, Cuban or Cajun/Creole, where chefs tended to dampen down flavors to suit the Irish palate.

When Daniel came out to serve the food, he was limping.

'What happened to you?' Todd enquired.

'Twisted my knee while playing beach volleyball earlier.'

'Nice job, Dad.' Todd shook his head. 'You know, you're not as young as you think you are.'

'I don't know what you're talking about. I'm in my prime,' his father insisted with a wink.

'Yeah, I forgot, you're Batman.'

Reilly smiled. It was good to hear the two bantering.

She looked at the feast Daniel was laying on the table and nearly jumped out of her seat. 'Oh, my God . . .' she gasped, unable to believe what was she was seeing. 'Is that . . . corn bread?' Homemade Southern-style *American* corn bread was her absolute favorite and she hadn't tasted the stuff in almost three whole years. She practically launched herself at the plate, grabbing a thick piece and biting down into the buttery, melt-in-mouth crumbly texture. Heaven . . .

Todd chuckled. 'Wow, you really have been away too long, Steel. Don't think I've ever seen a girl get that excited about food. Guess they don't do corn bread in Dublin.'

Reilly smiled happily through a mouthful of crumbs. 'No – they don't, not like that. And they don't do stone crab, or coconut shrimp or creole spices like this . . . mmm.' She sat forward in her chair, dipping the corn bread into the spicy rice stew, unable to remember the last time she'd felt so contented.

'So now you know the way to this girl's heart is through her stomach,' Daniel chided, raising his wine glass to her and Todd for a toast.

Then he turned to his son. 'Well, like I said, I wanted to talk to you about the memorial,' he continued, his tone softening. 'Alice decided that she wanted to hold a service next week. Once the body's released, she'll have Holly cremated. She doesn't want to do an actual funeral.'

'I see.' Todd blinked and looked away quickly, seeming to be struggling with his emotions. Reilly guessed there hadn't been a lot of time for grieving over the last few days and the mention of the memorial was making the loss of their close family friend all the more real.

'She's asked if you might read something at the service,' Daniel continued, 'and I told her I'd ask.'

'Sure. Of course I will.' His son's reply was hoarse.

'So how are things at the lab?' Daniel asked then. 'You guys any closer to finding answers?' The question was casual, but the atmosphere instantly shifted.

Reilly opened her mouth, prepared to play peacemaker, when Todd surprised her.

'You're right, Dad,' he ran his hand through his hair. 'What you said yesterday. Priorities are shifting day by day. The mayor is putting pressure on the department to find this missing screenwriter guy – says it's bad for tourism – and the DA's now trying to suggest that some of these deaths aren't related, because we simply don't have enough evidence to convince him otherwise.'

'Is there anything at all we can do?' Reilly asked, realizing the depth of the frustration Todd was feeling. 'Not officially, of course, but anything that might help take the load off with Holly's investigation – grunt work, even?'

She knew better than most that grunt work was the bane of most forensic departments, yet could often be the most fruitful.

Todd thought about her question for a moment. When he finally answered, he sounded cautiously hopeful. 'Bradley pulled Emilie off of trying to track down suppliers for the cameras as it was just too time-consuming given the current workload. It's probably a long-shot, but do you think you could try that? I can get you details of the makes and models, but not the equipment, obviously.'

'Of course.' Reilly completely understood chain-of-custody issues and she wouldn't dream of directly handling evidence in such a scenario. But tracking down suppliers was completely above board, and she and Daniel could carry out such work easily if his office provided the tools.

Daniel looked heartened. 'No problem, son. And anything else you can think of – within protocol, of course – you name it.'

'I will.' The three glanced at one another, each aware that they were agreeing to a kind of unspoken pact.

Later, after a hearty meal and a hefty slice of key lime pie, Daniel announced that he was going to bed, leaving Todd and Reilly alone at the table.

She looked up at the night sky, her eyes tracing familiar constellations. Despite the changes in location, the same shapes were still there. Strange how some things could be so much the same and so different at the same time. She'd enjoyed the food (especially the corn bread), the few glasses of wine she'd consumed were giving her a nice buzz, and the warm evening air and relaxing sound of the waves were making her feel heady.

It was finally starting to feel like a vacation.

'I'm glad you and your dad get along so well,' she commented idly. 'It's nice to see.'

Todd laughed, and she couldn't help but hear a hint of disbelief behind the tone. 'Reilly, how long have you known my father?' He stood and stepped down to the edge of the pool. 'You can't tell me that in all these years you haven't figured out his relationship with me.' He gave another bark of a laugh. 'And here I thought you were supposed to be the smart one.' Then he suddenly pulled his shirt over his head and tossed it onto a nearby sun lounger. 'I want to go for a swim.'

Before Reilly could respond to the sudden shift in conversation, Todd stripped off his dress pants and, wearing only a dark pair of boxers, dove straight into the water.

He popped back up to the surface, his face now sporting a daring grin. 'Well, Steel?'

All right, Reilly decided, why the hell not. She kicked off her shoes and stood. Then quickly, so she couldn't second-guess herself, she pulled her sundress over her head and dove in as well.

The cool water was like silk on her overheated skin. She'd been away from warm weather for far too long. When she broke through the surface, she found Todd staring at her, an appreciative look in his clear blue eyes.

While her sporty dark blue underwear covered more than most bathing suits, she found herself flushing. She wasn't sure how she felt about Todd looking at her that way. It had the potential to become very awkward, very fast.

As much to defuse the moment as anything else, she decided to address his previous rhetorical question. 'I do, by the way, have you and your father figured out.'

'Oh, really?' Todd seemed mildly amused. He swam toward her. 'Enlighten me.'

Reilly waited until he was just a foot away before answering, her voice coming out more at ease than she felt. 'You two butted heads even before the divorce, so when your mom said that it was his fault, you believed her. When you finally found out the truth – that she was the one who cheated, the one who wanted to leave – you stopped hating your father and started trying to be like him.'

Reilly had heard the divorce story years before, but was just taking a stab at the analysis. As she said it though, it made sense. 'Just like your father, you're too proud to admit you were wrong, so you try to make him proud of you. But because you two are so much alike, you still butt heads and you end up resenting him for you trying to prove yourself.'

'You missed one thing.' Todd's smile appeared frozen. He swam over to the edge and lifted himself out. 'You forgot to add into the mix the perfect little protégé prodigy who aced every test, solved every crime and did it all while charming juries and lawyers alike.'

Reilly was startled by the hurt in his tone as he said this. Was Todd . . . jealous of her and Daniel's relationship? Like she'd explained to Mike, it had always been more of a father/child thing than anything romantic, but now she wondered if perhaps it had been too much like that, and at Todd's expense. 'I never—'

'I know . . .' The moonlight glistened on the drops of water running down Todd's body. 'It wasn't your fault, isn't your fault, I get that. You were needy, maybe an emotional orphan with an absentee father, I don't know. Looking for a father figure no matter the reason. My dad just happened to forget that he already had a kid who needed guidance.' He picked up his clothes. 'I have to get going. Lots to do tomorrow.' With that, he disappeared into the house, leaving Reilly treading water.

'Yeah, so this isn't going to be awkward at all,' she muttered. She ducked back under the water and swam a few laps, her arms cutting through the water with graceful precision.

So much for breaking bread.

Chapter 14

Reilly set aside the laptop Daniel had had delivered to the beach house from his office earlier and stood. She stretched her arms over her head, bending backward until her spine popped, and she let out a moan of satisfaction.

Despite her misgivings about getting involved in the investigation of Holly Young's murder, she couldn't deny that it felt good to be back in the saddle again.

Hell, she wasn't the vacation type anyway.

Still, trying to track down anything on the camera information Todd had provided was proving annoyingly fruitless. As far as she could tell, the cameras found at the scene of Holly's death and the others could've been bought anywhere from a local electronics store to online; without a serial number, they were virtually untraceable.

She let her gaze wander around the living room.

A certain Quantico mentor had taught her that, for some people, the best way to come at a problem was from the side. If she let her brain focus on something other than the problem at hand, some outside stimulation such as music or painting, or even appreciating the surprisingly stylish furnishing of that same mentor's home, and his impressive books collection, the rest of her mind would continue to work the problem. It had served her well back in Dublin as she'd actually hit on quite a few answers to problems while cooking.

As Reilly's attention moved away from Daniel's book-shelf, her eyes fell on the picture on a side bureau next to it and she smiled. Todd's college graduation. Daniel and his ex-wife Stella stood on either side of their son, all animosity set aside as they beamed at the camera. For all of their problems with each other, the one thing Todd's parents had always agreed on was how much they loved their son. Reilly could almost feel the pride radiating off of them both.

Pride . . .

Something that Todd mentioned before suddenly came back to her. According to his computer expert, the killer had been sending footage of the murders to an email address.

They also knew he'd spent a lot of time painstakingly staging each murder. For maximum dramatic effect, Todd had said.

Was the video footage for the killer's sole entertainment, or was he sharing his work? Reilly's intuition was telling her that such a creative type was unlikely to pass up the opportunity to broadcast his 'talent'.

Which made her think about something else; something about the recent boiling-water death that had been niggling at her.

Reilly returned to the laptop on the couch and started a new internet search.

This time, she typed in a few key words unique to Holly and her boyfriend's murder, grimacing as she did so.

There were some seriously sick people out there, she decided, as the search returned over 1.5 million hits. Reilly skimmed each of the descriptions, her stomach churning as she read through the listings. Some were legitimate news stories, including one or two short references to the recent murder, but others were websites and jokes and . . . wait.

She stopped, her cursor hovering over a link to a video clip, debating whether or not she wanted to do this.

No, she didn't, but someone had to. Reilly clicked on it and waited as the video loaded, a chill settling deep into her bones. Again, something had been niggling at the back of her brain since she'd heard the horrific details of Holly's death, and now she thought she understood why.

Her roommate in her Quantico freshman year, Ellen, had been obsessed with horror movies. Reilly had tried to avoid them as much as possible. With her past, she didn't need a horror movie to tell her just how twisted the world could be.

But despite the care she'd taken to switch off as much as possible, there had still been times when she took in the odd showing. A piece from one particular movie – a clip of which she was about to click on now – had happened to be on during one of those times.

At the time, Reilly remembered being mildly repulsed by the movie, but it had seemed so far-fetched that it hadn't bothered her as much as some of the others Ellen had watched.

The internet video had finished loading and started playing. As a chained-up woman struggled and called out for help, Reilly couldn't help but notice the similarities between the blond actress in the movie and the late Holly Young.

'Damn,' she whispered, every hair on her body standing on end.

Images mixed in her head. The photographs from Alice Young's house interchanging with the face of another, more familiar, little blond girl. The violence of a young woman being torn asunder. The blood pooling on the floor beneath Reilly's own mother's body. The actress's screams emanating from the computer . . .

Reilly let out a shaky breath and squeezed her eyes shut. As she'd been told to do when the memories came knocking, she repeated the little poem her shrink Dr Kyle had taught her years ago.

'. . . Lay you down and take your rest; Forget in sleep the doubt and pain; And when you wake, to work again . . .'

The words and rhythm soothed her, helped her collect herself, and she opened her eyes. Her mind cleared and she could focus again. She knew well that her mind's greatest asset was also its greatest weakness.

She had an eye for detail, a brain that processed information in a way that most people couldn't understand. The downside to that was that it was often hard for her to turn her brain off, to move beyond a problem before it was solved.

When something particularly bad stuck, it was nearly impossible for her to get it out. Dr Kyle had understood that in a way no one else had. After numerous hits and misses with various treatments, finally the solution presented itself. Give the brain something else to ruminate on and it would let go of whatever it had been holding on to. Hence her decision to go into crime scene work, where there was something to think about, something to puzzle over, every waking hour.

She muted the volume on the laptop and, after taking a deep breath, let the movie clip play through one more time.

'A killer with a taste for the dramatic . . .' Todd's assessment of the murder scenes popped into her brain once again. That was an understatement.

Reilly wasn't entirely sure how much to tell them, or even how to do it. Part of her wanted to protect anyone from ever having to see what she'd seen. Just the memory of it was enough to make her feel nauseated all over again.

She'd avoided Daniel for most of the day, heading out for a ten-mile run on the beach when she heard him arrive back from the grocery store, then taking her time in the shower, wishing she could wash away the memory of what she'd seen as easily as she could the sand and sweat.

She'd told him that after her shower she was going to take a nap, blaming residual jet lag. She wasn't sure if he'd believed her, but it was either that or try to keep her expression under control and she didn't think she was that good an actress. She needed to tell him and Todd at the same time. This wasn't a conversation she wanted to have once, let alone twice.

Despite her claim, Reilly didn't nap at all; she couldn't have even if she'd wanted to. Instead, she spent the hours before Todd was due to arrive examining the video clip for anything that may have been missed. A notebook lay next to her, filled with her scrawling script. Questions. Observations. Details. So far, not much else that could help. This killer was definitely meticulous in his staging.

Only after she heard a car pulling into the driveway did she emerge from the bedroom, hoping she looked disheveled enough to allay any suspicions that might distract them.

She set the laptop and notebook on the coffee table and sat on the couch, tucking her feet underneath her. The smell of reheated Cuban food was almost enough to tempt her. Unfortunately, her mind was still too filled with the gruesome images she'd seen to consider eating.

'Anything new?' The question was out of Daniel's mouth before Todd shut the front door behind him.

For once, Todd didn't take offense at his father's brusque tone. 'We finally got a hold of the 911 call reporting the first murders.' He took the beer Daniel offered him, looking like he needed it. 'Male, nothing really unique about his voice. Sounds in the background indicate that the call was made near the crime scene, which fits with the scenario the caller described. Problem is . . .'

'Because it was a burner, it looks more like the killer actually placed the call.' Daniel finished the statement.

'Exactly.' Todd gulped down half of the beer before continuing with a quick summary of everything they'd learned. It didn't take long.

Reilly waited until Todd was finished before she spoke. 'I found something.' Her voice was quiet.

'You tracked down suppliers for the cameras? That was fast,' he said, eyes widening in surprise.

Reilly shook her head and took a deep breath. She spoke slowly, choosing each word carefully. 'I wasn't sure how exactly to tell you this other than to just come out and say it. There's this slasher-horror movie from 1986, called *The Hitcher*. At one point, a female character is chained between two trucks.'

The expressions on Todd and Daniel's faces told her that they immediately understood the significance, and she forced herself to continue. 'At first, I thought maybe the killer got the idea from the movie.'

'At first?' Todd echoed, nearly choking on the words.

'In the original film, the camera pans away when the truck . . .' Reilly swallowed, fighting down the sour taste in the back of her throat. 'The clip I found online, there's a cut from the movie to . . .' She forced the words out, 'There's a cut to the filmed murders.'

She watched as her words registered. The color drained from the faces of both father and son, and she saw her own nausea reflected on their faces. She twisted her fingers together almost to the point of pain and waited for the men to say something, though she had some idea of how they must be feeling.

Earlier, when she'd played back that short clip from the movie, she'd spotted another in the listing below, the part where viewers who liked this also liked that. It was titled 'Extended Cut'. Playing this one, the familiar camera pan away that happened in the movie abruptly stopped, to be replaced with something that looked far too real to be fake.

Reilly had bolted from her seat, tossing the laptop aside. She'd barely made it into the bathroom before her lunch made a reappearance. It was one thing to see the aftermath of a horrific crime, but quite another to watch it in full Technicolor.

She had remained sitting on the cool tiled floor while screams echoed from her laptop speaker, each one piercing through her head. No matter how talented the actress, there was always a quality that couldn't be faked, something that couldn't be held back at that moment when screaming was all that could be done, when it was no longer a conscious choice but an involuntary reaction.

While the first glimpse had told her what she needed to know, she still had to play it again to really see exactly what was there. And there it was again. Where the original clip had panned away from the victim, the film had been spliced with video of Holly Young's death intercut with her boyfriend Aaron's.

The difference in quality of film alone told her that the original film and the new material had been shot with different equipment, decades apart.

'You're telling me,' Daniel said, his voice hoarse, 'there's a video online where people can actually watch Holly . . .' He stood abruptly and Reilly wondered for a moment if he was going to be sick.

'It's not just her, either.' She forced herself to keep going. 'I suspected that if the killer had set up the first scene as some kind of homage to a well-known movie, maybe he'd done the same with the second one.' She opened her laptop. While horrific in and of itself, this was going to be the easier of the two clips for the Forrests to watch. 'This was just posted online yesterday. The original movie's called *Deep Red*.'

Reilly didn't watch the clip as it played through. She didn't need to. The images she'd seen today would be replaying through her mind enough on their own. She kept her eyes on Todd's face. She didn't know enough about the second murder to be one hundred percent certain that the details matched.

Todd uttered a low curse and her heart clenched. 'I'm guessing that means I was right? That's the most recent victim?'

'Down to the fucking heating coil in the tub.' Todd slumped back in his seat. 'The son of a bitch isn't just imitating movies, he's adding to them.'

Chapter 15

'Fuck!' Bradley spat.

'Yeah, that's pretty much what I said.' Todd leaned back in the office chair the following morning. He rubbed his hand over his face, eyes bloodshot and burning from lack of sleep.

He'd considered calling Bradley immediately after Reilly had shown them the videos last night, but had ultimately decided that he'd need a clearer head to be able to explain the significance of what she'd found, and how best to pass the information on to the investigative team without stepping on toes.

He hadn't gotten much sleep though, his conversation with Reilly running round and round in his head. Finally, he'd given up and called Bradley from the car and met his superior at the lab before anyone else arrived. An empty bottle of energy drink sat next to his computer.

'You do know the DA's going to have our asses if they find out where this information came from,' Bradley said as he sat down. He held up a hand when Todd opened his mouth to speak. 'I'm not stupid. I know you've been throwing your dad's office a bone or two to help with his own investigation.'

Todd exhaled. He knew where Bradley was coming from and normally he never wanted to be the one to bring in extra help, insisting that they could handle it themselves, but this was different. This was Holly. He was always just going to do what needed to be done.

He was also relieved in a way, too. The confirmation of the existence of a serial killer with such a gruesome and distinctive MO meant that it was a dead cert the department would be calling on the services of their on-call criminal profiler. Which meant that his dad's office would soon be cleared to work with them, there would be more eyes and ears on the case and Todd wouldn't have to worry about breaking protocol.

If everything his father always said about 'Saint' Reilly was true, there was a good chance she could be a godsend on this case. A part of him knew he'd been unfair to her the other night with that crack about her being his dad's favorite. It was stupid and he'd been a little bit drunk, but the truth was he envied the unconditional respect and affection Daniel had always had for Reilly Steel right back from their academy days.

Still, that wasn't Reilly's fault, and the fact was she'd been nothing but helpful since her arrival. Finding those video clips was a major breakthrough, no matter how horrifying and upsetting ... Todd's stomach clenched afresh. He looked at his partner.

'About the videos ... ?'

'Already thinking about it.' Bradley was reaching for the phone. 'I'm going to call Detective Reed to update him – and then get the Cyber Crimes Unit to try and trace the clips' origin. I'm sure Peni will be thrilled.'

'Is there any way ... ?' Todd wasn't quite sure how to ask the question. 'Do you think it would be at all possible to get the murder clips taken down? It's just, knowing that there are people watching ...'

'Let me talk to Peni and I'll see what she says,' his colleague assured him. 'Don't worry; this guy's got no chance of getting an Academy Award.'

The man took a deep breath and closed his eyes for a second. He had to focus.

He wasn't entirely sure he could orchestrate the complex scenario he wanted to try next. He had total faith in his own abilities, but there were some drawbacks to only using practical devices. While simplistic enough in theory, the execution – pun only partially intended – was going to be more difficult. And, as anyone in his line of work knew, there was only one solution to mastering a difficult prospect.

Practice, practice and more practice.

He'd found the latest girl wandering around downtown, looking for all the world like the dumb blond he needed.

Once he'd told her what he did for a living, again it hadn't taken much convincing to get her to go for a drink with him. Slipping the clear liquid he'd purchased back home into her cup had been almost too easy. Figuring out how to get her to stay standing had been a bit more difficult. He'd finally had to tip the mattress at enough of an angle that it was more or less propping her up.

It had made tying her hands a bitch, but he'd finally managed.

Her eyes were just starting to flutter open when he lifted his bow.

Archery had made such a big comeback over the last few years that he couldn't resist at least trying to recreate one of the many death-by-arrow sequences he'd seen.

Problem was, he hadn't shot a bow since summer camp when he was twelve. He could've practiced with a paper target, he supposed, or even a corpse, but he had to take into account that a live target was going to squirm.

He nocked the arrow and drew back, a familiar feeling of excitement coiling in his belly at the sight of the young woman's widening eyes, at the fear on her face. He held the position as he spoke to her.

'I'm going to try to make this as quick as possible,' he explained. 'Though I do apologize if it takes me a few tries. I'm a bit rusty.'

The string stung his wrist as he released the first arrow. It embedded itself in the mattress with a muffled thump. A thin trickle of urine rolled down the inside of the girl's leg, mimicking the tears coursing down her cheeks.

'Hmm,' he murmured, then adjusted his stance and picked up his second arrow. He sighted more carefully this time before letting it fly, then cursed as the string stung him again.

A meaty thwack and a spurt of blood accompanied the muted scream. The cords on the young woman's neck stood out as she screamed into her gag. Her face was red and she tugged at the ropes keeping her in place. Although, he guessed that wasn't entirely true. Technically, the arrow in her stomach was now keeping her in place.

'Not bad,' he said, critiquing his own work. Second shot and he'd only missed by a few inches. He'd been aiming for her heart, of course.

He'd save the eye for last. The arrow he'd shot quivered as the girl thrashed, but it had lodged deeply in her torso, just a bit above and to the right of her bellybutton. He was pretty sure there were some vital organs there. She wouldn't last much longer. He needed to hurry if he wanted her to still be alive when he tried to put a shaft through her eye.

He reached for another arrow.

Third time's a charm.

Chapter 16

Things started to move very quickly into gear once the investigative team learned about the movie clips, and that it looked like they had a serial killer on their hands.

As anticipated, the department chief Captain Harvell formally sought Daniel's assistance with the case and requested an immediate profile. Conveniently ignoring (or perhaps unaware of) the fact that the investigative team had already been offered one.

'So I talked to Reed and Sampson about getting the footage off the internet,' Bradley told Todd, following the interdepartmental briefing to discuss next steps. 'They're going to see what they can do but . . .'

'But what?'

Todd knew what the investigator was going to say. Still, he waited to hear it firsthand, anger bubbling up inside him.

'Todd, to be fair, we're all stretched to the limit with this new information. Julie said she'd talk to the DA about getting a warrant to pull the videos, but the investigation will naturally take priority . . .'

'So anyone can still go online and watch Holly die?' Todd knew he was getting close to crossing the line, but he didn't care. This was wrong. And while he used her name, it wasn't just about Holly. It was about the family and friends of all of the victims so far.

'She said she was going to do what she could,' Bradley repeated.

'Bullshit!' Todd slammed his hands down on the table. 'An hour, maybe two, that's all it would take. But because Holly and Aaron and that poor kid in the bathtub aren't rich and famous like that screenwriter, they don't matter. And no one seems to care that once this hits the news, these families are never going to have a moment of peace. Could you imagine knowing that, with just a few keystrokes, you could be face to face with the brutal death of your child, your friend, as it happened?' Todd's voice cracked. 'And those assholes won't take the time out of their busy day to do their fucking job.'

'Todd,' Bradley said; his voice held a warning note.

'I can do it,' Peni said easily. Both men turned to look at the computer expert. She shrugged. 'I already have to be inside the site code to see what I can trace. While I'm in there, it wouldn't be too difficult to kill the links.'

'Seriously, you can just delete stuff from inside?' Bradley asked.

She winked at him. 'Yup. Any site at all. Been there, done that. Parking tickets can be a bitch.'

'I'm going to pretend I didn't hear that,' Bradley replied, though there was a smile in his voice. 'And I will also pretend to be surprised if those videos miraculously disappear.'

When Reilly and Daniel pulled into the Tampa Police Department parking lot that morning, it was already full despite the fact that the sun was only just now starting to peek over the horizon.

Apparently, they were calling everyone in.

Captain Harvell, a gruff-sounding man in his mid-fifties with thinning hair, greeted them at reception. 'Thank you for coming at such short notice, Dr Forrest.'

'Happy to help.' Introductions were made and, ever the gentleman, Daniel held the door open for Reilly as they followed the captain through to the briefing room.

'I've got the full investigative team together so you can outline the more salient points of your profile and how it holds up against the new information,' the captain told them. 'It doesn't have to be long. Just anything our people can keep in mind as they're talking to witnesses, potential suspects, and putting together evidence.'

Going into the briefing room, Reilly looked around and among those gathered inside she recognized Detective Mark Reed, Todd's partner Bradley and, of course, Todd himself.

None of the investigative team looked particularly happy, though she really couldn't blame them. She wasn't too cheered about being up this early in the morning either and she knew from how experience how much detectives hated behavioral specialists telling them how to do their job. She smiled fondly, thinking of Detective Pete Delaney in Dublin and his open animosity toward the behaviorist the Irish police usually parachuted in, Reuben Knight.

Captain Harvell began making introductions. 'I'm sure most of you already know Dr Forrest from his previous work with the department. This is his associate Reilly Steel, former San Francisco field office and on leave of absence from her current post in Ireland, I understand?'

'From Dublin, yes.' Reilly smiled tightly, hating to be the center of attention. She hadn't wanted to come along but Daniel had insisted, given she was the one who'd made the breakthrough in finding the video footage and discovered the killer's MO.

'Based on Dr Forrest's initial profile of our unsub, and his supplementary private investigation on behalf of Holly Young's family, I've asked that he outline some salient points for you to keep in mind throughout the course of this murder investigation. Please give Dr Forrest and Ms Steel your undivided attention.'

The captain stepped back and Daniel began to speak, his soft dulcet tones as always commanding attention seemingly without trying.

'Let's talk about what we know so far. Analysis of the recent crime scenes shows that we need to separate the intentional from the unintentional deaths when trying to understand the motivation and mindset of our killer.

'When looking at the timeline, the unsub killed the couple on the beach with chloroform and a rock, then partially hid the bodies. He then took Aaron Overton and Holly Young from the same section of beach. Halfway to the location where he would set them up to die, he was stopped by Officer Carlos Sanchez. After killing the officer, he moved on, setting up the scene the police found after he called it in. Cameras have been found at this and a subsequent scene,' Daniel's voice grew stronger, more confident, as he spoke.

'This suggests that the killer is meticulous when it comes to the intentional deaths. He had every detail in place for each kill scene. The first three were out of necessity for him. The others were all part of what he considers his "art". He is ruthless, shows no remorse for his actions, even though he understands that murder is wrong. He just believes that the ends justify the means. Bold and willing to take risks to get what he wants, he most likely has an obsessive personality and, once he gets an idea in his head, he has to act on it. He's a narcissist and a perfectionist with a dramatic, creative flair.'

'What's the best way to spot these personality traits?' one of the officers asked.

Reilly noticed Daniel indicate that she should answer that. She fixed her eyes above the heads of the detectives. When she was in college, she'd nearly panicked when she'd found that she had to take a public speaking course. Only by learning to avoid eye contact and find a fixed point above the audience's head was she able to get through it. She called on those techniques now as the familiar butterflies threatened to flutter around in her stomach.

'If, for example, you've interrupted something that he's doing, he's going to be agitated, unable to focus until he gets it done,' she replied. 'But the easiest thing to do is to get him talking about himself. If you suggest that he's not good enough or smart enough to have committed the murders, he may slip up because he wants to prove how great he is.'

The captain turned to Daniel. 'Thank you again, Dr Forrest. You too, Ms Steel.'

'No problem,' Reilly replied, shaking his hand.

'Here's hoping we'll catch up with the son of a bitch very soon.' Captain Harvell walked with Reilly back to the doors. 'Thank you again. You two have a good day.'

As they headed back to Daniel's car, Reilly couldn't help but think that the captain's sentiment, while well meant, was somewhat misplaced.

While monsters like the one they were chasing roamed the streets, how was it possible for anyone who knew about it to have a good day?

Chapter 17

Later that morning, Todd waded through the sea of humanity filling the lobby of the Millennium Hotel in downtown Tampa.

A man in a suit waved him over. Detective Mark Reed's salt-and-pepper hair was cropped short, almost military style, and his eyes were the color of faded jeans. He didn't stop for pleasantries. 'Crime scene's this way.' He led Todd behind a partition and through a metal door.

Todd blinked rapidly, his eyes adjusting to the lunchtime sun streaming directly into the alley. His nose twitched. Cat piss. Why was it every alley in the world smelled like garbage and cat piss? And the heat wasn't helping.

He cursed Bradley once again for sending him here of all places. A report had been filed earlier about a patch of blood found in the alleyway. As this happened to be the same hotel in which the missing screenwriter was staying, the department called the CSI unit to check it out.

Todd was already pissed enough that the guy was taking resources away from Holly's murder, but he had his orders. Though he'd brought along one of the interns to do most of the dirty work.

As he surveyed the scene, he tried to get his conscious mind to switch off and put his brain into work-mode. The heat of the sun crept higher in the sky, but none of it mattered. Everything faded away. The background noise. The people around him. The young woman currently yelling at Detective Reed. All he saw, heard, smelled, everything was compartmentalized and analyzed. Anything out of place was a potential clue.

Something reflecting the sun's light caught Todd's eye and he crouched down. He reached into his kitbag and took out a pair of tweezers to lift the item from the alley debris. He held it up, not entirely sure what he was looking at. Smooth on one side, and jagged on the other, it wasn't like any of the other gravel around it. A pale orange color, it glinted in the sunlight. It might end up being nothing, but Todd wasn't going to take the chance on missing anything. Especially when finding this screenwriter guy seemed to be such a fucking priority. He slipped the find into a pre-marked bag and continued on.

By the time he reached the blood spatter, his intern had finished photographing the scene and was taking samples of the blood. Todd crouched beside her, the muscles in his legs protesting the awkward position. The rich coppery scent of blood filled his nostrils. Underneath it, the stench from alley Dumpsters in the Florida heat, and the faint aroma of sweat.

'Not a whole lot of blood,' he commented to Reed, who'd come up alongside him.

'But no footprints or tracking, so it doesn't look like it's from a fight,' the detective replied.

Todd's eyes flicked up to the nearby wall. 'Nothing on the wall, so probably not a hit to the face. Maybe the perp threatened your writer guy with a knife and nicked him when he didn't move fast enough?'

Reed seemed unimpressed by Todd's assessment. 'Find anything helpful?' he asked.

'I'm not sure.' He turned his attention back to the crime scene. 'It looks like most people use the alley as an ash tray. I doubt any of the butts I collected are going to have perp DNA. Most of the footprints stop just outside the door, where there's still some shade, so I'm guessing that's where most of the smokers stand. I only counted a few out here.' Todd indicated the more open area of the alley. 'I'm betting some of those are going to belong to your missing writer. If we're lucky, one of the others will match the perp. Unless he wore gloves, in which case we're back to square one.'

Todd straightened, noticing some background noise. He glanced over his shoulder as a particularly long string of expletives was directed toward the officers at the tape.

The culprit was a young brunette, pretty enough to be one of the many aspiring actresses hanging around, hoping to be talent-spotted. So much for Hollywood glamor. If anything, the place stank of desperation with so many wannabe locals about, pleading to be discovered and propelled to stardom. As if.

But he wondered what was making this particular girl so agitated.

'Sheldon's daughter,' the detective informed him. 'The screenwriter. She's been all over our asses since the guy went awol.'

This surprised Todd a little. He wasn't a movie fan and thus had never heard of Drew Sheldon, but for some reason he hadn't pictured the guy as old enough to have a daughter, never mind bring her along to a festival with him. Maybe there was more to his disappearance than met the eye?

Mark Reed turned back to view the full scene. He pointed toward the door. 'So the writer comes out for a smoke and the kidnapper's waiting.' He motioned closer to where the blood was drying. 'The perp somehow draws him further out, probably to get Sheldon further away from the door.'

Todd picked it up. 'Once out here, the kidnapper pulls a weapon, most likely a knife based on the blood pattern. He threatens the guy, and nicks him. Then the two of them leave by the street entrance.' He turned toward where the police were gathered.

'Where the kidnapper had a ride waiting,' Mark finished. 'No one stopped them, no one reported anything strange. With the festival going on, there were double patrols in this area. I guess that's why the DA's so pissed. The department's getting reamed for letting this happen.'

'For this, but not for the movie murders?' Todd couldn't help himself.

The detective scowled. 'Hey, I just do what I'm told.'

'I get it.' Todd made sure his words implied just the opposite.

But he wondered now about a connection between the film festival and Holly's murderer's obvious movie penchant. The murders had started around the same time as the festival came to town. Could the perp be directly involved in the movie business?

His mind raced and he struggled to sound indifferent as he tried to draw out the detective for more details.

'Maybe we should go talk to some of the other people at the festival. See if anyone in particular would benefit from Mr Sheldon's sudden absence?' he fished, though he wasn't particularly interested in the screenwriter's whereabouts. Unless it really did have something to do with the murders.

'Among the things found in Sheldon's hotel room was a letter from a producer he was working with, Toby Carpenter,' Mark told him. 'Apparently, he and Sheldon were in a bit of a tiff over some new movie. We're going to talk to Carpenter now.'

'I can take the letter to the lab if you like, get it analyzed,' Todd suggested, finding the in he was hoping for, and suddenly taking a brand new interest in the disappearance of Drew Sheldon.

* * *

'You could be on to something,' Reilly heard Daniel say into the phone, and she wondered if Todd and the investigative team had made some kind of breakthrough.

When he got off the phone, he filled her in on the conversation with his son.

'Todd thinks the film festival being in town might be too much of a coincidence and given what we've just learned about the killer's MO, I agree with him. The cops are all over this missing person investigation, but nobody seems to be asking these guys questions about a possible rogue film-maker in their midst.

Reilly looked at him, recognizing that tone. 'Thinking about flashing that investigator's badge around the film festival, Agent Forrest?'

Daniel picked up his keys and gave her wry smile. 'We can pick up yours at the office on the way.'

They decided to operate under the guise of investigating Drew Sheldon's disappearance so as not to raise any suspicion. Todd had passed on the name of the film producer rumored to be in disagreement with the screen-writer and, having carried out some background information on the guy, they figured he was as good a place to start as any.

Based on the way Toby Carpenter was now leering at her, Reilly suspected that the rumors she and Daniel had heard were true. Even after she'd introduced herself as an investigative consultant, the fifty-something executive producer had only taken his eyes off of her breasts to flick down to her hips once or twice. Although, she figured she was a bit older than his usual fare.

'We've heard that you and Mr Sheldon were in a dispute regarding a movie,' Daniel said, the expression on his face clearly communicating that he didn't appreciate the way Carpenter was looking at his associate.

'Not really.' The producer didn't take his eyes from Reilly. 'I just told him that if he didn't change the lead female role to a younger character, I wouldn't produce the film.'

Reilly scowled. She hated the movie business habit of giving older men romantic interests young enough to be their daughter. 'Isn't Bruce Reynolds playing the lead role? He's forty-two. Just how young did you want his romantic interest to be?'

'Honey,' Carpenter said, leaning forward, 'after that whole fiasco on *Leno*, Sheldon did a rewrite where Reynolds gets killed off in the first ten minutes. The character's older brother comes in to avenge the murder and falls for his former sister-in-law.'

'So Sheldon was making all of the changes you wanted then?' Daniel asked.

Reilly wasn't sure if he was trying to draw the producer's attention from her or keep her from saying something she'd regret. Either way, it worked.

'Of course.' Carpenter shrugged. 'In fact, I have a whole group of girls coming in to audition for me tomorrow. Why would I want Sheldon gone?'

'Maybe because he told you that he'd never write for you again, you hypocritical ass-hat,' said a voice from behind Reilly and Daniel that made them turn.

A tall, slender young woman stood with arms crossed, glaring at Carpenter. Late teens, long dark hair and startling blue eyes, she was exactly the type of girl Carpenter usually went for. 'Now, now, Kai, let's not air our dirty laundry in front of outsiders,' Carpenter said, his tone condescending.

'Shut it, Carpenter.' The girl turned her attention to Reilly and Daniel. 'Are you two looking for my dad?'

'If you'll excuse me.' With one last full-body ogle directed first at Reilly and then at Kai, Carpenter turned and walked away.

Reilly shuddered. 'I feel the sudden need for a shower.'

'Tell me about it,' Kai said.

'Your dad's Drew Sheldon?' Daniel asked.

The girl nodded and stuck out her hand. 'Kai Sheldon. He brought me with him this year to meet some people. I want to get into the industry.'

'Screenwriting or acting?' Reilly asked.

'Neither.' Kai shook her head and tucked a long strand of hair behind her ear. 'Stunts.'

'Really?' Daniel didn't even try to hide his surprise.

Reilly smiled indulgently at him. He sounded like her own dad. 'Kai, can you think of anyone who'd want to hurt your father?'

'You mean besides the slimy son of a bitch who just left?' Kai shrugged. 'It's hard to say. Working with these people is like being in one giant high school, complete with the backstabbing and partner-swapping. Dad tried to stay out of it as much as possible, but there were always people pissed about something.'

'Why did your dad decide to cut ties with Toby Carpenter?'

'Like I said, Dad never liked to get involved, especially with rumors, but when Carpenter offered to put me in one of his films if I had sex with him, that was the last straw.'

'When did you tell your dad what Carpenter did?' Daniel asked.

'I didn't need to,' Kai said. 'My dad was standing right there.'

'Oh.' Reilly and Daniel exchanged glances.

'Yeah.' Kai nodded. 'Look, that night, I went up to my room early. Dad was supposed to check in before he went to bed. He never did. The last time I saw him was here in the lobby after he told Carpenter he was through working with him.'

'OK, thanks.' Daniel pulled out a card and handed it to Kai. 'If you think of anything else, please give me a call.'

'I will.' Kai's expression changed, the tough girl melting away to reveal a worried child. 'Please, just find my dad.'

'We'll do our best.' Reilly felt guilty. The poor girl had no idea their focus was on something entirely different.

As they watched Kai walk away, Daniel said, 'Somehow, I don't think someone like Toby Carpenter has any idea what's going on in the real world. He certainly wouldn't know anything about our killer.'

'I agree,' Reilly said. 'Who's next?'

'Well, I don't know about you, but if I had just been killed off in a movie that was supposed to relaunch my torpedoed career, I might have a point to prove,' Daniel suggested, and Reilly figured out where he was going with this angle.

Could their killer be an actor with a grudge, bent on carrying out his own particular brand of revenge?

Chapter 18

He sat in the silence of his room. He'd had a productive week and deserved some time to sit and reflect. He sipped at the expensive Scotch in his glass. Things were starting to fall into place, and it was about time too.

Everyone in the business was all about the overnight successes or the legacies.

No one cared about the people like him who worked their asses off day in and day out. He'd worked extremely hard to get to this point and had put in his dues in every respect. And still he had to bow to somebody else's vision, dance to someone else's tune.

Well, no more. He'd always been certain of his abilities, and now was the time to show the world how talented he truly was.

A glisten on the floor caught his eye. In hindsight, he regretted stomping the ring into pieces. He'd just been so frustrated the other day and that old prop had seemed to mock him, reminding him that he was a hack. Now, he could see it for what it really had been: a reminder of just how far he'd come.

As the amber-colored alcohol warmed him, he thought back through his recent body of work, as well as the scenes he'd used for practice, the ones that hadn't turned out quite right. He'd decided to abandon the arrows idea for the moment – it was just too tricky. Not to mention messy.

Perhaps he should have recorded everything, for posterity of course.

He could even use it as a tutorial for anyone wishing to learn from him.

When he'd first decided to take on this project, he knew he'd need to start slow to perfect his technique. First, he'd dabbled with assault to practice his editing, and then had moved on to the bigger stuff.

While that couple at Belleair Beach had been his first foray into the world of chloroform, they hadn't been his first kill. That honor had gone to a skinny teenage hitch-hiker who'd called himself Rory.

That one hadn't been anything fancy. No camera, no elaborate staging. Just a quick and messy stabbing to prove that he had the stomach for it. The blood had been a real bitch to clean up though. In the end, he'd gotten frustrated enough to leave the car in a bad section of town with the keys in the ignition.

He'd gotten better with the next one. The girl hadn't been more than fifteen when she'd tried soliciting him.

He'd been interested in a different sort of performance though. She'd even played along until she'd realized that he wasn't acting. A raincoat and axe had served to make her his first movie homage. It had helped him understand the complexities of staging a scene with a less than willing participant.

When he'd begun his research to decide what movies he wanted to improve, he'd had to take into account the nature of each story's antagonist. For example, he wouldn't be recreating anything from *It* even though the idea of ripping off a victim's arm was compelling. He hated clowns. Always had. They scared the shit out of him.

Movies like *Nightmare on Elm Street* and *Alien* also had to be eliminated due to being logistically impossible without CGI. And what was the point of realism if special effects had to be used?

And of course the typical 'phone call coming from inside the house' babysitter-slash-sorority-house-slash-slumber-party-slash-prom-horror flicks were also out of the question. Too many unknown variables. Besides, he hated working with teenagers.

When he'd started choosing his initial scenes he'd begun with the ones that didn't require the antagonist to be on screen. Once he'd completed a couple of small acts, he'd moved on to the big one, the one he'd been waiting to use when he finally announced himself to the world.

And what a debut the new and improved *Hitcher* had been.

He'd originally intended to improve on movies that pissed him off, the ones that had inexplicable fan bases or were huge blockbusters while other more deserving films were ignored.

Hence his most recent creative endeavors, though in truth that jaw-crunching scene from *American History X* needed no improvement, iconic perfection as it was.

Still, fun to recreate.

Now, as he mused on the recent realization that he actually liked being in front of the camera as well as behind it, he considered some of his previously disregarded scenarios.

The hook-handed bad guy of urban lore had appeared in numerous frat-fests, including *I Know What You Did Last Summer* and its godawful sequel. Perhaps, if he was feeling particularly adventurous, he could even try *Silence of the Lambs*? He smiled. Then again, perhaps not; even he wasn't willing to go as far as to consume human flesh. And since the entire point of this exercise was that everything be real, changing out the meat would be a cop-out. Perhaps another scene from the movie would work better, something with a little less cannibalism?

Although, he thought as he drained his glass, maybe it would be best to wait to do a reboot of such a classic. That particular one was a tough act to follow; maybe a bit more experience might be a good idea before tackling such an iconic role.

He wasn't completely narcissistic, after all.

That being said, he had a letter to write . . .

*   *   *

As Daniel and Reilly consulted the festival schedule to see where Bruce Reynolds might be, he asked. 'Did you see the guy on *Leno*?'

She remembered that she hadn't paid much attention to it at the time, but the actor's public meltdown had been reported in the Irish media too. High-profile star begins ranting about how his psychic had confirmed his past lives as none other than Abraham Lincoln and Gandhi. Yeah, that'll cross oceans to be a headline.

Later the actor's public relations people had claimed Reynolds had been suffering from exhaustion and over-medication for a sinus condition. While subsequent interviews had been done with poise and little excitement, the man's career had yet to recover.

'Says here, he's supposed to be signing autographs.' Daniel pointed on one of the festival maps posted every few feet. 'Here.'

As they wove their way through the crowd, Reilly made a mental note to boycott Toby Carpenter movies in the future. She'd dealt with her fair share of lecherous men – it kind of came with the territory being a woman in a mostly male field – but this had been the first time that she'd felt like someone had actually succeeded in undressing her with his eyes.

Daniel pointed. 'Right there.' He flashed his investigator's badge at the security guard and stepped behind the table.

'Mr Reynolds?' Reilly asked.

'No comment,' Bruce grumbled as he scrawled lazily across a head shot. The woman he passed it to looked disappointed. Reilly couldn't say that she blamed her. Finding out that one of your celebrity idols was a douchebag in reality was never easy.

'We're here about Drew Sheldon.' Daniel put his badge closer to Bruce's face.

'Oh, that again.' Bruce leaned back in his chair, looking up at Daniel with an insolent grin on his once handsome face. The last few years of hard living hadn't been kind. 'I heard he's missing.'

'He is.' Daniel kept his voice mild. 'Know anything about it?'

Bruce laughed. 'Like I already told the cops, I barely have enough money to pay my bills. I certainly wouldn't waste a dime of it to pay someone to take him out.'

'Who said anything about him being taken out?' Daniel asked. 'As of now, he's considered missing. Unless there's something you'd like to share.'

Bruce shrugged. 'Only that I wouldn't see any reason to keep a hack like Sheldon around.'

'Hack?' Daniel said. 'From what we understand, Drew Sheldon is one of the most sought after writers in the business.'

'Yeah, because he'll bend over and take it.' Bruce's smile disappeared. 'He cares more about money than about the integrity of his work. The guy'll do anything to make a buck.'

'Whereas you're in it for the craft?' Reilly indicated one of the movie posters on the table. Bruce Reynolds's biggest blockbuster had been slammed by the critics as being 'so brain-dead that a zombie toddler could've produced a finer piece of work'. Reilly had seen it while on a blind date back in Dublin. The guy had loved it. That had been their only date.

'Look, what do you want?' Bruce's swagger dissolved into petulance. 'I already told the cops everything I know.'

'I know that you had a reason to be angry at Sheldon, to want revenge. After all, he wrote you out of what was supposed to be your comeback role.' Daniel was smooth.

'Maybe I do have a reason to be angry,' Bruce said, 'but I don't have the money to do anything.'

'Doesn't mean you couldn't have done something yourself,' Reilly said.

Bruce snorted. 'Yeah, right. I only play the action hero. I'm not much of an action guy in real life.'

Not really any shock there, Reilly thought. Then, taking her cue from Daniel, she changed her tone. 'On an unrelated note, we've also been hearing rumors about someone posting movie inserts online – taking famous movie clips and splicing in their own newly shot footage. Have you heard anything about that?' She deliberately left out the fact that the clips in question were famed murder scenes.

'Movie inserts . . .' Bruce looked more interested than worried. 'Hadn't heard, but that sounds like a good idea to me.' He shrugged. 'Have you seen some of the crap that gets called "classic" these days? Whoever it is, if you find them, give 'em my number. I could use the work.'

'Will do,' Daniel said, meeting Reilly's gaze, which she took it as a cue to move on.

'And as for people who had issues with Drew Sheldon, you should be checking out Wesley Fisher,' Bruce said, now giving a dazzling smile to the pretty thirty-something who approached his table.

'Who?' Daniel asked, turning to him once again. He glanced at Reilly and she shook her head. She didn't recognize the name either.

'Wesley Fisher,' Bruce repeated. He added a note under his signature and gave it the girl.

Reilly rolled her eyes as she read over his shoulder. His room number. Typical.

'He's another director here at the festival,' Reynolds went on. 'Thinks he's the next big thing but can't get anyone to watch anything he does. Probably because it's even worse crap than what's already being peddled around here. I do know he was trying to get Sheldon to write for him. Match made in heaven if you ask me,' he added sardonically. 'Sure to have the straight-to-DVD crowd salivating.'

'Thanks.' Daniel looked over at Reilly and she nodded, silently agreeing that they weren't going to get anything else out of the actor.

Finding Wesley Fisher in the hotel turned out to be much harder than finding the other two. Fitting his image as a little-known director, he didn't seem to be on any schedules. Finally, following a tip-off from Fisher's co-producer, they tracked him down at the front desk where he was arguing with the concierge.

'Sir, for the last time, we are not upgrading your room. We are completely booked this week for the festival. I'm sorry.' Though the pencil-thin man looked anything but.

'Wesley Fisher?' Daniel cut in and the man at the desk gave the investigator a grateful look.

'Who wants to know?' Fisher was average in every way. Sandy-brown hair, brown eyes, just under six feet tall. Absolutely nothing about him was remarkable which, in a hotel full of movie bigwigs, was in a way a bit remarkable in and of itself.

'I'm Daniel Forrest, this is Reilly Steel.' Daniel showed his badge. 'We're looking into the disappearance of Drew Sheldon.'

'Of course.' The attitude in Fisher's voice vanished, replaced by concern. 'I'd heard he was missing.'

'And we heard that you might have had a problem with him.' Reilly deliberately phrased her statement to provoke a response. Something about Fisher's concern struck her as false.

Fisher gave a half-smile. 'I wouldn't go that far. Drew and I had our disagreements, but nothing more than two creative minds trying to collaborate on one vision.'

'So he was going to write a screenplay for you to direct?' Daniel asked.

Fisher shook his head. 'No. We tried for a few days but decided that our creative vision was just too different. We parted on good terms.'

'Do you know anyone who might not have been quite so willing to let things go?'

The director considered the question before answering. 'It's hard to say for sure. In this business, simple misunderstandings are blown up into feuds, disagreements into vendettas. I do know Toby Carpenter was arguing with Drew on the first day of the festival.'

'How do you know?' Reilly tried to keep the suspicion from her voice. Fisher's answers came easily, without a trace of guile. But for some reason, she didn't trust him.

'I heard them. Actually, everybody heard them. They were in the middle of the lobby having a shouting match.' Fisher shrugged. 'Then again, Toby doesn't really seem like the type to kidnap someone. He's more of a "ruin their reputation" type of guy.'

Reilly caught Daniel's eye and he nodded slightly.

'One more thing,' Reilly said. 'There are some other rumors going around about someone messing around with classic movie scenes.'

'Really?' Fisher asked. 'What do you mean, "messing around"?'

She chose her words carefully. 'Crosscutting new film together with old.'

'Hmm.' He cocked an eyebrow. 'Interesting. What does Drew's disappearance have to do with that?'

'Just covering all angles, Mr Fisher,' Reilly replied smoothly, giving nothing away. 'So what kind of movies do you direct? Sorry to say, I don't think I've heard of you before.'

Fisher smirked. 'Let me guess, you like those soppy chick-flicks where boy meets girl, there's some misunderstanding or lie that breaks them up, then there's a big emotional scene where they get back together.'

Reilly blinked. Not exactly the response she'd been expecting from someone who'd tried to be overly pleasant and helpful so far. She smiled. 'No, I'm more of a mystery fan, actually. I like figuring out who did it.'

'Well,' Fisher said, returning the smile, the corners of his eyes tightening, 'good luck with that. And be sure to let me know if there's anything else I can help you with.'

'Sure.' Daniel looked back and forth between Fisher and Reilly, a puzzled expression on his face. As he and Reilly moved away, he said, 'You were pretty rough on him even by your standards. Any particular reason for that?'

'I don't know. I just think there's something off about him.'

'This is the movie business, Reilly. There's something off with almost everyone here,' Daniel joked.

'Hey, are you the investigators looking into the disappearance of Drew Sheldon?' asked a middle-aged man, interrupting the banter.

'That's right. And you are?' Reilly held out a hand.

The man shook it; a firm, confident shake without lingering. His eyes were intelligent, his gaze appraising without leering. 'Jason Stuart, I'm a casting director. I was scheduled to work with Drew on his next project. Kai told me you were here, said I should talk to you. She doesn't have much faith in the cops.'

'So you and Mr Sheldon got along well?' Daniel asked.

Jason shook his head. 'That's what's odd. The last time Sheldon and I worked together, he was furious about the actress I cast as the heroine in *Chase the Wind*. Said I should've refused Carpenter's request for a recast. He told me that, if he had his way, I'd never work on another of his films. Then, this week, he was acting like it had never happened. I just went with it. In this business, you learn not to argue when things are going well.'

'Mr Stuart,' Reilly said, 'is there a specific reason you sought us out? Most people haven't exactly been eager to talk to us.'

'Well, like I told the detectives, I think I was one of the last people to see Drew before he vanished,' Jason said. 'We were having a smoke in the alley, talking about this new project he wanted me to work on. I finished my cigarette and headed back inside to meet up with a . . . friend. Drew stayed out for another.'

Based on his hesitation, Daniel seemed to deduce exactly why he was so eager to go back inside. 'And your friend can confirm that you were with her for the rest of the night?'

Jason nodded. 'She can. When I left Drew, there were only a couple of other people in the alley with him.'

'Who else?'

'Wesley Fisher and Paul Lennox, his co-producer, as far as I can remember. And a couple of other guys that I faintly recognized but don't know. There are so many hangers-on in this business that faces tend to blend into each other.'

A buzz cut into the conversation. Daniel reached into his pocket and pulled out his phone. 'Forrest. Hold on a minute.' Holding the phone at his side, he spoke again to the casting director. 'Thanks for your help, we appreciate it.'

Reilly followed Daniel through a set of double doors and out into the late afternoon heat. She took a deep breath of the heavy, muggy air as Daniel spoke to whoever was on the phone. In a way, she guessed Daniel was right. The whole Hollywood scene was definitely something she didn't understand.

'It's Todd. Their computer expert just tracked down one of the people who posted an admiring comment beneath the YouTube video of Holly's murder.' Daniel's prior good humor had vanished. 'Seems like our killer has been splicing films for a while. Old bar brawls and fight scenes. They've been popping up online for a couple of months and he's got a nice little following. So irrespective of whether this guy is already involved in the movie business, he's certainly on his way to going mainstream.'

Reilly cursed. If they didn't catch up with this guy soon, they could have a string of copycats looking for their fifteen minutes.

Daniel seemed to be thinking the very same thing, and the expression in his eyes suddenly made him seem far older than he was. 'We need to find this guy, Reilly, and fast.'

Chapter 19

The following morning Bradley dropped a newspaper onto Todd's desk. 'Take a look at this.'

'What?' Todd looked up from his workstation. He'd been working on getting trace from the rock at the beach used to kill the movie-maker's first male victim. So far, the only things he'd found were pieces of the same orange cotton fibers that had been in the victims' mouths. The killer had kept the towel wrapped around his hand when he'd picked up the rock. Impulsive but smart.

'He wrote to the *Tampa Bay Times*.'

Todd picked up the newspaper and the words leaped out at him in stark black and white. He found himself reading out loud, as if the verbalization would create some semblance of sanity to the moment:

I am writing to tell the city of Tampa not to fear. I am not looking to create a state of panic. While there

*has been unfortunate collateral damage, I am not
killing indiscriminately.*

*Those who appreciate the true art of film making
will come to respect the nature of my work, and the
statement that I am trying to make.*

*As I continue to work on my project, I will send
periodic updates so that the less evolved audience
can understand what I am trying to accomplish.*

'Narcissistic son of a bitch . . .' Todd shook his head.
He looked up at Bradley. 'When do we get the letter for
analysis?'

'It was an email, apparently.' He leaned back against
the counter. 'Detectives already have the IT department
tracing it. And another thing,' he added tiredly, 'it's not
Drew Sheldon's or the kidnapper's blood from
yesterday.'

'How do you know for sure?' Todd asked, interested
despite himself. Even though it wasn't the crime scene he
was focused on, the Sheldon one had been his. 'The blood
type in the alley was the same as on the medical records,
wasn't it?'

'Yes. But it didn't matter according to the tox screen,
because whoever this blood is from had so much amobar-
bital and alcohol in their system that they would've been
comatose, if not dead.'

'Couldn't the kidnapper have drugged Sheldon, though?
And maybe he already had alcohol in his system?' Todd
suggested.

'Not this much,' Bradley said. He turned toward Todd. 'Stand up.'

He did as asked, a puzzled expression on his face.

'You be Sheldon.' Bradley picked up a pen from the table. 'If I'm the kidnapper, I'd have to have a syringe with a highly concentrated dose to even get close to what I'm seeing here. Now, to cause the blood we saw in the alley, I'd have to create a wound bigger than one I could make with a needle, so I'd need a knife too.' He picked up a ruler.

'So you have a knife in one hand and the syringe in the other.' Todd's eyes narrowed. 'You'd need to put the knife in your dominant hand, which would leave the syringe in your weaker one.'

'But for the drugs to be in your system, I'd have to inject you first, wait a few seconds to a couple of minutes, depending on the injection site, and then cut you.'

'If I'm Sheldon . . .' Todd saw the problem as Bradley swung down with his left hand. He reached up and grabbed his wrist. 'I've just walked out to talk to you for some reason, so I'm facing you when you try to inject me. I grab your wrist. It's not your dominant hand, so I can stop you.'

'And if I try to use the knife with my free hand . . .' Bradley brought his other arm forward. 'Even if I could manage to only nick you while struggling with my other hand, there's no way for you to already have the drugs in your system.'

'And if your initial attack resulted in you successfully injecting me,' Todd said, 'I'd automatically grab for the syringe and yank it out.'

'Unless I knock you out, there's no way for me to pick up the syringe and still keep you under control.'

'But if you'd knocked me out, there'd be drag marks at the scene leading to your car. Which there weren't.' He was thoughtful. 'But that would be the only way to be able to come back for the syringe. If I'm not unconscious, keeping me locked in the car while you went back to get the syringe wouldn't be very smart.'

'Especially since the department had doubled police patrols for that area,' Bradley stated. 'Would it be worth it to go back for the syringe if there was a chance of being caught?'

'There's no scenario that allows for either Sheldon or the kidnapper to be both drunk and drugged without leaving behind a method of drug delivery, or someone being unconscious,' Todd mused. 'And since there's no evidence of someone falling or being dragged, it's safe to assume that they both walked to the vehicle under their own power.'

Bradley nodded. 'Which can only mean that the blood belongs to someone else.'

Detective Julie Sampson motioned to the suspect on the other side of the glass, currently being held by the Tampa PD in connection with the 'movie-maker killings' as they were now being called.

'Meet Brett Kubiak,' the female detective said to Daniel and Reilly. 'Twenty-year-old film student at NYU, home in Florida for a study break.'

The detectives had picked him up via a comment beneath the online clip of Holly's murder. 'The kid the cyber-crime geeks found yesterday gave us Kubiak's real name, said they'd been communicating online for a couple of months.'

Reilly studied the dark-haired young man in the inter-rogation room. He was decidedly unkempt and almost too thin, the bones of his wrists visible under his pale skin. He didn't look especially dangerous, but she knew that looks could be deceiving.

How many times were serial killers described as quiet and charming when in reality they were making suits of human skin?

'Kubiak's screen name is The Acolyte,' the detective said. 'Our techs have been working on connecting him to other videos, and so far we've identified him as having commented on several of the spliced movies, always complimentary and encouraging.'

'The Acolyte,' Daniel murmured. 'Interesting name choice.'

'What do you mean?' the detective asked, but before Daniel could answer, their attention was drawn to some-one entering the interrogation room. The interview was about to begin.

A tall detective with thinning black hair whom Reilly hadn't seen before took a seat in front of Kubiak. The kid didn't even look up.

'So, Kubiak, you like horror movies?' the interrogator asked.

'Sure.' The kid kept his eyes on the table. 'And long walks on the beach at sunset.'

'Don't be a smartass.' The detective stood up, put his hands in his pockets and began to pace. 'You're in a lot of trouble.'

'For what?' Kubiak barely sounded interested, much less concerned.

'Did you watch a film online that showed a girl getting ripped asunder and then comment that you were "looking forward to more"?'

'It's a movie,' Kubiak said, shrugging. 'And last I checked, freedom of speech includes posting comments on public Internet sites.'

The detective stepped up right next to the suspect. 'You know what I think?'

'Very little, I would assume.' Kubiak leaned back in his chair and crossed his arms over his chest. 'But go ahead.'

'Funny.' The detective didn't take the bait and Reilly wondered if he had always been that laid-back or if it was an acquired habit. He continued: 'I think you set up and filmed that murder, then couldn't help yourself and had to brag.'

Kubiak finally looked up, his expression carefully blank. 'I'm flattered, but it wasn't me. This guy has been working for months. Find the other videos and you'll see I was nowhere near where they were filmed.'

Julie Sampson's voice turned Reilly's attention away from the interrogation. 'What do you think, Dr Forrest?' she asked. 'Could he be our guy, or are we wasting our time?'

Daniel's jaw was set and Reilly knew what he was going to say. 'No, I don't think it's him. He admires the person who did the work, that's why he posts the comments. He wants the actual killer to see that he appreciates the "art" of what he's trying to achieve. Kubiak may secretly want to emulate the murderer, but he hasn't done anything other than watch.'

'What makes you think he wants to emulate the killer?' the detective asked.

'The name he chose for himself,' Daniel replied. 'It means disciple or follower.'

Chapter 20

'I've never seen anything like this.' Assistant Medical Examiner Dr Matthew Perez's skin had taken on a pale, waxy appearance.

Todd couldn't blame him. The violence of Holly's and the other murders had been bad, but this was somehow different.

Maybe because of the damage to the face. There was something depersonalizing about seeing someone's face like that, something that had once been normal looking so completely non-human.

'Do you understand the sheer force it would take to do this to someone?' The assistant medical examiner took a step back and gathered himself.

Given the severity of the violence, Todd was mildly impressed with the young man's quick recovery time. 'Could it have been a kick in the back of the head?'

'A kick?' The young man shook his head. 'No, at least not in the traditional sense.' Dr Perez pointed to the shattered remains of Anton Williams's jaw. 'The detectives said he was found face down on the sidewalk?'

Todd nodded. 'It looked like he'd put his mouth to the edge of the curb and . . .' he swallowed hard, not wanting to finish the sentence.

He recognized the setup of this one too. *American History X* was a good, if disturbing, movie about a vengeance-seeking white supremacist. There was a particularly memorable (for all the wrong reasons) black-and-white scene in which Edward Norton's skinhead character makes an attempted thief – a young African American man like their victim – pay by making him 'bite the curb', before stomping on the back of his head to break his neck and jaw.

Resulting in the same horrifying scenario they had here, though the movie had thankfully cut away before showing the end results.

'That sounds about right,' Perez said, when Todd outlined the comparison to him. 'There are burn marks on his torso consistent with a cattle prod of some kind. More concentrated electricity than a taser. It'd be enough to make him harmless, but not so much that he was completely unconscious. If he put his mouth on the curb . . . this injury was caused by abrupt, solid pressure against the back of his head. It would've caused his jaw to dislocate . . .' The doctor swallowed hard.

'Basically, a slam-down with the flat of a foot rather than a kick with the toe.' Bradley wanted to clarify.

'Exactly.' The doctor's attention was fixed on the remains.

'So we should be able to get a foot imprint from the head then.' Bradley's voice had lost all of its usual chirpiness. In fact, Todd noticed that his partner looked a bit green.

'I would think so.' Dr Perez picked up a pair of surgical scissors and cut off the filth-stained T-shirt.

Afterward, once they'd finished running the scene, Todd made a call as he and Bradley headed back to the car. He spoke softly into the phone. 'You know what this means . . .'

'It's moved beyond murder for the sake of art,' Daniel replied on the other side. 'This time the perp chose a brutal, hands-on murder. The *Hitcher* re-enactment was horrible, but he didn't physically cause the moment of death. The *Deep Red* one gave him a taste for it, but even the disfiguring was different; the victim would've died even if the water wasn't boiling. With this one, the route to death chosen was direct, brutal, essential, and for the first time our perp had the starring role in it.'

Todd didn't like where it was all going. 'You think he's going to keep picking stuff like this?' As Bradley looked back at him from the car to see what the delay was, he held up a hand to indicate that he was on his way.

'Quite possible, because it's not just about adding to or emulating movies anymore,' his father said grimly. 'I think he's enjoying himself.'

*　　　*　　　*

'So . . .' Reilly's tone was thoughtful as later at the beach house she and Daniel talked through their progress, or lack thereof. She began with the film festival interviews from the day before, trying to establish whether anyone they'd spoken to could be ruled in or out as a possible kidnapper or killer. 'We have a salacious producer who has a thing for young aspiring stars. He didn't really seem to know a lot about the world outside of his own private bubble, though.'

'Is he a good enough performer to fake his ignorance?' Daniel asked. 'Someone that self-centered would be narcissistic enough to equate his work with film greats. The question is, would he have been able to deny knowledge when asked directly or would he have wanted to take credit?'

Reilly considered it, then shook her head. 'I don't think so. The ego's there, but I don't think Toby Carpenter has the maturity to hide anything.'

Daniel nodded and took a sip of red wine. 'What about the other two – the director and that pompous actor Reynolds. Anything stand out for you?'

She wrinkled her nose. 'Both have flagging careers that could have inspired the desire to try something crazy. I know in the past that Reynolds has expressed a desire to try his hand at directing. Most actors do. And both he and Wesley Fisher came across as collected enough to have pulled off hiding whatever they knew.' Reilly sighed. 'And then there's that casting director. He's one of the last people to have seen Sheldon, but he volunteered to talk to us.'

'I think the producer we can pretty much discount,' Daniel said. 'And the casting director, since he gave us an alibi. The other two might know something, but I don't know if they'd be better suspects for the kidnapping or the murders. Both had grudges against Drew Sheldon.' He stood up and crossed to his refrigerator. 'Maybe the best solution is to send the whole damn lot of them back to LA.'

Reilly smiled. 'Sounds good to me.'

'So I'm thinking maybe something light for dinner this evening.' Daniel changed the topic of conversation. 'Chicken salad?'

'Oh,' Reilly replied, trying to sound nonchalant. 'Todd's actually coming to pick me up in about twenty minutes. We're going to get something to eat.'

'You and Todd are going out to dinner?'

Reilly could hear Daniel's amusement loud and clear. She sighed, pushing back her own mixed feelings about the idea. 'To discuss the case.' She kept her words firm.

'Got it.' She could almost hear his smirk. 'You know it's been good having you around,' he added fondly. 'And, just so you know, that job offer is open-ended. If for any reason you decide that you want to call it quits with Dublin, all you have to do is say the word.'

'Thank you,' Reilly replied, her feelings actually quite mixed at that idea. There was no denying that she was loving being back in the States, and she thrived on the challenge of working alongside Daniel. The weather was so bright and warm and her general demeanor had improved no end. She wondered now if her unusually somber and lackluster mood of late might actually have been some kind of SAD-induced thing, brought on by a three-year deficiency of vitamin D.

Or might her improved mood also be something to do with Todd's growing appeal? Reilly wasn't sure and she still couldn't quite figure out if he'd phoned earlier to ask her out to dinner really to discuss the case, or for any other reason.

Either way, she found she was looking forward to it perhaps a little more than she should have been.

She excused herself to her room, wanting to take a quick shower before Todd arrived. She told herself that it was just to wash away all of the day's work-related grime, but that didn't stop her from adding a spritz of lilac-scented body spray as she heard Todd's car pull up outside.

'Have fun at dinner.' Daniel grinned as she emerged from her room. 'And don't forget what I said earlier.' He waved at the pair as he headed out back onto the deck, his own dinner in hand.

'My dad giving you a hard time?' Todd gave Reilly a knowing grin as they walked out to his car, a Mustang Shelby.

'Actually, he keeps offering me a job.' She decided a simple explanation was best. No need to bring up any other implications.

They were pulling out of the driveway when he asked, 'And are you going to take it?'

'I don't know,' she said truthfully. 'If you'd have asked me a year ago, I would've said no way. Now though, things are different.'

'Really?' Todd glanced at her. 'How are they different?'

'They just are.' Reilly's tone let him know that the discussion was closed. She hadn't wanted to talk to Daniel about her recent misgivings about Dublin so there was no way she was going to tell Todd. She changed the subject. 'So, does Reed have any new suspects? Seeing as the Kobiak thing seems like a dead end.'

'I called him for an update earlier,' Todd snorted, 'for all the good it did me. His response was something along the lines of "You do your job and let me do mine".'

'I figured as much,' Reilly said. 'So how good is Reed – at his job, I mean?'

Todd used the remainder of the journey to fill Reilly in on the various personalities and quirks of the people with whom they worked. Some she'd guessed, others were a huge surprise, such as Bradley Ford's weakness for musicals.

As they walked up the path to the door of the restaurant, Reilly passed by close enough to get a whiff of Todd's aftershave. Armani, she realized, instantly cataloguing it.

The restaurant looked plush and welcoming, and actually much classier than she'd expected, given that many of the restaurants in Clearwater Beach were of the more laid-back barefoot and beachfront kind. Not that Reilly would have minded that either; from what she could tell, as well as offering terrific views most did great seafood along with the best American classics.

'Two, please,' Todd said to the smiling hostess who motioned for them to follow her. They walked through the main dining area and outside to an open-air wooden terrace perched right above the waterway, twinkling fairy lights strung from surrounding posts above the cosy patio tables. Reilly was almost sorry they'd arrived after dark as she imagined it would be a beautiful place to watch the sunset, and she made a mental note to revisit the restaurant to do just that.

Once they were seated at an intimate table for two directly overlooking the water, Todd switched to asking Reilly about her own life. 'You've been in Dublin for the last couple of years, right?'

Reilly nodded. 'Almost three, actually.'

'And you're in forensics there too.' Todd took the proffered menu.

She waited until the waitress had taken their drink orders to answer. 'Yes, I head up the GFU, the Garda Forensic Unit.'

'A senior investigator?' Todd sounded impressed. 'I mean, after the Hicks case, I would've expected that here, but in Dublin . . .'

'My reputation preceded me.' Reilly couldn't help but grin. It was actually nice to hear a response that for once wasn't incredulous. She'd had more than one man imply that she'd earned her position for a different skill set.

It had been only her second official case since graduation, back when she'd been an intern with the San
Francisco field office. A local senator, Eldon Hicks had
been the prime suspect in the strangulation of a call girl,
but there hadn't been any forensic evidence linking him to
the crime scene. It had been Reilly who'd found and identified trace on the senator's shoes as being from the park
where the girl's body was found. While the discovery had
been enough to gain some attention from her colleagues,
the moment everyone remembered was what had
happened at the trial.

Todd gave a smile that wasn't like his usual sardonic
one. This one was deeper, somehow more solid. 'Did you
really tell the defense attorney that he was dumb?'

Reilly couldn't help the grin that played over her
lips. Back then, she'd barely looked out of high school,
even though she was in her twenties; like most men,
the defense attorney had underestimated her. He'd
implied that she was too inexperienced to properly
analyze the two trace samples and, well, she'd lost her
temper. And when Reilly lost her temper, she didn't
shout. She just lost the filter between her brain and her
mouth.

'I believe my exact response was, "Normally, I would
say that a person's appearance holds no bearing on their
intelligence, but in your case, I'd say that's a correct
assessment. You are as dumb as you look."'

'How did you not get fired?' Todd's question was punctuated with his laughter.

'If the prosecution had lost, I probably would've been,' Reilly admitted.

'Dad talked about that case for weeks.' Todd glanced up as the waitress returned. 'He was so proud of you.'

Reilly squirmed in her seat as Todd ordered his meal. Until their conversation the other night, she'd never thought about how often Daniel had talked about her at home.

How Todd must have felt, hearing his dad talk about the accomplishments of someone else, especially when Todd and Reilly were close enough in age and in the same field. He must have felt like the two of them were being compared.

Then add in the pressure of a father as revered as Daniel Forrest . . . No wonder Todd came across as so touchy all of the time. It was a defense mechanism.

She felt his gaze on her as she gave her order – fillet steak cooked 'Pittsburgh medium'. It was such a revelation to have the server get exactly what she meant, unlike the ones in Dublin who couldn't possibly know that the term referred to medium on the inside but crispy on the outside. Yet an employee of any US steakhouse restaurant worth its salt would understand immediately.

And as she and Todd chatted easily about everyday stuff distinctly unrelated to the case, she couldn't deny the warmth that spread through her at the notion that he could be attracted to her. Just because she couldn't deny it didn't mean she had to act on it, or even like it. She had a job to do and she didn't need such a diversion interfering with her ability to help with the investigation.

That's what Reilly told herself as all throughout their dinner she noticed the heat and admiration in Todd's eyes.

By the end of the meal, she'd almost convinced herself that it was true.

Chapter 21

Morning came, and with it Holly Young's memorial service. Reilly had tried to clear her mind (as well as the effects of the couple of late-night margaritas she'd shared with Todd) beforehand with a run, but it hadn't worked. When her stomach was still in knots after three miles, she'd turned around and headed back. There was no point in pushing herself when it wasn't accomplishing her goal.

Daniel had been in his shower when she'd returned. Now, as she tried to decide how best to style her still-damp hair, she heard him behind her. 'You don't have to come to the memorial, you know.' He stood in the doorway to the guest room. He was already dressed in his suit, looking uncomfortable.

Judging by the number of times Reilly had seen him in a suit and tie, she was willing to bet it was the event that was making him uncomfortable, not the attire.

Not that she could blame him. Things like this were never easy. If anyone understood that, it was her. She had never really been a big fan of cemeteries, even before half of her immediate family ended up in one.

She'd certainly never understood people who thought it was somehow mysterious and alluring to hang out around gravestones, to be seen to be grieving, as if grieving itself wasn't enough.

For her, a cemetery meant one thing: she was visiting her mother's and sister's graves. Nothing alluring about that.

'If you're going to be there for Alice Young then I'm going to be there for you.' Reilly tried not to let her own anxiety seep through. She didn't want to go. Didn't want to sit in some church while a pastor extolled the virtues of a young woman she didn't know and tried to make sense of a senseless death. But she meant what she said: someone needed to be there for Daniel.

At the service, she sat between Todd and Daniel, resisting the impulse to reach over and take Daniel's hand when she saw how tightly he was clenching his jaw. She recognized that expression well, had used it herself – the desperate attempt to hold back tears, to be strong when everything inside wanted to break, was already broken.

A grim determination to find the man responsible filled her afresh.

And she didn't just want the guy found, Reilly realized as she looked at the grieving mother, she wanted him to pay.

*   *   *

Later that day, Todd frowned as he entered the bedroom.

The living room had been trashed, the floor filthy with debris. The bedroom, by contrast, was relatively empty. The only things inside the eight-by-eight room were a bare mattress, the body and the arrows holding the body in place.

He swore to himself, sorry that he hadn't taken Bradley's offer of taking the day off after the memorial service this morning. If he had he could have avoided this.

The victim was young, probably early twenties, Todd surmised. Pretty with honey-blond hair. Average height, average weight. She'd been stripped down to her bra and panties, but Todd was willing to bet that there'd been no sexual assault. A neat pile of clothes sat on the floor, splattered with blood. He snapped on his gloves. 'What do you think?'

'Robin Hood gone bad?' Bradley reached out a gloved finger to touch the end of one of the arrows.

'Robin Hood had better aim,' Todd countered absently.

There were three hits in total. One in the mattress (an apparent miss), another almost dead center in the torso, and the other . . . right through the eye-socket. Based on the volume of blood and the placement of the lower arrow, a few vitals had been lacerated and the girl had bled out. It was far from the most gruesome scene he'd seen, but it was enough to make Todd feel tired.

'Another one of our movie-maker's victims or just a pissed-off ex?' Bradley directed his question to Detective

Reed. 'Maybe a kid who's been watching too many movies?'

'No cameras at this one?' Todd asked. He carefully skirted a puddle of blood to get a closer shot.

'Nothing that implies a movie re-enactment so far.' The detective took a step toward the corpse. 'But there's something weird about this anyway. You don't see too many deaths by bow and arrow. Hunting accident with a cross-bow, sure, but nothing like this. Nearly twenty-five years on the force and I've never seen anything like this.'

'Maybe it's our guy after all.' Todd narrowed his eyes, looking over the scene again. There was a familiarity to the theatrics. A deliberateness to the placement of the arrows. 'Maybe he didn't film this because it wasn't the right scene.'

'But unless it's out of necessity, he seems to film all of the murders, does his whole edit and video stream thing somewhere else.' Bradley crouched down for a closer look at the floor. 'He always has a reason to kill. It's either a scene he's set up, or to protect himself. This might look like it could be one of his death scenes, but there are no cameras. It doesn't look like there's a motive here.'

'Sure there is,' Todd said grimly. It had taken him a minute, but he knew what had happened here.

'And what's that?'

He snapped a picture of the body. 'Practice.'

He took a step back and admired his make-up job. This scene had been in the back of his mind for some time, but he'd thought it too childish. It shouldn't have been easy to find the right shade this far from Halloween, but when he'd run across it at a craft store, he'd known it was a sign that he had to do it.

And of course it had been all too easy to find his cast member. With the festival in town it was like shooting fish in a barrel. This one seemed to have a little more spark than the other airheads he'd been working with though, and he wondered if she actually had the makings of a true celluloid star after all. Too bad they wouldn't get to find out.

He set the black hat on the dark-haired girl's head and straightened her dress. He'd never understood why this movie had been such a hit with families. Personally, it had given him nightmares for weeks. He still couldn't watch it. Even the songs made him cringe. The sequel had been even worse. And the stage play? He shivered and then scowled.

Time to get this done.

'Wake up.' He grabbed the girl's arm. If he was being truthful this death scene was less about art and more about overcoming childhood fears. Then again, weren't most movies just writers, actors and directors working out their own various issues?

Her eyes widened when she saw him approach and she screamed, the sound muffled by the gag in her mouth. He'd take that out in a minute, once he gave her the stage directions.

'In a moment,' he murmured, pitching his voice low, 'I'm going to take out the gag and let go of your arm. If you scream, if you try to run, I'm going to use this on you.' He pushed back his jacket to reveal the cattle prod. Part of him kind of hoped she would try to run. 'I'm not going to ask you to undress or touch you at all. I just want you to stand right there and don't run. Do you understand?'

She nodded frantically and his grip on her arm loosened. He pulled her to her feet and waited to see if she'd try to break away. When she didn't, he released her arm and reached behind her to untie her gag. As he pulled away the tie, she whimpered, but didn't scream. He held up the make-up wedge. 'I have to finish this first.'

As he covered the last of her face with the stage make-up, he wished all actors were this compliant. Her entire body was trembling but she never tried to run, didn't complain as he tilted her head this way and that.

Yep, definitely a fighter.

It was a pity he wouldn't be able to use her again.

He took a step back and paused, his hand ready to draw if she tried to escape. She didn't move, just stood where he'd left her, bottom lip trembling, tears coursing down her cheeks. When he reached his spot behind the camera, he pulled on a pair of gloves and bent to pick up his bucket.

The expression on her face said she thought she knew what was coming. One couldn't exactly be dressed as she was and not expect to get liquid thrown at her face. She didn't realize that it wasn't water until it hit her and she screamed.

Her hands went to her face as the acid melted the green make-up alongside her flesh. He couldn't help but grin as then, with no prompting from him, she screamed. A tortured, helpless screech; brilliantly theatrical in its delivery. Not too unlike the actual one from the movie.

He watched her crumple heavily to the ground and smiled.

One less childhood nightmare to worry about.

Chapter 22

Back at the lab, Todd realized he'd been staring at the wall for nearly twenty minutes. He and Bradley hadn't spoken for the entire ride back from the crime scene.

As soon as they'd arrived, he'd hurried to the bathroom and relieved his churning stomach of what little he'd eaten that day. He was fairly sure that Bradley had done the same. Even if he hadn't, he accepted the ginger ale Todd had purchased from the vending machine and started drinking it almost right away.

No one else had been in the lab when they'd come in but that hadn't been surprising. The only cars that had still been in the parking lot were theirs and Emilie's. Everyone else had finished for the day.

'Go home.' Emilie's voice drew both Todd and Bradley's attention. He turned toward the younger technician.

'What?' Todd was startled.

'I don't know what was at that crime scene, and I don't want to know.' Her voice was firm. 'But you look like hell. Get out of here. Do whatever you need to do to relax – go get a beer, whatever, and we'll tackle the evidence tomorrow.'

Out of the corner of her eye, Todd saw Bradley nodding. 'She's right, Todd. You should start again tomorrow, with a clear head. It's been a shitty day.'

But Todd didn't want a beer, and he certainly didn't want to go home to his empty apartment. After what he'd been through that day, he wanted – needed – to spend time around people he cared about.

Saying a reluctant goodbye to his workmates, he got in the battered Mustang and drove in the direction of Clearwater Beach.

Reilly drew her arms tightly around her shoulders, even though the chill she felt had nothing to do with the temperature. The memorial service and subsequent visit to the cemetery had brought too many memories back to the surface and she knew she'd been unusually quiet afterward.

Todd had arrived shortly after dinner, looking tired and defeated – and Reilly, still feeling slightly uncomfortable after their dinner last night, had exchanged pleasantries before the awkwardness got to be too much and she'd excused herself to the guest room.

She'd showered and tried to sleep. Her body had been – and still was – exhausted, but her mind hadn't stopped racing. No matter how hard she'd tried to sleep, she hadn't been able to stop thinking that there had to be something more she could do to help track down the movie-maker and stop even more bodies piling up. The guy seemed relentless, she thought, recalling Todd's account of the callous brutality of the latest murder with the arrows, and the other awful scene from *American History X*.

After that one, she'd briefly considered the possibility that there might be some kind of racial supremacist message behind the perp's actions, but seeing as he'd been indiscriminate with his victims up to then, and they'd found no link between any of them, this was probably a long shot. With the kind of movies chosen, the sick bastard didn't seem to be sending any particular message other than he considered himself to be some kind of 'artist'.

After nearly an hour, she'd given up on the sleep venture and reached for her laptop.

Now, at midnight, she was deep into the world of online snuff sites, not exactly the kind of thing that Hollywood dreams were made of. She'd seen a lot of messed-up things in her time, but her opinion of human-kind was slipping ever further downhill as she dredged through fantasies that turned her stomach. Now she was sure she wasn't going to get any sleep tonight. Or eat anything for the next week.

She clicked on another link, this one promising the 'long-awaited completion of one of the greatest horror scenes of all time'. As it started, she glanced at the title.

The Texas Chainsaw Massacre. Another one of her room-mate's favorites. She remembered now why they hadn't been roommates for very long.

The moment she saw the cut, her heart started pounding. She'd found another one. And, as she watched, something else about this film caught her eye. She grabbed her phone and was dialing Todd's cellphone number before she realized the time. Was he still here at the house or had he travelled back to Tampa to spend the night?

'Reilly . . .' Todd's voice held a note of concern, but no sleep. 'I'm just down the hallway. What's going on?'

'Meet you downstairs in five.'

Throwing on a T-shirt and a pair of shorts, she tiptoed down the wooden staircase, hoping not to wake Daniel. Two insomniacs in one house were enough.

Todd was already waiting, clad in a white shirt and boxers.

'Have you ever seen *Texas Chainsaw Massacre*?' she asked, without preamble.

He swore, immediately understanding.

'I just found a spliced clip from it,' she said.

'So we're looking for a lot of small body parts this time?' Todd sounded as if he were going to be sick.

Reilly didn't blame him, but bypassed any comment. While he'd made an important point, there was something else about the finding that directly affected the investigation. 'Those skin cells you found on the gloves from before, didn't you say that Emilie pointed out that there was something wrong with them?'

'Well, they were old, she said. Not as in the person they originated from was old, more like they'd degenerated over time.' Todd's voice held the question he didn't ask.

Reilly's tone was grim. 'In the movie, the killer—'

He finished the thought, his voice full of unashamed horror. 'He wears a mask made of human skin.'

'In just a short period of time, he's moved from setting up the scenes to being an active participant.' Reilly wrapped her free arm around her bare knees and hugged them to her chest, feeling a sudden chill despite the Florida heat. 'I don't think these were his first murders, but they were the first he'd filmed directly carrying out the killings, and I think he likes being in front of the camera. He's escalating, Todd.'

'So what's his end game?'

She shook her head, her gaze staring at distant shadows in the darkness. 'I don't know, but it can't be good.'

Chapter 23

He entered the storage unit and pulled down the door behind him. Then strode across the narrow space to where his prized acquisition was sitting, and wrinkled his nose as he grew closer.

The man's fear hung in the air, far fouler than the inevitable waste that came with being kept in an enclosed space for a few days. For someone who had created some of the most memorably horrific scenes ever to grace the big screen, Drew Sheldon didn't seem to have much fortitude.

'Are you finding the accommodation more to your liking now that you've realized I'm not going to kill you?' He sat on the room's lone chair and faced the middle-aged man on the cot. 'Though, I must say, Mr Sheldon, you're looking a bit the worse for wear. I know this isn't exactly the Hilton, but I did provide you with a bucket of water, soap and clean clothes.' His gaze ran over the unkempt creature whose own daughter probably wouldn't have recognized him. 'Have some respect for yourself.'

Sheldon glared back at him. The writer's dark eyes were bloodshot, his gray hair matted with dirt. His clothes were filthy, half of his nails ragged and broken.

He had expected a slew of questions when he'd arrived. An attack wasn't possible thanks to the thick chain he had purchased at a local hardware store, but an attempt wouldn't have been out of the question.

He'd considered not using a chain, but he had to be sure Sheldon wouldn't escape.

The writer was essential to the plan.

He felt bad that Sheldon's ankle would be raw by the time they were done, but the only other option that had come to mind involved a piece of wood and a sledgehammer. He had opted for the less violent solution. Although, the irony of hobbling a man named Sheldon did appeal to his dramatic side. He'd always been a big fan of the work of Stephen King.

Drew Sheldon didn't say a word. In fact, he looked a bit petulant, which amused though didn't surprise him. Most big-wigs in Hollywood considered themselves so important that they would react to a situation like this with a sullen, narcissistic mentality. Oh, well, small talk wasn't necessary, just polite.

Time to move on.

They had a lot to do and it was only a matter of time before either the detectives or that profiler guy and his blond sidekick he'd seen at the hotel started connecting the murders to the missing writer.

Amazing it was taking them so long, actually. Then again, was it really that much of a surprise? He knew how easily the ball was dropped when personnel were scarce and resources were stretched. Happened in the movie business all the time. 'Since you don't seem interested in chatting, I'll just cut straight to the point.' He crossed his legs and got comfortable. 'I've brought you here to write me a script – an original screenplay.'

Sheldon's eyes widened, then narrowed. Whatever the writer had been expecting, a job wasn't it. His voice was shaky, but his words were defiant. 'Like hell I will.'

He grinned, glad Sheldon was regaining some of his feistiness. The writer was petrified – and who wouldn't be – but at least this attempt at strength meant this was going to work. If Sheldon had been too scared, his writing would suck. After all, it would be difficult for him to come up with a brilliant script while pissing his pants.

'We'll come back to that then,' he said with a wave of his hand, dismissing Sheldon's words. 'Let me show you some of my previous work; let you get an idea of what I can do.'

He could barely contain his excitement as he fixed his flash-drive into the tablet he'd purchased just for this purpose. He'd been dying to show someone his work all at once. He hadn't gotten to watch a reaction to any of his films in the flesh, though he had enjoyed reading the comments online, validating what he already knew: the fact that he was more than capable of creating what an audience wanted.

He laughed every time he thought of the cops' tech people desperately trying to take down his clips, only to have them pop back up again in just a few hours.

'Take a look at this.' He started the first video and watched Sheldon's face with eager anticipation.

Ten minutes later, he was stepping back, disgusted, as Sheldon dry-heaved into the bucket that had been serving as his toilet. He scowled. Maybe Drew Sheldon had been a mistake. Apparently, he couldn't appreciate art.

'If these aren't to your liking,' he said, unable to keep the sneer out of his voice, 'perhaps my next one might better suit your fine palate.'

He started walking toward the door. 'Until then, I'll just let my new improved movies play. Keep in mind, sir, that you only have two choices: writing my script or watching that pretty daughter of yours star in one of my masterpieces.

'And I guarantee you,' he added ominously, '*my* stunt people don't survive.'

'You've got to be kidding me.' Reilly shoved herself back from her computer and grabbed the coffee Daniel had just dropped by her desk.

They'd been at the office in Clearwater since the early hours, trying to make sense of the mounting evidence gathered from the increasingly prolific movie-maker's crime scenes. It was now late afternoon and Reilly was just beginning to flag, when she'd hit on something related to what she'd discovered last night.

'Found a lead on the *Texas Chainsaw* thing?' Daniel asked.

'Yes, but you're not going to believe from where.' Reilly stood up and crossed to the printer, grabbing the sheaf of paper that she'd just run off. 'We'll need verification from the locals, but I found this article.' She handed the document to Daniel.

'California?' He took the printout and quickly skimmed through it.

Reilly nodded, explaining even as Daniel read. 'Several body parts were found in a landfill in Southern California, not enough to make an entire body, but the coroner said they looked like they could be from up to four different victims. And judging by what they did find, most likely homeless. Cut marks to the bones indicated that the victims were dismembered by chainsaw.'

'So our man started in California and ended up here?' Daniel nodded sagely as he came to the same conclusion Reilly had when she'd seen the location.

'The film festival again,' she said. 'It has to be connected, I'm sure of it.'

'Perhaps these murders and the kidnapping are connected by more than just film. Maybe Drew Sheldon was tired of being just a screenwriter and wanted to move behind the camera?'

'And maybe he wasn't kidnapped at all,' Reilly said, her mind racing. 'Maybe he just wants the authorities to think that someone took him, as cover for when he's out making his own movies.'

'Could be,' Daniel said. 'But that's a lot of maybes.'

'You don't agree?' she said, frowning.

Daniel was typically circumspect. 'I just have a hard time believing that a man would bring his own daughter to the same place he plans to go on a killing spree. I agree that it's increasingly possible someone at the film festival is involved, perhaps practicing on home turf and then going public here.'

'Either way, it's a good lead.'

'What's a good lead?' Todd entered as Reilly spoke. He looked tired and she guessed that the brutality of the latest murder was taking its toll on him. 'It better be something because this asshole's getting too cocky for my liking. He sent an email to the department this morning, "explaining" that the archery thing was a botched attempt. A botched attempt? A kid ended up speared to a bed, for Chrissakes!' He put a hand through his hair.

'Sit down, son.' Todd complied and Daniel handed him a cup of freshly made coffee.

Then he read through the email the killer had sent, uttering four short sentences aloud.

'*I have proven my skills in the area of gratuitous violence and now show that I can match the greatest of film-makers. Fans of the genre have acknowledged my superiority and have asked for more. Until the demand for my work disappears, I will continue to provide society with what they want. As other artists have not fulfilled society's needs, I will do so proudly.*'

Daniel considered the words, both the stated meaning and the one hidden, the subconscious meaning of what the killer was saying, Reilly knew.

'He's narcissistic,' he stated. 'Most likely has been involved in the artistic community or has been shunned by it, either for poor work or inferior quality. He sees himself as an ostracized creative, misunderstood by those around him, and he's using these murders as the way to prove to the world that they were wrong about him.'

'Hell of a way to prove a point,' Todd muttered. Then he asked Reilly about what she'd found.

She indicated the laptop on the desk. 'Based on what we learned last night – the possible *Texas Chainsaw* connection – I've been searching for unsolved murders where skin was missing from victims,' she explained quickly. 'I couldn't find anything in Florida that fit. So I expanded the search to include news articles from other states. I figured if there was something that strange, it'd make the papers. And I was right. I got a hit in Southern California. Your dad and I were thinking it more and more likely that our killer is someone from the film festival, and not just because of the timing. If the detectives question—'

Todd held up his hand. 'I've already passed the information along about the skin to Detective Reed, but I think we need to keep this particular discovery quiet for now.' He glanced at his father, who looked thoughtful. 'The California connection, I mean.'

'Why?' Reilly looked from Todd to Daniel and back again, confused. She was missing something.

'Because once a murderer crosses state lines, the Feds get involved,' Daniel reminded her. 'They'll come in and take over.'

'But that means more resources, surely?' Reilly still didn't understand. The Tampa PD already had too much work and not enough people to do it. How could bringing in outside help be a bad thing?

'It's been too long since you've worked in the States,' Todd said. 'The Bureau doesn't play well with the locals, and Reed and Sampson will freak.'

'Todd . . . for goodness' sake . . .' Reilly tried to reason with him.

'I want *us* to nail this guy.' His voice was hard. 'I don't want some gorilla Fed coming in and screwing everything up.' He looked at his father. 'No disrespect intended.'

Daniel put his hands up. 'None taken, I know how it works,' he said. 'And I also know that if the Feds do come in, it means we're all well and truly out.' He looked at Reilly. 'In this situation I agree with Todd. We promised Alice we'd take this guy down.'

Reilly opened her mouth to argue; then shut it again. She could understand their point of view to some degree. If being part of the team that caught Holly's killer would alleviate some of Todd and Daniel's helplessness, then she couldn't blame them. And as long as they were making progress, and unless she saw any evidence of the investigation being compromised, she'd just do her job and leave the interdepartmental relations to Todd. It wasn't like it was her call in any case: she was a guest here.

And she'd never cared much for politics anyway.

Later that evening at the beach house, she and Daniel sat in silence through two television shows that she wasn't familiar with, and didn't even try to follow.

She barely noticed when Daniel said he was going to bed; her attention only returned when the news announced it would be headlining a story about the recent murders: 'Leading news tonight – as it has been for the past week – the killer, a self-confessed movie maestro, has claimed another victim. Little is known other than that the victim was a male African American and was discovered outside a half-finished housing complex near Hillsborough Avenue.'

'Maestro . . . they gave him a goddamn nickname . . .' Reilly shook her head, exasperated.

'And in related news, an unnamed source at the TPD has confirmed that the killer sent an email, unsigned, to the department earlier today.'

She sat up straight and sighed, wondering where this supposed confidential information had come from, even though leaks were unfortunately rife in police enforcement all over the world.

The late-night newscaster's voice was smug, as if he had personally tracked down the killer and extracted an interview. 'In the email, the killer talks about another recent victim – an as of yet unidentified woman found in an abandoned house on the city's south side. He explains that the victim had been targeted merely for rehearsal of a particularly difficult scene. The movie maestro apologizes for, quote, "taking a life without producing a piece of quality work" and signs off by promising that his next re-enactment will be unforgettable.'

Unforgettable for all the wrong reasons, Reilly thought darkly. The news bulletin continued. 'No word from our DA or local authorities as to how close they are to an arrest.'

'Because they really want you to announce it to everyone, including the killer, that they're closing in.' Reilly glowered at the newsreader, thankful Daniel had already gone to bed and hadn't heard her talking to herself.

'In other news,' the reporter went on, 'there have been rumors that Hollywood screenwriter Drew Sheldon, scheduled to be in town for the Tampa Film Festival, is not, as authorities have led us to believe, absent from the line-up but has in fact been kidnapped. With the alley next to the Millennium Hotel reportedly cordoned off as a crime scene, one can speculate that it was from this point that Sheldon was taken. Between the recent rash of murders and Mr Sheldon's disappearance, citizens of the Tampa Bay Area can only wonder just what our law enforcement authorities are doing with their time. No one from the department has been available to take our questions.'

'That's because they're all out doing their goddamn jobs.' Reilly scowled and reached for the remote. Jeez, media really were the same all over the world.

No one wanted to catch this bastard more than Todd and Daniel though. She stood up, deciding to try and get some shuteye. She wasn't sure if she'd be able to sleep, but she was going to try.

If they were going to catch this guy, they all needed to be at the top of their game.

Chapter 24

Maestro. It just had a certain ring to it. Son of Sam, Jack the Ripper, Hollywood Maestro. It could work. A chosen few knew his industry moniker, of course, though none of them knew his real name.

He was an artist, not an idiot.

And speaking of art, he needed to decide on something for his next creation.

After his last re-enactment had gone so well, he'd briefly considered purchasing a clown suit and taking a machete to it, but that wouldn't work because he wasn't supposed to be mixing genres or creating entirely new scenes with iconic characters.

Unfortunately, that meant that addressing his adolescent fear of clowns would need to wait. He would do it though. Clowns and then that stupid Jabberwocky that had caused him to sleep with a nightlight for six months.

He'd then considered going a bit more old-school to make a lasting impression. One of the off-screen death scenes that had always niggled at him was from a source that probably would've surprised most people.

This killer had taken out hundreds, maybe even thousands, of innocent victims, all of whom died off-screen. Once he really thought about it though, he realized that using the Angel of Death from *The Ten Commandments* was probably a bad idea.

First of all, he had no idea where he'd get so many kids at such short notice, and the idea of killing a bunch of infants did turn his stomach, even if it was for artistic reasons.

But the deciding factor was a bit simpler than that. The resulting outcry from completing such a film would completely overshadow what he was trying to do. Aside from all of the people who'd label him a monster for killing kids, every right-wing kook in the country would start on a religious rant. That was the last thing he needed.

No, the Maestro wanted to be appreciated, not reviled.

So he moved on.

He was still saving a couple of options until he had the perfect casting, but maybe he could dip into *Se7en*. He was fairly sure he could find a pregnant blond and the right-sized box, but without the reactions of the other characters, it just didn't have the same impact. He could've been chopping the head off of any blond. The significance would be lost.

Although, beheading did sound like a good idea. Censored films always did them the very same way: the victim, the cut away to the executioner and the fall of the axe, the roll of the head. Such a cop-out. And these days, with special effects taking the place of stunts and the abundance of vampires and zombies, decapitation was as common on screen as gun shots.

All this meant was that he shouldn't use just any old beheading. He needed something special. Something *memorable*.

Two movies popped into his head simultaneously. One male victim, one female. Both with deaths unique enough that, with the right costume and set-up, they couldn't be mistaken for anything but what they were.

The latter would be a perfect sign-off piece before he began his own work with Sheldon. What better way to usher in a new era than to recreate the deaths of two characters based on real-life people, and use two iconic films to do it?

The Maestro smiled. The setup for this one needed to be just right for both parts, but it was going to be well worth it when he was done.

Now, he had one other thing to do before he could call it a night.

He'd never considered himself a particularly articulate man. He tried, of course, but most of the time he thought he sounded stilted, pretentious even.

It didn't help that he was so much smarter than the people around him. It was difficult to put so much brilliance into words. As a result, he generally found himself rewriting his letters several times until they were letter perfect – no pun intended.

He reread the second draft of his new missive with a critical eye. It was always hard to find the right balance of soul-baring without giving away his true identity.

'What makes a particular film or scene stand out? Is it the writing, the directing, the acting? If popularity is the basis of judgment, it would seem that the audiences choose the most gratuitous, disgusting, shocking piece of filth possible and tell all of their equally unsophisticated friends . . .'

The Maestro stopped. He probably should rethink the accusing tone.

He wanted to bring the public to his side, not alienate them.

Besides, he had to admit that making movies was much more fun than he'd originally thought it would be.

'I don't know about you guys, but I could use a drink,' Bradley announced as he put aside the arrow he'd been examining. Two sets of surprised eyes turned his way. 'Look, we've been working our asses off for the last week and more. And I know I'm not the only one who could do with a bit of a break.'

'Do you really think now is the best time to drop everything and go get drunk?' The edge to Todd's voice was sharp.

'Todd,' Emilie began, putting a gentle hand on his arm. 'I don't think that's what Bradley was saying. And he's right. You're going to burn out if you try to keep going like this.'

'I'm not suggesting we all go out and get wasted.' Bradley's voice softened. 'I'm just saying that we've all been putting in insane hours this week. Let's go out, have a drink and go home. Get some real sleep tonight, and come back focused and ready to keep working.'

'All right,' Todd reluctantly agreed. He put the most recent victim's shirt back in its bag.

They moved to a bar down the street often frequented by other law enforcement and by the time the team had ordered their second round of drinks, the tension had all but melted away. Even normally quiet Emilie had loosened up. Todd and Bradley listened with amusement as she shared a story about her first time counseling at summer camp when she'd been mistaken for a camper out past curfew.

'So the security guard, looking very pleased with himself, escorts me in to see the camp director, who just happens to be my aunt.' Emilie's tale was interrupted when an overly intoxicated young man bumped into the table.

'Excuse me,' he slurred. His face broke into a large smile as he ran his eyes over Emilie. 'You're pretty.' He put his hand on her shoulder.

She shook it off, trying to be polite. 'Thank you. Have a good night.'

'I wanna have a good night with you,' he continued, reaching for Emilie's face.

Long fingers clamped around the man's wrist and Bradley yanked the young man away from Emilie. 'I don't believe the lady's interested.' His voice was firm.

'And who're you? Her father?' The young man leered at Emilie. 'Guess I shouldn't tell you what I want to do—'

The rest of the sentence was lost as Bradley's fist connected with the man's jaw. He shook his hand as the man tumbled to the floor.

Todd raised an eyebrow, taken aback by this unusual display of violence. He looked from his partner to Emilie. Was there some kind of budding office romance going on here?

'Dean,' Bradley called out to the bartender. 'You'll want to get some guys over here to throw out the trash.' When he turned, Emile was staring at him with some kind of wonder in her eyes. He shrugged and smiled. 'I can't stand men who don't know how to treat a lady.'

'And on that note,' Todd said, glancing at his watch, deciding he wasn't going to stand in the way of true love, 'I should get going. I really like that idea about catching up on some sleep.'

'You're probably right,' Bradley said. He picked up his coat and turned to the younger technician, leaving Todd in no doubt whatsoever that his suspicions were correct. 'Want to split a cab, Emilie?'

As they said goodbye and went their own way, Todd castigated himself for not having noticed his colleague's growing closeness when it was right under his nose, though he guessed they were all working so hard, he'd been focusing on little else but the investigation.

Still, if he'd missed that, what else had he been missing lately? Was Reilly right about bringing in outside help and letting the FBI take over? Were he and Daniel too caught up in their own grief, more immersed in finding vengeance for Holly than being able to methodically examine the facts as they presented themselves? Or too pigheaded to accept anything other than their own theories? In short, was he really doing everything he could to find Holly's killer?

Not for the first time, Todd doubted his ability to see the wood for the trees.

Chapter 25

The slightly nasal voice of the nine-o'clock newscaster in the background once again talking about the movie killings caught Reilly's attention.

'The recent spate of horrific murders remain unsolved, and as usual, neither the police nor the DA's office have issued a statement, leaving many to wonder just how much actual work is being done to catch the killer. Or if the authorities are simply waiting for the Maestro to strike again.'

Reilly shook her head, exasperated. The perspiration on her skin was drying, leaving her feeling clammy and gritty. Definitely one of the things she *hadn't* missed about the warmer climate. 'You'd think the media would know better by now.'

'I think it's less about knowing better and more about just not caring.' Daniel took a sip of his wine. 'And about what they can get out of it in entertainment value rather than what's right.'

'Makes them not much better than the killer himself then, doesn't it?' Reilly commented darkly. The more tired she got, the loopier she became.

'You know reporters just get pissy when the cops don't tell all,' he said, turning toward her.

'I know,' she muttered. 'Doesn't mean I have to like it. But . . .' She looked up at Daniel as the thought struck her. 'What you just said about caring more about what they can get out of it, rather than what's right.'

'What is it?'

'It's Todd.' Reilly had been debating whether or not to tell Daniel about her concerns. 'He's putting himself under so much pressure to solve this case that I think he's losing sight of the big picture. Like refusing to bring in outside help.'

Daniel considered her statement for a moment before responding. 'When Todd came to tell me that he wanted to go into the forensic field, it was said as a kind of challenge, like he expected me to try to warn him off, to tell him that he wasn't going to be good enough for it. Since then I think every one of his achievements has been accomplished with a chip on his shoulder. He's letting his grief over Holly turn into this need to fix things on his own.'

'It's not working though, is it? We need to do something.'

'What you need to do right now is get some sleep.' Daniel's tone was amused. He stood up. 'Let Todd work things out on his own. We can keep an eye on him to make sure he doesn't cross any lines, but other than that, there's nothing anyone can do. He's a Forrest, after all.'

'Meaning pigheaded to the last?' Reilly raised a smile. 'I'll head for bed in a few minutes.' As Daniel walked into the kitchen, she tucked her feet up underneath her and closed her eyes, wanting to just rest up for a moment. When he came back, she'd get up and go to bed. The thought was still in her mind as the darkness crept over her.

It had all been a bad dream, Reilly realized, as she walked into her house. Her mom and sister were right there, laughing, talking, joking. She rushed forward, wanting nothing more than to put her arms around them both, hear them breathe, see them smile.

Even as her skin touched theirs, she felt them start to cool under her touch. Despite this, she clung to them, knowing that if she pulled away, she would see the chalk-white flesh, the sightless eyes. If she didn't look, then it hadn't happened . . .

Her eyelids were stone heavy, but she forced them open anyway. She had to stop that incessant buzzing alarm. Reilly sat up as her hand closed on her phone. She turned off the alarm and was halfway to the bathroom before she realized that she was still wearing the clothes from the night before. The best she could figure, as she climbed into the shower, was that she'd fallen asleep on the couch and Daniel had carried her to her room.

The thought brought forward a memory. It was fuzzy, clouded by sleep and grief, but she knew it was true. After her mother's funeral, after everyone else had gone home, back to their unbroken families, Reilly and her dad had sat up together on the couch until, finally, she had succumbed to her exhaustion. She'd only barely been aware of her father as he'd carried her to her room, but she'd never forgotten the feeling of being safe and loved.

It had been that memory she'd clung to in the days afterward when Mike had abandoned the family, seeking solace in the bottle. No matter what happened, she always had the knowledge that he loved her.

As she searched through the closet for something to wear today, her phone rang. She glanced down at the name and smiled.

'Chris, hi!' Reilly switched to speakerphone. She was delighted to hear from him, but the cheeriness in her voice sounded forced even to her own ears. She shook her head, trying to get rid of the cobwebs.

'Hello, stranger.' Even though it wasn't all that long since she'd last heard it, the Dublin accent sounded almost alien to her. 'How's the tan coming along?'

She smiled balefully. If only . . .

'Hope I didn't phone too early and wake you up or anything, but it's lunchtime here—'

'No, it's fine, I was up,' Reilly interjected. 'How's everything there?'

'The same, up to our necks in it as usual. It's not the same without you, though,' he added fondly. 'We all miss you, of course, but Kennedy in particular is bereft without you. Don't think Gorman appreciates his particular brand of humor as well as yourself.' He laughed, referring to Jack Gorman, the GFU colleague who was covering for Reilly throughout her enforced leave.

She laughed, oddly touched to hear this. 'Well, if he calls him "blondie" and makes *Baywatch* jokes about him too then I don't blame him. Tell him I said hi.'

'I will, of course. So while it's always good to hear your voice,' Chris went on, 'there's actually a reason I'm calling.'

'I thought as much.' Sounded like the lab had finally found something on the powder.

'Well, you'd probably know more about this than I do, but seems the stuff on the table was antimony.'

Reilly's eyes widened. 'Seriously?' Antimony (sulphide stibnite) was a metallic substance, produced mainly in China and used in alloying metal and tin. The initial jump her mind made regarding the metalloid was related to alloying used in fire retardants, and also for bullets and ball bearings. Though, trying to think about it from the perspective of the powdered form she had encountered, she recalled that in Egyptian times the component had been used in cosmetics as a form of eye make-up, and even today was still popular among Goths. The metallic form was harmless from what she could recall. But the stibnite component was extremely toxic.

Then Reilly thought about the violent vomiting episode she'd suffered at the hospital in the aftermath of her return to consciousness. Severe nausea inhibited absorption into the bloodstream, which is likely why the hospital had been unable to identify the compound in her blood.

'What about the victim; is that what killed her?' She thought back to the crime scene in Dublin where the victim had lain spread-eagled across the bed, hands bound, wrists raw from the struggle to free herself and/or the writhing to vomit. Her suspicions since had been that it was kinky sex mixed with drink and drugs gone wrong, whereupon the partner had gone running. The subsequent discovery of a hard-to-come-by toxic material that no one in their right mind would take as a recreational drug put a different slant on it.

'Karen Thompson believes that the girl didn't specifically die from antimony poisoning, but it doesn't mean she didn't ingest the stuff – she had also been violently sick, remember?' Chris said. 'The extreme stress of being ill and bound may have just caused her respiratory system to shut down.'

'Wow.' Reilly ran a hand through her hair, not sure how to feel. 'Did Julius – I presume it was Julius who ran the analysis – say anything else?'

'It was Julius, yes, and only that he believed your blackout was the result of a strong nervous reaction to the stuff – we all know how well that nose of yours operates,' Chris added lightly.

'Not well enough this time,' she muttered. 'Well, thanks for letting me know. I hope the discovery gave you some kind of breakthrough in the case.'

'Well, it's something, but it's mostly got O'Brien worrying that there's someone going round out there trying to pass the stuff off as cocaine. Anyway, enough about work; how's beach life? You must be getting bored of sitting around by now.'

'Actually . . .' Reilly quickly filled him in on the moviemaker investigation, or the Maestro, as the media now liked to call him.

Chris was incredulous. 'You're working a murder investigation – in Florida? But how?' Then he got it. 'Of course. Forrest.' His tone was full of disapproval. 'I can't believe the guy dragged you into something like this when you're supposed to be taking it easy. Christ almighty.'

'It's not like that.' She explained how one of the killer's first victims (that they knew of) had been a close friend of Daniel's. 'He asked for my help – how could I say no? You'd do the very same thing and you know it.'

'I'm not so sure – sun, sea and sand sound pretty nice from where I'm standing. It's lashing rain out again today; spring, my foot.' Then Chris's voice softened. 'Look, I know what you're like with things like this. A dog with a bone, as Kennedy says. Just try and keep your involvement as low-key as possible, OK? We want to see you back in one piece here very soon.' Then he paused. 'You *are* coming back, aren't you?'

Reilly's insides tightened. A week ago it would have been an easier question to answer, but now she wasn't so sure.

She laughed, trying to make her voice sound light. 'Sure I am, unless of course O'Brien decides I'm more trouble than I'm worth.'

Chris's voice was warm in return. 'Reilly, I think we all decided that a long time ago, but we still want to keep you.' The words touched her more than she could imagine and she actually felt herself bite back tears. It had felt like a very long time since she and Chris had shared such an easy, comfortable conversation. 'Listen, I'd better go,' he said then, getting ready to end the call. 'Stay safe and hurry back.'

'I will,' Reilly replied, eyes shining as she held the phone close, and suddenly missing the cold damp country across the Atlantic from which she'd been so sure she needed to escape.

Chapter 26

'For the love of . . .'

Everyone in the lab stopped what they were doing and looked toward the door of Bradley's office, waiting. Less than a minute later, the man himself entered the lab looking more bewildered than angry.

'Something happen?' Todd asked, as if no one had heard the string of expletives that had followed the original exclamation.

Bradley glared at him. 'You and Emilie head to this address.' He thrust a piece of paper at him. 'You're not going to believe what movie the sick fuck acted out this time.'

'What is it?' Todd asked, curious despite the growing feeling of dread.

Bradley shook his head. 'You're going to have to see it to believe it.'

As the senior investigator walked away, Emilie looked over at Todd. 'What do you suppose he meant by that?'

'Beats me,' he said. 'But we'd better get going.'

When they reached the crime scene, an abandoned warehouse on the outskirts of the city, Todd immediately knew that something about this one was different. The cops standing outside the building all wore the same slightly befuddled expression that Bradley had been wearing.

The ones inside merely pointed Todd toward the center of the building without a word. His curiosity growing with every step, he kept his eyes on the yellow police tape.

He stopped just inside it, his brain suddenly unable to process the simple command to move forward. It took him a moment to comprehend exactly what his eyes were seeing.

A crumpled shape dressed in a shapeless black garment, the material deteriorated in places. A puddle of green goo on the concrete beneath. A pointed black hat. And the unmistakable smell of chemicals and charred flesh.

'Oh, my God . . . no fucking way . . .' Mouse-like Emilie (whom Todd had never before heard swear) pretty much summed it up.

Todd pressed the back of his wrist against his nose and took a step back. The fumes were becoming overpowering. He could feel himself growing light-headed as his body warred between gasping for air and not wanting to take in the toxic fumes.

Mark Reed was suddenly between him and Emilie, a filter mask in each hand. 'You're going to need these.'

'Thanks.' Todd fixed the mask over his mouth and nose, the tension in his chest vanishing as he drew in a clean breath.

Emile spoke again. 'Did he seriously just melt the Wicked Witch with acid?'

Detective Reed's voice was grim. 'Which means we're either looking for a girl from Kansas, or a pack of flying monkeys.'

'Nitric acid,' Bradley announced later, as he looked up from the test results.

'That's good, isn't it?' Todd turned his head. The latest victim's hat sat nearby on the lab bench. 'We can trace it to where it was purchased?'

His colleague shrugged. 'Depends. If the killer purchased it here in the city then maybe, but it's not like it's all that uncommon. I'll see what I can find, but I'm not holding my breath.'

'What about the costume?' Todd asked from where he stood next to the main table. The victim's actual clothing had been neatly folded a few feet away from where she'd died, very similar to the archery victim. Emilie was currently examining them for any trace elements the killer may have left. 'Any luck on that?'

'Well, the dress was pretty much destroyed,' the younger girl said. 'But the tag in the hat said it was bought at a Halloween store. I'm still trying to find it. I think it's one of those seasonal ones. He didn't wear latex gloves under the black ones this time, but the acid was strong enough that any kind of skin or DNA I get is going to be corrupted.'

'Pull it and bag it anyway,' Bradley instructed her. 'If they get an arrest, the detectives might be able to use it to prompt a confession. The killer might not realize that we don't have anything.'

'We might actually have more luck with the make-up,' Emily continued, and Todd's eyes narrowed as he turned the canister over. 'It was bought locally. Some store called Crafty Creations.'

Bradley picked up the phone. 'I'll ask the detectives to get us a sample for comparison. They can also question the employees at the store, see if anyone remembers some-one buying green stage make-up.'

Todd frowned down at the empty can. 'I'm going to run a spectral analysis of the chemical composition.'

'We already know where the stuff came from, so why does it matter what its chemical make-up is?' Emilie asked.

'If I can break down the specific chemistry of the nitric acid, we might be able to use that to trace where it was manufactured; from there we could get where it was purchased. Batches have chemical signatures that are unique to each one as well as to certain manufacturers. But, to get the analysis of the acid, I need to be able to eliminate anything that might have contaminated it. Basically, the remains and the make-up.'

'How long will that take?' Bradley asked, the impa-tience in his voice making his words sharp.

Todd bit his tongue before he could ask his senior colleague if he had any better ideas. They were all on edge. It wasn't Bradley's fault that the lab hadn't found any leads, but he would be the one with the brass in his ear.

Keeping his voice as even as possible, he said, 'Probably a day or so. I'll start on the samples I have here while we wait for the detectives to bring the others, OK?'

'Fine. Meanwhile,' Bradley muttered, pinching the bridge of his nose, 'we get to sit here and hope the sick fuck doesn't strike again.'

The Maestro hated to admit it, but the investigators on his case – well, cases – weren't as stupid as he'd originally thought. First, there was that old guy and his hot blond sidekick sniffing around, then some hard-faced brunette cop who'd given him the same disgusted look every woman gave him, even when he promised to make them stars.

Perhaps it was time to send the Powers That Be a major message. The only real question was what to use next.

'Any suggestions?' He looked down at Drew Sheldon.

The screen writer was huddled on his waste-stained cot. The glare he gave wasn't nearly as tough as the previous ones, but some spirit was still there. The notebook and pen sat next to him rather than across the room where the writer had thrown it every time the Maestro had given it to him. He considered the change a step in the right direction.

'I've heard good things about *Henry: Portrait of a Serial Killer*.' He kept his tone conversational. No need to freak the man out even more. 'Have you ever seen it?'

Sheldon shook his head, not meeting his eyes.

The Maestro continued. 'It actually starts with a series of still-shot intercuts. They never show how the murders occurred, just the bodies afterward. There are enough ideas there to take care of the investigators and a couple of detectives.'

'If they're getting close,' Sheldon's voice was hoarse, 'doesn't it make more sense to just run? You can get away while they're looking for me. I won't say a word.'

'I'm sure you won't.' He picked up the notebook and handed it to Sheldon. 'Because as soon as you start writing, you're in it with me.' He leaned down, ignoring the foul stench. 'It's time for you to make a choice. I picked you because you're the best, but if you don't work with me, it doesn't matter how good you are.'

The Maestro straightened and stepped away. He could feel the writer's eyes on him as he began to pace. 'You have two options. Either you begin to write an amazing screenplay for me, something that people will still be talking about in fifty years, or I use your daughter to recreate one of the scenes from *Se7en*. I'm thinking of casting her as Lust.'

Sheldon swallowed hard. The Maestro could almost hear the dry clicking in the writer's throat.

'I take it that's a film you've seen.'

He didn't want to have to start all over again with another writer, but time was growing short, especially if someone had figured out the connection between Sheldon's disappearance and the murders. There'd been nothing in the news about a connection, but the Maestro couldn't risk it. Being questioned twice in the last week had made him suspicious of just how much was known.

'I'll do it.' Sheldon's shoulders slumped. 'Just tell me what you want.'

'Very good.' The Maestro could feel the grin spreading across his face. It was time to begin the next phase of his plan. Next time he wouldn't need to use someone else's work for the investigators and detectives.

He could use something entirely original.

Chapter 27

'Where is everybody?' Reilly asked as, only a couple of days later, following a frantic call from Captain Harvell, she and Daniel approached yet another crime scene. The killer was now seriously escalating and the department was panicking.

'I think a better question is why they had to put up a tent around the body.' Daniel sounded like he didn't want to know the answer to his own query.

The dread grew with each step that took her closer to the sterile white tent. It reminded Reilly of the quarantine areas she'd seen in movies, which of course was what made it particularly frightening with this serial killer. As Detective Reed approached them, she could see his grim expression even in the dim evening light. She really didn't want to hear what he had to say.

'Please tell me our killer didn't decide to go with a scene from *Outbreak* or *Contagion* this time.' Daniel spoke as soon as the detective was close enough to hear. 'I'm not really that fond of quarantine.'

'He didn't put that up. We did,' Detective Reed stopped in front of them rather than falling in alongside them, forcing both to stop too.

Alarm bells started to go off in Reilly's head. Whatever was inside that tent had to be more graphic than anything the authorities had seen so far. And since they'd already had one person torn in two, another boiled, someone melted by acid and a face demolished, Reilly was positive that she didn't want to know what lay inside the tent.

And she certainly didn't want to see it.

The detective went on: 'Trust me, this is one we don't want reporters sneaking a picture of. We've got a perimeter set up, but figured better safe than sorry.'

'Is that where all the uniforms are?' Reilly asked. She scanned the area again, seeing only the faint outlines of people at the edge of the park.

'We've got a few at the entrance to the tent, but everyone else is making sure no one gets close.' Detective Reed ran his forearm across his forehead. 'Not that anyone wanted to be near this.'

Reilly's unease ratcheted up a notch. She'd never seen a detective sweat quite so much, at least not in this way. Compared to the 105-degree day, the night's low 90s was nothing for Florida. This wasn't normal perspiration from the heat, this was something else.

'What's in there, Detective?' Daniel asked, his tone

suggesting that he didn't want to know any more than Reilly did.

And he'd seen a lot in his fifty-odd years.

'Have you ever seen the movie *Braveheart*?' Reed asked. 'You know how they keep the camera on Gibson's face and hands during the execution scene?' He pressed the sleeve of his jacket against his lips and didn't say any more.

Reilly heard Daniel swear, but was unable to say anything herself. She'd always hated that movie. It was great up until the ending, whereupon her imagination had filled in the blanks and made her ill for days.

She still couldn't watch it, just because she knew what would be coming. It was a scene she always thought of when she heard people talk about how kids today were desensitized to violence. Executions like that back then had been a form of public entertainment.

Apparently, the Maestro shared the same twisted mentality as the people of that particular era.

Reilly inhaled deeply through her nose, just close enough to catch a whiff of decay carried on the night breeze. She was prepared. She could do this.

And she continued to tell herself that as she and Daniel followed the detective to the tent.

'He's taken more victims in two weeks than most serial killers do in their entire lifetime and we're no closer to catching him now than we were when he started.' Mark Reed was pacing, but Todd ignored the detective, choosing instead to focus on the trace analysis he was running from the *Braveheart* murder scene. Everyone knew the senior investigator's habit of pacing and ranting when he was frustrated.

'You and Julie make any headway with the film festival people?' Bradley stood and cracked his back. He'd been hunched over his microscope.

Reed sank into his chair and tossed a nearby empty Chinese food box into his trash. 'Complete dead end from what I can see. As is what happened to that screenwriter.'

'Actually . . . I may have something on that.' Emilie's voice was soft.

Todd started. He'd almost completely forgotten about the redhead in the corner.

While she was always quiet, the last few days – especially that *Wizard of Oz* scene – had really taken a toll. Her smile was a shadow of its former self and, like the rest of the investigative team, lines of weariness showed at the corners of her eyes. She dutifully put in her time, staying over whenever she was asked, but the joy that had been on her face the first time Todd had met her was gone. Was it this sense of shared horror, he wondered, that had recently brought her and Bradley together?

'That strange splinter that you found in the alley,' she said to Todd as all eyes turned toward her, 'it's amber.'

'Amber?' he echoed. What was amber doing in the alley outside a Florida hotel?

'Actually, a really rare form of amber,' Emilie clarified. 'Only available from a handful of places in the country.' She held a piece of paper out to the detective. 'I made a list. The closest one to here is in Miami.'

'Thanks. I'll go call Julie.' Reed ran his hand through his hair as the technician went back to her station. 'The DA's all over the department for not having found this psycho yet. But at least the media outcry about the murders is forcing the department to split resources more evenly between that and the Sheldon thing now.'

'No ransom demand for Sheldon yet?' Todd had been concentrating so much on the murders that he hadn't paid any attention to the missing screenwriter case since returning from the crime scene a few days earlier.

'Nothing.' The detective shook his head. 'As much for the daughter as for the negative publicity, they're telling the public that Sheldon's still considered a missing person, but word is the department is looking for a body, not a survivor.' He headed for the door. 'Thanks again for this. Keep me updated if you find anything else.'

As the detective exited the lab, Todd spoke up, giving voice to the theory that had started to bounce around in his head. 'There was nothing in that alley that indicated a murder. Not really even any signs of a struggle. A small amount of blood. No bone fragments, evidence of a shooting. Nothing to suggest a body had fallen. Sheldon wasn't killed in the alley,' he said.

'But why would a kidnapper take someone like Drew Sheldon only to kill him somewhere else?' Bradley asked.

'It's not a matter of money because there's been no ransom. And it's not like middle-aged men are targeted for sex crimes, at least not in the kidnapping sense.'

'Then why snatch Sheldon in the first place?'

A curse from the other side of the lab drew everyone's attention, effectively ending the conversation about the missing writer.

'Sorry,' Peni apologized. She'd been putting in almost as many hours as the investigators, running traces on five different computers. 'I thought I had the slippery little weasel, but he bounced his signal again. There's no way that he saw me coming because two others changed . . .' She stopped.

'What?' Bradley asked, sitting up straighter.

'Three of them changed even though I was only getting close on one.' Peni frowned. 'Why didn't I see it before?'

'See what?' Todd glanced at Bradley but he looked just as confused.

'He's using a routing program to change the origin points on each feed. I didn't catch it because they weren't using any distinguishing pattern that I could see. Too many variables.' Peni turned to Todd and Bradley. 'The program alternates when it bounces the signal to another server. Maybe three minutes the first time, nine the second, fifteen the third. Another may be set up to switch every four, eight and sixteen minutes.'

'So each feed has its own set of instructions as to when it changes the signal.' Todd frowned, not sure if he was understanding correctly. He was good at research and understood the machines he used on the job, but any sort of intricate computer work was beyond him.

Peni nodded. 'Because the amount of time between each shift change is based on that feed's particular algorithm, it looked like they were all changing randomly – as if a person were doing it rather than a program.' Her voice took on an admiring note. 'Pretty smart.'

'Does this mean you can't trace it?' Bradley asked.

'Please,' Peni scoffed. 'I said it was pretty smart, not up to par with me. All I need to do is pick apart the signals, and search for the commonalities between the different feeds.'

'Well, you're soon going to have another feed to add to your trace,' Detective Reed announced as he re-entered the lab, his tone jaded. 'A jogger in River Park just found a decapitated female.'

'Another decapitation?' Todd couldn't believe what he was hearing. First, *Braveheart*, now . . . what?

Bradley nodded at Todd to go, who dutifully grabbed his things.

'Am I the only one,' Emilie asked, as he headed for the door, 'mentally going through other movies featuring decapitations and wondering what the hell you're going to find now?'

'Same here.' Todd exhaled heavily. 'I'm starting to wish I hadn't watched so many violent movies growing up. Or –' he frowned as he recalled the Wicked Witch's horrible demise – 'any movies at all.'

Chapter 28

'This guy's really starting to piss me off,' Detective Sampson greeted Daniel and Reilly as they ducked under the crime-scene tape. 'This is a weird one.'

'How can it get any weirder than what we've already seen?' Daniel asked.

Reilly wasn't sure she wanted to know, and the female detective didn't answer, just stepped aside so she and Daniel could see the body.

Well, that was new . . .

The victim had been a tall redhead, but that wasn't what made this so strange. The opulent dress of red velvet not only didn't belong in a city park, it didn't belong in this century. The way the body had fallen into the grass had prevented the majority of the dress from becoming too . . . messy.

The same, however, couldn't be said for the head. Half of the woman's auburn hair was caked with blood and her fair skin, chalk-white in death, was in startling contrast to the dried blood on her face.

'What in the world?' Daniel stopped short.

Reilly kept walking, trying to stay out the way of Todd, who was already on site and processing the scene. He nodded a terse greeting as she skirted the pool of blood, approaching from the victim's feet. A pair of ugly, old-fashioned shoes peeked out from beneath the full skirt. Reilly's eyes narrowed as she scanned the costume. Something about this looked familiar.

When it clicked, she swore under her breath and straightened. She knew why she recognized the dress. 'It's Mary, Queen of Scots.'

'What?' Todd paused from photographing the victim's head. Seeing an antiquated costume on a decapitated victim may have been a bit strange, but it was hardly on the level of the other things they'd seen from this killer.

'I try not to watch too many horror movies . . .' Reilly took a step to the side to allow him a clearer shot of the torso. 'But I've always liked historical films and books. Particularly those about English royalty.' She motioned back to Daniel.

'What is it?'

Reilly pointed to the head. 'Tall with auburn hair and beheaded. Queen Mary.'

Daniel's forehead wrinkled. 'But I thought our killer did fiction. I know *Braveheart* is based on a real person, but it's far from historically accurate.'

'There is a movie though,' Reilly replied. 'Most people consider it the first, quote, horror film, unquote, even though it's about a historical figure. In 1895, an eighteen-second, black-and-white film called *The Execution of Mary, Queen of Scots* showed an actress dressed as Mary kneeling in front of an executioner. The executioner lifts the head for the crowd and the screen goes to black. That's the same style of dress worn by the actress who played Mary.'

'How in the world do you know that?' Todd looked and sounded so impressed that, despite herself, Reilly gave a small smile.

'Like I said, I know some English history. But while I was researching horror movies, this one popped up too; that's why it's so familiar to me now.'

Todd crouched down again and used a pair of tweezers to pluck a few hairs from the back of the dress. Judging by their length and color, Reilly guessed they surely belonged to the victim, but better safe than sorry.

Daniel looked thoughtful. 'Until now, our killer has picked well-known, relatively recent movies or ones with a cult following. Using something like this is his way of bragging, showing off his knowledge of classical work.'

'So he's a real film buff – we kinda guessed that,' Todd said darkly. 'Not just some guy who goes down the multiplex every now and again.' He looked at his father. 'Makes the festival connection even stronger.'

Daniel nodded. 'I'll talk to Sampson, ask the detectives to rework this angle. Good information, Reilly, thank you.'

'The dress,' she said to Todd, indicating the costume. 'It's distinctive individuated evidence. You should definitely be able to get something from it; trace where it came from. This isn't some cheap knockoff.' Her face was grim. 'Whoever made that costume knew what they were doing.'

At Todd's request, Reilly agreed to update Bradley at the lab while he talked with the assistant ME about the best way to transport the victim's head.

She scrolled through his phone contacts, accidentally going too far and having to backtrack. She raised an eyebrow at the sheer number of female names and then shook her head, feeling stupid. Who Todd had in his phone wasn't any of her business. She tapped Bradley's name.

The senior investigator answered on the first ring. 'Todd, what've you got?'

'It's Reilly Steel,' she began, taking a few steps away from the crime scene. 'Todd asked me to call you.'

'What's up?' The informality spoke volumes as to how tired Bradley was.

'He's just finishing up at the scene,' she said, before giving him a quick overview of the crime scene and the implications of this particular theme. 'The costume looks like it's going to be your best bet to find this guy.'

'Costume?'

'The victim was dressed like Mary, Queen of Scots. Looks like the killer went pretty far back in his movie catalog to find this particular sequence. You might want to have your computer expert looking for *The Execution of Mary, Queen of Scots* as the next clip.'

'What'd you say?' Bradley's tone sharpened, suddenly alert.

Reilly gave a further explanation, puzzled by the abrupt change in tone. 'When I was researching, I found a really old movie about the execution of Queen Mary. He might be trying to re-enact something else, but I'm pretty confident that's the one.'

'OK, thanks.' The rustle of papers nearly drowned out Bradley's words.

'No problem.' Reilly hesitated, then asked, 'Is everything all right?' Granted, she didn't know the investigator very well, but on the couple of times she'd met Bradley, he'd come across calm and unruffled, not at all like the distracted, frazzled person she was talking to now.

'Fine.' Bradley seemed decidedly preoccupied. 'I just need to check on something. Tell Todd I'll talk to him later.'

Silence.

Reilly looked down at the phone in her hand. Seriously, he had hung up without a goodbye? She turned toward the approaching footsteps, unsettled by the abrupt end to the call.

'You OK?' Todd wore an expression of concern when she rejoined him and Daniel. He yanked off his gloves and tossed them into a nearby biohazard bucket.

'I think Bradley has a lead,' Reilly said absently. She handed Todd his phone, her forehead still furrowed with confusion.

Todd's eyes lit up. 'Great. What is it?'

'He didn't say.' She shrugged, trying to shake her feeling of unease. 'Just said he had to go and check something out and he'd talk to you later.'

By the time Todd returned to the lab, the sun was past its peak, the temperature was in the high nineties and Bradley wasn't there. Both Peni and Emilie were hard at work, only looking up when Todd announced that he'd brought lunch.

Emilie took a bag but didn't open it, the expression on her face slightly sick. The redhead looked even more pale than usual and Todd couldn't really say that he blamed her. This was a lot of grisly deaths for anyone to take in, much less someone who'd been on the job less than a year.

Peni's appetite apparently hadn't been affected. She grabbed the bag Todd offered, tucked her feet up underneath her and began to eat. Around a mouthful of turkey on rye sub, she announced that she'd narrowed down the area where the killer was sending his video footage.

'Once I separated all of the feeds and analyzed their change pattern, I was able to start the process of backtracking.' She pulled up a map and indicated an area of almost fifty square miles. 'I know it's still not close enough, but we're getting there.'

'Very good.' Todd nodded his approval.

'While I was waiting,' Peni said, 'you know how Sampson and Reed are looking into that list of film festival people? I found an article published about a year ago, where one of the actors on the list bashed the movie industry for the recent outpouring of, as he put it, "slasher gore porn" that had no true artistic merit.'

'Which actor?' Todd asked, curious.

'That nut-job Reynolds.' Peni took another bite of her sandwich and spoke around it. 'He even went on to say that if Hollywood didn't start producing more quality films, it was going to be up to him and people like him to take up the slack.'

'Doesn't that imply that he'd be the last one to commit these murders?' Emilie asked. She took a tentative sip of the tea Todd had brought her. 'I mean, if he thinks horror movies are trash, why would he want to add to them?'

Todd was helpless to understand what it meant, if anything. Behavioral analysis wasn't really his forte. He'd run it by his dad later, see what he thought, as he knew that Reynolds was one of the people Daniel and Reilly had interviewed before.

Still, he had a theory of his own. 'Whoever our killer is, I don't think he's carrying out re-enactments because he likes horror,' he said. 'I think he's actually more like a child reacting to being told that he has to do something he doesn't want to do. Kind of the "Well fine, if that's what you like, that's what I'll do and I'll do it better than anyone else" approach.'

'Shouldn't we tell Bradley to let the detectives know that they should be looking into Reynolds then?' Emilie asked.

'It's certainly an angle.' Todd nodded and took another gulp of his sweet tea. 'Speaking of Bradley, what do you know about this lead of his?'

'What lead?' Emilie looked at Peni who shook her head, just as puzzled as the other woman. 'He didn't mention anything.'

'Where did he go then?' Todd asked as he opened his salad. He'd never been a fan of greens, but he didn't think his stomach could handle anything solid at the moment.

Peni answered this time. 'We figured you'd know,' she said. 'About an hour ago, he rushed out of his office and went out. Looked like he was in a hurry. Didn't stop to tell us anything.'

'He didn't say anything about following up on some movie called *The Execution of Mary, Queen of Scots*?'

'Nope.'

Todd was curious. What could've been so urgent that Bradley would have run out without talking to his team? Whatever it had been, it had to have been important enough for the senior investigator to behave completely out of character. Well, for whatever reason, at least it sounded like his partner had a decent lead.

Something they all badly needed at this point.

Chapter 29

The Maestro couldn't believe his luck. He'd been pondering over his casting options for his first truly original scene when the perfect leading man had just happened by.

He'd been around long enough to have heard stories of things like this happening. Kismet. Fate. Whatever you wanted to call it. Didn't matter.

All he knew was that he'd still been making blocking decisions and waiting for inspiration about who to cast when the perfect specimen had simply presented itself.

At first, he'd been concerned that his lead of choice would prove to be too strong, but like everyone else, the man had underestimated him and the cattle prod had once again proved to be a worthy investment. Now, the man was bound and gagged in the trunk of the car. He supposed he would need to get rid of the car soon enough, but for now it would serve his purpose.

The docks appeared deserted, but he looked around anyway. It wouldn't do to get caught now. Not when he was so close. Not when he'd spent so much time today setting everything up. He'd used an assumed identity to rent a slip that afternoon and purchased a run-down speedboat under a totally different name – Fred Krueger – which the young man who'd set everything up had found amusing. Clearly a kindred spirit.

The box in his back seat, however, had been a bit more difficult to obtain. Fortunately, his contacts had let him get what he needed. He knew it had been a risk, but what was life without a little risk?

He carried the box to the boat first, walking gingerly down the rickety pier. If he dropped it, things would not end well for him. Fortune was with him, however, and he reached his antiquated little boat without incident.

He set the box at one end of the boat where he could easily tip it before sending the boat on its maiden voyage. His trip back to the car confirmed that he was indeed alone, and his anxiety was quickly replaced by excitement. One of the reasons he'd chosen this particular spot was that most of the boats weren't worth stealing, which meant his wasn't out of place and security would be light.

Cattle prod in hand, he opened his trunk. His captor blinked blearily, but didn't seem to be enough in control of himself to fight or run. Still, the Maestro was cautious as he pulled the man from the trunk. With one hand, he dragged his prisoner down the dock, the other hand still gripping the end of the prod, poised to strike if necessary.

'Congratulations,' the Maestro said as he shoved the man onto the boat. 'You're going to be a star.'

It wasn't until nearly three-thirty in the early hours that Todd had dropped onto the couch and fallen into a deep but restless slumber. Then he'd woken at five and hadn't been able to get back to sleep.

Now, he let the warm water wash away the sweat and grime of the day before and tried to gather his thoughts. When he climbed out of the shower nearly thirty minutes later, he felt a bit better, though still tired. It didn't matter. He'd pretty much counted on being tired until Holly's murderer was found. Wrapping a towel around his waist he went through to the small kitchen to start a pot of coffee.

He'd just finished getting dressed and was reaching for the coffee when his phone rang. He grabbed for it, his mood instantly darkening. Early-morning calls were never a good thing, especially not for CSI. They almost always meant a body.

Another one, was it even possible? This guy was relentless, fearless even.

What was he trying to prove?

'Todd?' Mark Reed's voice sounded strange.

'Another movie one?' Todd decided to beat him to the punch. He poured the aromatic liquid into his 'My Other Car Is A Time Machine' mug.

'I'm afraid so.' The detective cleared his throat, but there was something in his voice that put Todd on high alert.

'Mark?' He felt his stomach suddenly turn to ice. Something wasn't right. 'What's going on?'

'Some fishermen this morning found a boat . . . and a body.'

'And?' Todd knew there was more, something the detective was finding hard to say. After everything they'd seen, Mark wouldn't be acting so weird if it was just another body.

And what scene was being re-enacted this time? A boat . . .

'The body they found . . .' Mark's next words were so soft that Todd almost missed them. 'What?' Todd shook his head, forgetting that Detective Reed couldn't see him. 'No . . . You're mistaken.'

'We found his badge and ID on the body,' the detective said, his voice somber. 'But we need an official identification from a third party not directly involved with—'

'Where is he?' Todd interjected woodenly, his throat working as the words echoed in his head, their meaning lost.

'Dr Kase has him now,' Reed said, sighing and sounding old. 'I'm so sorry, Todd. He was a good guy.'

'Thank you.' Todd's reply was automatic. His mind was still reeling, arguing that it couldn't be true. It was so surreal it felt like something from out of a . . . He stopped the thought before it could get any further.

'Don't worry. We're going to get this fucker,' the detective said, before he hung up.

Todd stood in the center of his kitchen, mug in hand, dressed in his usual slacks and white button-up shirt, for several minutes. He didn't move, didn't speak, did absolutely nothing to indicate the depth of the turmoil raging inside him.

'Fuck!' he screamed, throwing his mug at the wall. It shattered, coffee spraying everywhere. He slammed his hands against the counter, his next scream one of inarticulate rage. He turned, needing to do something, to destroy something, needing some outlet or else he'd explode. He swung at the wall, fist crunching through drywall.

The pain bloomed bright and hot, cutting through his anger. Todd sank to the floor, his bloody hand resting on the towel. Then he buried his head in his hands, lost.

Chapter 30

Her feet were rooted to the spot and nothing she could do could get them to move. She wanted to run, to stop them, but she was helpless to do anything other than watch as she saw the crimson bloodstain pool onto the floor. She opened her mouth to scream, to call for help, but she couldn't make a sound . . .

The last person Reilly had expected to be calling her at quarter after six in the morning was Todd.

This wasn't going to be good. As soon as he said her name, she knew it would be beyond not good, but whatever this was, it was worse.

She sat up, reaching for the lamp as dread filled her, displacing her usual confusion after a nightmare.

'The killer . . .' Todd's words were halting, punctuated with what sounded like sobs. 'He . . . last night – this morning – he . . .'

'Todd, you're scaring me. What happened?' Reilly

reached for her robe, a sudden chill coming over her. She had the urge to tell him that she wanted to take back her question.

'It's Bradley.' Todd's voice cracked on his friend's name, and she instantly knew what he was going to say next. Even as she was shaking her head, trying to deny it, he confirmed her fears. 'Some fishermen found his body this morning.'

'Oh, my God, Todd, I'm so, so sorry.' Reilly felt her own tears slip down her cheeks. She hadn't known Bradley well at all, but she knew how close he and Todd were.

Bradley had been more than a partner. He'd been Todd's friend and mentor. He was to Todd what Daniel was to her and she could only imagine too well how her friend was feeling.

'Detective Reed called me,' Todd said, his voice still shaky. 'He needs me to officially ID the body.'

The unspoken request was there, hanging between them. What Todd was being asked to do . . . no one should have to do alone. Reilly knew that all too well.

'Do you want to pick me up or will I meet you there?' She wiped her hand across her cheeks. She needed to be strong for Todd.

'I'll come and get you but I don't want to see . . . anyone else,' Todd said, meaning Daniel.

Reilly understood. 'I'll be waiting on the porch. Just pull into the driveway and I'll be ready.'

She crossed to the closet and started flipping through clothes. She'd showered when she'd gotten back to the house last night, but she needed a little bit of time to process what had happened before she could be of any help to Todd. It would be a good twenty minutes before he made it over from his place anyway.

When she emerged from her room fifteen minutes later, her hair was still wet and her eyes were red, but she was composed.

Daniel looked up in surprise from where he sat with the morning paper and a cup of coffee. Reilly sighed. Of course. He had always been a morning person and she should have known better than to think she could sneak out before he rose.

He was about to offer her a cup but one look at her face and his expression grew grave.

'What's wrong?'

She reached for the coffeepot and poured herself a cup. 'Todd is going to be here in a few minutes. I need to go with him down to the city morgue.'

'Another one? For Chrissakes.' Daniel slurped down his coffee. 'Give me a couple of minutes to freshen up.'

She dumped more sugar than usual into her drink. She needed the boost. 'If you don't mind, Daniel, I think he'd rather keep this one private. He needs to ID a body. Bradley Ford is dead.'

As she climbed into Todd's car, she couldn't help but notice that he seemed to have aged ten years since she'd last seen him. She didn't try to offer any condolences or ask how he was. Those were stupid questions; of course he wasn't OK. Instead, she just gave him a half-smile and squeezed his hand.

At times like this, human contact was about the only comforting thing.

They rode in silence, looking out the window but not seeing the lingering colors of sunrise, the early-morning commuters. Her mind was elsewhere, back in the past, remembering things that she'd rather forget.

The sharp, antiseptic smell that couldn't quite cover up the odor of death.

The police officer who walked at her side, asked where her father was.

The cold grays and whites that seemed to personify the morgue.

Reilly shook her head as Todd pulled into the parking lot. It had taken her years to free herself from those memories. Now they only came in times of stress. Well, if anything counted as stressful, it was this case. The return of her nightmares proved that.

'Before we go in there . . .' Todd broke the silence. He stared straight ahead as he spoke. 'I just want to thank you for coming with me.'

'You're welcome.' Reilly put her hand on Todd's arm. 'This isn't the type of thing you want to go through alone.'

The somber expression on Dr Kase's face when she and Todd entered the mortuary said far more than just the death of a colleague. Reilly's stomach churned. This was going to be bad.

A figure covered with a white sheet lay on a stainless-steel table in the center of the room. Reilly wanted to look away from it, to not think about what was under that sheet, but her eyes kept being drawn back.

'Are you sure you want to be the one to do this?' Dr Kase asked. 'His sister said she would come down tomorrow. It's just a formality for the records.'

'Better me than someone in his family.' Todd set his jaw, a determined light in his eyes. 'I'm not going to make them look at something I can't face.'

Dr Kase nodded. He crossed to the table. 'I have to warn you though, it's bad.'

'How . . .?' Todd stopped, and cleared his throat, as if summoning himself to hear the worst. 'Do you have a cause of death?'

'I haven't started the . . . examination yet,' Dr Kase said, picking his words carefully.

He picked up the sheet but didn't yet fold it down. 'But based on the surrounding environment, I'm fairly confident that death was caused by anaphylactic shock brought on by numerous stings.'

Reilly frowned.

'Stings?' Todd asked. 'What surrounding environment? I was told he was found by some fishermen. I assumed he was in the water.'

The doctor let the sheet flutter back down. 'Detective Reed didn't give you any details?'

Todd shook his head. He hadn't exactly been in a fit state to process anything.

Kase took a moment before explaining, the muscles in his face working for control. 'A few men decided to go fishing early this morning. Before their boat had gotten more than a few yards from the docks, they spotted a half-submerged speedboat. Inside was a body, a camera in a waterproof container and a tipped-over box. The body was covered with fire ants.'

What little color had been left in Todd's face slowly drained away and the coffee that Reilly had drunk roiled in her stomach. She was now certain that she didn't want to see what was beneath that sheet.

'Show me.' Todd's words came out sharp, but neither Reilly nor the doctor commented or tried to stop him. She didn't think she could say anything at all.

Dr Kase nodded and pulled back the top of the sheet.

Reilly didn't want to look, but part of her refused to let Todd be the only one to bear the burden. Bile rose in her throat at the sight of the once handsome features now swollen and distorted, but she wouldn't let herself turn away.

'It's Bradley Ford.' Todd's voice was flat, his face tight and pinched as he delivered the formal confirmation of what they already knew.

Reilly held in her sigh of relief when the doctor covered the face once more.

'Who'd they call to the scene?' Todd asked. 'From CSI. Please don't tell me it was Emilie.' Reilly didn't quite understand what he was getting at here, though she did agree that the younger technician shouldn't have had to deal with something like this on her own.

'Todd, they're not going to let your team investigate this.' The doctor's voice was strangely gentle. 'This thing has gone too far; the FBI's going to take over now.'

'Like hell, they will.' Todd's mouth flattened into a line, and Reilly automatically put a hand on his arm. 'I'm going to find this bastard.'

Dr Kase sighed as if he'd expected this response, but didn't press the issue. 'I am sorry about Bradley, Todd. He was a good man.'

'Yes,' Todd said. 'He was.' He looked at Reilly, his expression stony. 'I've got some calls to make, stop this thing from slipping out of our hands. And there's one I need you to make.'

'Me?' Reilly was taken aback. What could she possibly do to affect investigative jurisdiction?

'I need you to convince my dad to call in a few favors to keep us on this case.' The bitterness in his words told just how much they cost Todd to say. Reilly could see that he didn't want to ask for her – or his father's – help, but finding the killer was superseding his desire to do this on his own. He didn't have the connections that Daniel did, nor the clout to ask for special treatment. 'I'm not giving this to the Feds.'

Chapter 31

The Maestro applauded as he entered the storage unit, the sound echoing off of the metal walls and creating a cacophony of admiration. The noise startled a cry out of Drew Sheldon as the writer jerked upright. He was fairly sure that Sheldon had just pissed his pants. Not that it mattered. He didn't need clean pants to keep writing.

'Well done, Drew, well done indeed.' The Maestro clapped Sheldon on the shoulder and chuckled when the writer flinched. 'Your first scene went over beautifully. Using the water to drown the ants was genius. After all, wouldn't want the little bastards running away, now, would we?'

He crossed to the chair and sat down. Excitement coursed through him. He was – he searched for a word – giddy, so much so that he barely noticed how badly the place smelled. Maybe he should bring some air freshener the next time. 'Now, how much work have you gotten done today?'

Based on the flash of fear in Sheldon's eyes and the slack jaw, he guessed the answer. He scowled, his previous happiness evaporating as his temper flared. Why did no one appreciate his vision?

'Apparently, I wasn't clear, so let me rectify that.' He leaned forward and was pleased to see Sheldon jump back. 'I'm not looking for a single scene. I want a full script. Beginning to end, filled with provocatively horrific death scenes. You're not done until I have my screenplay. And if I don't like it . . . well, you just may find yourself starring alongside your daughter in one of the scenes you wrote.'

Sheldon's face drained of color.

'Now, before you start, I have something else I need some assistance with.' He sat in his chair and pulled a piece of paper out of his pocket. 'I've been writing letters, short snippets really. Because this was my first foray into original work, I need this letter to be perfect. A clear thesis and statement of intent.'

Sheldon uttered a long string of profanities that involved committing several acts that were illegal in most states.

'Charming.' The Maestro rolled his eyes. 'Now shut your mouth and listen. I'm going to want an honest opinion.'

He smoothed out the paper and read: 'Many of you will have heard about my latest project and perhaps you suspect I have borrowed this idea from another film, but I did not. This fine piece of work is original, as will be the rest of the work I share with you from here on out. I will try my best to continue to produce artistic and merited work worthy of a receptive audience.' He looked expectantly at Sheldon. 'What do you think?'

Sheldon crossed his arms defiantly.

The Maestro sighed and nodded. 'I suppose you're right. It needs more work. Thanks for the feedback.' He stood up, grinning in anticipation. 'You get started on the next few scenes and I'll work on another draft of my letter. I'll be back later on to discuss casting and locations.' He stuck his hands in his pockets, whistling as he stepped out into the warm, muggy air.

Things were certainly looking up.

Reilly wasn't entirely sure how she was supposed to handle this. Todd had called Emilie and Peni into the lab to tell them about Bradley's death.

Now the two women were sitting at their usual seats and Todd had pulled his chair over to them, leaving Reilly on the outside. She didn't know what she was supposed to do while the others talked and offered each other comfort.

She wasn't part of the team and hadn't really known Bradley well enough to join them and it felt awkward – not to mention an invasion of privacy – to watch.

Finally, she decided to see what information she could gather to add to what they already knew. Since she was the least emotionally involved, there was one thing she shouldn't have anyone else doing. She just didn't want to do it either.

Steeling herself, Reilly stood up and went over to the nearest laptop. She knew of at least one movie with death by fire ants, but wasn't sure if that was going to be right. After all, the movie had been set in a jungle, not a boat off the coast of Florida.

Still, it was better than nothing.

'So what do we do now?' Emilie sniffed, the poor girl sounding distraught. 'If we're not going to be allowed to work on the case.'

'Until I hear otherwise, it's still ours,' Reilly heard Todd say firmly.

Daniel had said he'd do what he could to try and keep the investigation within the local jurisdiction but couldn't make any promises. Reilly had passed the information along to Todd and his response had been the one he'd just given to Emilie. Until the Feds arrived to take over, the Tampa CSI team was still involved.

'But we don't have anything to review.' Emilie took a shuddering breath as she gathered herself.

'That's not entirely true,' Todd replied. 'Dr Kase has . . . the body, so anything that was brought in with it, we have.'

Reilly could see how hard it was for Todd to refer to his friend as 'the body' and 'it', but she understood what he was doing. They all had to do it, separate the victim from who they were when they were alive. If they saw every victim as a person, they wouldn't have lasted long in this job.

'Emilie.' He handed an evidence bag with Bradley's clothing in it to the redhead. 'Analyze these, see if there's trace – anything we can connect to our killer.' He turned to Peni. 'Keep working on the IP addresses and start searching for the new video footage.' The computer expert looked suitably distressed and Reilly spoke up.

'I'm on that,' she said. Todd turned toward her, the expression on his face saying that he'd completely forgotten that she was there. Then he looked grateful.

'OK, thanks. I don't think any of our guys need to see . . . that.'

'I'll let Peni know if I find anything she needs to take down,' Reilly continued. 'She can stick with the IP addresses if she prefers.'

'Thank you again.' Todd's voice softened.

'What are you going to be looking at?' Emilie asked Todd.

'I've got some bugs to check out.' Todd held up a container. Inside the murky ocean water floated several ants. 'The Feds apparently decided to wash down everything and suck up the ants and the water together.' He rolled his eyes.

'They compromised the clothing?' Emilie frowned, the expression foreign on her usually smiling face. 'They could have washed away trace particulates, changed chemical compositions . . .' She looked frantic.

'I guess they were more worried about a few bug bites,' Todd said darkly. 'Which is why I want *our* team on this. Let's get to work.'

It was the longest day Reilly had had since arriving in Florida. The longest one she'd had in years, actually. Every search was fruitless as she watched the same footage over and over again, all unchanged.

It wasn't until Todd finished his analysis on the ants that she began to suspect that maybe she was looking for the wrong film.

'*Solenopsis invicta*,' he said triumphantly, a little bit of life finally returning to his voice.

'What was that?' Reilly turned to look at him.

'The ant. It's the *Solenopsis invicta*, a highly aggressive species of the fire ant,' he told her. 'Commonly called RIFA, the red imported fire ant.'

'Just a minute.' Reilly pulled up a new browser window and typed a question into the search engine. 'Damn it.'

'What?'

'I was thinking the scene might have been from *Indiana Jones*, you know, the part where they . . .' She skipped to the important part. 'It's not the same type of ant. The ones from the movie, while not entirely real, were based on the *Dorylus* ant.'

'Maybe our killer couldn't get his hands on the right bug,' Todd mused.

'Or,' she said, 'maybe it's not the right movie.'

'Maybe,' he agreed, but she could tell his mind was racing. 'But I'll bet these ants aren't easy to come by. I mean, they're not like flies that you just go out and catch. If we can track down places that sell fire ants, maybe we can find out who bought them.'

'I may have something,' Emilie spoke up then. 'But I need a second opinion.'

Todd crossed to the other woman.

'You know those fibers you found on Anton Williams?' Emilie said. 'The guy who had his jaw broken? I think the ones I found on Bradley's clothes match.'

He peered into the right microscope and then into the left one. 'You're right, they're a match.'

'So the killer has some sort of uniform he wears when he kills?' Emilie asked.

'Or maybe,' Todd said slowly, 'they aren't from clothes at all.'

'We ran them through a hundred different tests. Wool. Not something used in any type of car upholstery,' Emilie countered.

'They could be from a blanket,' Reilly suggested, from where she'd been listening.

'Something that might be kept in the trunk of a car,' said Todd.

'Exactly.' Reilly nodded. 'Which means both Anton Williams and Bradley were taken from one location and transported to where they were found, just like Holly and Aaron. The other three scenes, the killer was already on location. Since we have the truck the first victims were moved in, he must've gotten his hands on another mode of transport.'

'Something with a big enough trunk for a person,' Emilie supplied.

'Which means we need to pull security footage around the docks and around the housing estate where

Williams was killed. See if we can find a match,' Todd finished.

'On it,' Peni piped up. 'Gives me something to do while I'm waiting.'

'Good work, Emilie.' Todd smiled down at the redhead and Reilly saw that the younger woman managed half of one back. While not back to her usual self, it was an improvement. 'Maybe we're getting somewhere,' he added, though his voice held no excitement, only grim determination.

Worried, Reilly watched her friend turn back to his workstation. His initial grief had vanished, leaving behind an almost robotic veneer.

She had a feeling he was going to crash, and soon.

Chapter 32

Todd wouldn't say it, but Reilly knew he didn't want to be alone that evening. She couldn't blame him. Besides, after everything that had happened today, she was dog-tired and didn't think she had the energy to drag herself back to the beach house, update Daniel on everything, and then be able to turn her brain off enough afterward to try to sleep.

Her nightmares were bad enough most of the time. She didn't want to think of what they'd be like after today.

On the way back to his apartment, inspiration had struck and she'd asked Todd to stop at a nearby Publix grocery store. He might not feel like eating tonight, but nothing soothed her like cooking and a nice Cuban chicken sounded like heaven. She'd cooked a lot in Dublin in the very early days when she'd had more time on her hands, but finding anything like Texas sweet onion or adobo there had been virtually impossible.

Now, as the chicken breasts were sizzling in the pan, she chopped the last of the onion, added the adobo powder and a few small sprinkles of oregano, cumin and black pepper. She padded across the kitchen to Todd's fridge to take out the mojo sauce she'd already prepared, even though she wouldn't need it until everything was done. The tile was cool against her bare feet, in direct contrast with the heat of the stove as she leaned over to stir the chicken and squeeze in more lime.

'Again, thank you for coming with me today.' Todd spoke up from the doorway where he'd been watching her.

'It was nothing.' She didn't look at him, keeping her eyes on the contents of the pan.

'No, Reilly, it wasn't nothing.' Todd took a sip of his beer before setting it on the counter. 'Seems like we've known each other forever, yet I couldn't ever describe us as being close, even friends. What you did, coming with me today, calling my dad, and making me come away from the lab tonight, as well as helping out on this whole thing when you're supposed to be on vacation – all of that is above and beyond. Just want you to know that I appreciate it.'

Reilly slowly stirred the food, letting silence settle over the kitchen. She knew she should just say 'you're welcome' and leave it at that, but part of her wanted to say more. There was a story that she rarely shared outside of the people who were involved, a reason she understood the pointlessness of words and the importance of a touch.

The same reason why she hadn't wanted to be alone tonight either.

'Did your dad ever tell you about my family?' She asked the question without turning around, her voice soft. If he'd gone back into the living room, he wouldn't hear her and she wouldn't ask it again.

He hadn't left. 'Only that your mom was . . .' he hesitated suddenly. 'Your mom died when you were a teenager, and you pretty much raised your younger sister because your dad didn't handle it so well.'

She could hear the curiosity in his voice, but he didn't ask. He didn't need to; Reilly was going to tell him. 'My mother didn't just die, she was murdered.'

'I knew that too. I'm sorry . . .' Todd began.

She poked again at the contents of the pan with the wooden spoon. As the food cooked, Reilly continued, working to keep her voice steady. She rarely told anyone about this, and for years hadn't been able to talk about it with anyone other than Daniel. And then Chris.

'Like you said, I had a sister, younger than me by almost four years. She was Mom and Dad's miracle baby. After me, the doctors said Mom couldn't have any more, so when they found out she was pregnant again, they were ecstatic. I was too. I loved Jess from the first time I saw her.'

Reilly closed her eyes, seeing her sister's face as clearly as she ever did.

'She was the one who murdered my mother.' Her voice was flat. 'Called me directly after it happened, possibly even before, I can't be sure. Either way, by the time I got there, it was too late.'

Familiar guilt surged through her. They called it survivor's guilt, but sometimes Reilly didn't feel like much of a survivor.

She took a deep breath. 'So I know what it's like to have someone you love taken from you violently, suddenly. What it's like to stand in that cold room and have to say the words that mean they're never coming back.' She turned to him. 'And I also understand what it's like to want to punish the person who did it – or worse, punish yourself for not stopping it.'

Todd stood silent for several seconds before asking, 'What happened to your sister?'

Reilly turned back to the pan. Almost done. 'Your dad didn't tell you?'

'No. All I knew was that you'd lost your mother. I didn't know anything about . . . how.'

She turned off the flame and poured the mojo sauce over the chicken, the aroma of lime and cumin as comforting as a warm Cuban breeze. 'A couple of years ago, she got out of prison, followed me and my dad to Dublin. Tried to kill him; me too, I suppose.'

'Dad never said a word.' She guessed he was a little hurt by this, though it was nothing new. Daniel rarely discussed a case and Reilly should have known that he would never have betrayed her confidence about the Jess situation.

'Main thing is, she didn't succeed on either count.'

'So is that why you went into this line of work originally?' Todd took the plate she offered him. 'Because of your mother, I mean.'

They moved to the living room and he settled on the couch, balancing his plate on his knees.

'I guess so.' Reilly could feel her cheeks burning. 'I never really talk about that to anyone other than my therapist.'

He looked at her softly. 'Then why me?'

She considered the question, eyes on her food. Then she turned to look at him. 'Because I'm a firm believer in having all the pieces of a puzzle before I try and figure things out.'

'What the hell is wrong with you?' The Maestro threw the notebook at Sheldon. 'Your first scene was brilliant. Creative, unique in delivery. But this? Complete drivel.'

'I did what you wanted!' Sheldon snapped. 'I wrote a new murder scene for you.'

'I wanted something inspired, something to set me apart from every other two-bit film-maker out there.' The Maestro paced, his fury building inside him. Why in the world had he chosen a hack like Sheldon? Sure, he'd got a couple of Academy Awards nominations, but everyone knew that was just politics and sucking-up.

'You want something so gruesome that no one will ever forget it,' Sheldon translated, unable to disguise the disgust in his tone.

The Maestro considered the statement for a moment and then nodded. 'I guess if that's the way you want to look at it.'

'I'm not giving you anything else you can use to torture and kill an innocent human being.' Sheldon managed to look almost dignified. Well, as dignified as someone could look when sitting in their own filth.

'And you thought writing a scene where a man shoots an intruder was the best way to do it?' His voice grew dangerously soft. 'I can have no survivors, no witnesses. And do you really think I'd use an actual criminal in the scene?'

'You know what?' Sheldon said. 'I actually don't care. I'm done helping you. Threaten all you want. There's no way you can get anywhere near my daughter.'

'I thought you might say that.' The Maestro crossed to Sheldon's cot, reaching into his pocket. He handed the contents to the writer. 'As you can see here, I have no problem getting close to your daughter. The joke of a security guard the hotel hired will do just about anything for a couple of hundred bucks.'

'You son of a bitch,' Sheldon whispered as he flipped through the stack of pictures. His face paled more with each one.

Kai eating her meals at the hotel with a distracted, worried look on her face.

Her angry, agitated expression as she yelled at a Tampa detective.

Her young face, relaxed at last as she curled up on her bed, unaware of the danger standing just a few feet away.

The Maestro sat on his chair, a smirk on his face. 'Now, in case you're wondering, I've done quite a bit of research into possible scenes I could use your daughter in.'

Sheldon's dark eyes blazed as he looked up at his captor. 'Don't you dare touch her.'

'You mean you don't want her to have the opportunity to do Jodie Foster's scene in *The Accused*?' The Maestro's grin grew. He had the writer exactly where he wanted him.

'You're one sick—'

'Write me a new scene. Two new scenes, as a matter of fact. Do that and your precious little girl might live to fail at her attempt to become a stuntwoman.' The Maestro stood. 'And make this one good. Write as if your life – and your daughter's – depends on it.'

The salt from the tears he'd hidden lingered on his lips, bitter against her tongue, and she pulled him closer. The rational part of her mind that would've said this was a bad idea had long since been banished by the part of her that ached to comfort him.

He'd started talking about Bradley in halting sentences, telling her about how when Todd had first been hired, he'd been cocky and arrogant, thinking that his father's name would automatically get him respect. How Bradley had called him on it, taken him to a crime scene where the remains of a drug dealer had been found inside an alligator, then laughed when Todd had thrown up all over his new shoes.

When the story turned to Bradley spending the weekend with him for support after Todd's only serious girlfriend had cheated on him, the tears had threatened to
spill over. He'd started to speak and his voice had cracked,
leaving him without words.

A sense of helplessness settled over Reilly and so she
did the only thing that she could. She leaned over and
kissed his cheek. She was still there when he turned his
face toward her. She wasn't sure who had moved first,
only that she blinked and then they were kissing.

His lips moved against hers with an almost frightening
urgency, his hands moving over her body, hesitating at
each boundary until she didn't protest. Their clothes left a
trail on the floor as they made their way back to his
bedroom, mouths never stilling long enough to question
the wisdom of what they were doing.

When he pressed her back against his cotton sheets, she
had a brief moment of clarity before her eyes met his, and
then she was lost again. She gave herself to him, wanting
nothing more than to give him time without pain, time
when he could forget everything but the feel of her body
beneath his.

He buried his face in her neck as he moved inside her
and she could feel his lips moving soundlessly against
her skin. She murmured words of comfort, stroking
her hands through his hair, down his back, holding
him as closely as anyone could be held. Their bodies
shuddered together, comforting pleasure washing over
them.

She held his welcome weight until he rolled them onto their sides; even then, she kept her arms around him. She waited for his breathing to slow before she closed her own eyes, secure in the knowledge that he would sleep now.

It didn't take Reilly long to join him, exhaustion claiming her so completely that this time no nightmares would touch her.

Chapter 33

A day later, the Maestro looked over the latest pages and smiled. Much better.

Setting up the networked computers had been a stroke of genius on his part. Not surprising, considering that he was one. Giving the writer access to a keyboard seemed to have prompted Sheldon's creativity once more.

The new scene was brilliant. So completely unsettling that he actually felt sick at the idea. In his opinion, that was one of the marks of a good murder scene.

The Maestro didn't understand why the writer felt guilty. It wasn't like he actually *did* anything. He'd barely be considered legally complicit. After all, no one blamed the lookout for the *Titanic* sinking . . . OK, so maybe that wasn't the best example.

He drained the last of his Scotch and pulled up a map on his computer. He had some shopping to do, as well as a little research. Once he had everything together, he'd go scouting for the perfect cast.

Finally being able to film scenes written with him in mind, without having to consult anyone else, and minus any of the usual Hollywood bullshit fucking things up – never mind having the opportunity to act as well as direct – was far more exciting than he'd ever dreamed.

Two days had passed and Reilly was still kicking herself for spending the night with Todd. She never did things like that.

The morning after, she'd managed to slip out before he woke, leaving him a note saying that she needed to call Dublin to check in with her boss. While untrue, she guessed he wouldn't be fooled into thinking that was the real reason she'd chosen to make her call from somewhere other than his apartment.

Back at the beach house over breakfast, she'd barely managed to compose herself before Daniel got up. If he'd noticed that she hadn't come back during the night, he didn't say anything, merely inquiring after his son and nodding in acknowledgment when Reilly had said that Todd was 'doing as well as could be expected'.

The entire day had passed without her seeing or speaking to Todd. Reilly couldn't help but feel that she should be out there with him doing something to bring Bradley's killer to justice. She'd prowled the house restlessly until Daniel finally told her to go for a run, a swim, anything to burn off the excess energy. After a ten-mile run and an hour doing laps in the pool, she was finally tired enough to sit down and pretend to read.

She'd been fine then, until Daniel had turned on the news to hear that yet another email had been sent to the police department. The newscaster had almost sounded gleeful as she'd read it:

I have heard many are calling me the Maestro. While this is not the name I have chosen for myself, I accept this title as it has been selected by my public. I am grateful for the positive reaction I've received from my audience, and hope for your continued support as I expand my horizons. Be expecting great things from me in the near future.

The reporter rounded up by saying, '. . . and with that the Maestro again flaunts the fact that the Tampa PD has yet to find him, and promises even more bloodshed.'

In that moment, Reilly had wished she had the opportunity to slap the snide smile right off the other woman's face. What had come next hadn't done much to curb the impulse.

'And in other news, screenwriter Drew Sheldon is still missing. With no apparent leads, Sheldon's daughter decided to step in front of the cameras this morning to make a plea for her father's life.'

The picture had cut to Kai Sheldon, whom Reilly and Daniel had met at the Millennium Hotel. The girl's face had been strained, the circles under her eyes dark, but her voice had been strong as she'd spoken. 'To whoever has my father, I'm asking, please let him go. If it's money you're after, please ask. I just want my father back.'

The screen had stayed on Kai but her voice had faded as the newscaster had talked over the visual: 'Sources in the police department have told us that Miss Sheldon's promise to pay a ransom was not sanctioned by the TPD and that she made the offer without their approval.' The picture returned to the anchor for the final comment: 'No word yet if Miss Sheldon's plea was successful.'

Reilly had turned it off in disgust and gone to take a shower, hoping it would ease some of her tension. It hadn't worked and she'd tossed and turned for most of the night.

The following day had been as awkward as she'd feared. Fortunately, Daniel was so busy sifting through the list of evidence from the previous two crime scenes that he hadn't seemed to notice Todd and Reilly tiptoeing around each other when Todd called in the office with a progress update.

They'd spoken only when necessary and avoided all forms of eye contact. She hadn't even looked at him when he announced that there would be a memorial for Bradley the next day, a small service at the little non-denominational church he'd occasionally attended.

Once his body was released, Bradley's family would be taking him back to Miami to be buried. It was also when the FBI would be stopping by the lab to pick up any evidence related to the serial killer.

Unless, of course, Todd added, Daniel came through in the meantime.

A heavy silence had fallen over the office at that point, an oppressive air that had threatened suffocation with every breath. Reilly had never felt under so much pressure. All she had been able to do was hope that Daniel would be able to push through a favor and keep Todd's crew on the case. She didn't want to see how he was going to react if he was told to walk away.

Then there had been Daniel's surprise at the beach house later that evening.

'I made the call Todd wanted me to make.' Daniel kept his voice low. 'The Feds are worried about the Tampa lab running things. Between Holly and now Bradley, Todd's personal stake in this is way too high; he shouldn't be working it at all. I can't step in and, really, no one else on the team should either. However, my contact at the field office agreed to let the team stay on the case if you run point and report to their special agent in charge. I recommended that as the best course of action.'

'I can't.' Reilly shook her head. 'I can't run a CSI lab here. I'm not . . .'

Daniel's hand closed around her wrist, the urgency in his voice harder than Reilly had ever heard before. 'You're former FBI and senior CSI in Dublin. Of course you can do it. The field office will issue the necessary credentials. If Todd doesn't want outsiders – and in truth, I'm not completely crazy about that myself given how far into this we are – then it's the only realistic option.'

'Daniel . . .' she started.

'Reilly,' he pleaded. 'Do you know what it will do to Todd if this is taken from him?'

She couldn't do it. She knew Todd would hate her for it, because effectively it *was* being taken away from him. And she also knew that any chance she had for something real with him would vanish the moment he found out that she was the FBI's go-between. Still, how could she say no?

'I'll do it,' she said.

'Thank you.' The two words were heartfelt. 'Now, come out to the living room. Agent Kent needs to meet you.'

Reilly frowned. The SAC was *here* at the house? Typical Daniel, pre-empting her response even before she knew the question.

The special agent in charge was not what she'd had in mind. The moment she saw the burly, balding forty-something scowling out of the living room window, she knew this was not going to go well at all.

'You must be Steel.' He gave Reilly the usual once-over and she could see him dismiss her. There was a man with serious women issues.

'Agent Kent.' She kept her voice polite and held out her hand.

He shook it, two brisk pumps. 'Look, I might as well tell you – I don't deal with the science geeks. You do your thing, give me what you've got and I'll decide if it's worth anything.'

Reilly bristled. She was in no mood to be patronized. 'Excuse me?'

'This wasn't my idea.' Agent Kent stared down at Reilly, his face hard. 'Forrest has influence at the Bureau and I was told to make this work. You were the only viable option.' He turned and headed toward the door. 'Like I said, you call, I make the decisions. The evidence from the Bradley Ford murder will be delivered to the Tampa lab first thing tomorrow.'

'We have a funeral in the morning.' Reilly's voice was sharp.

'And we have keys. Good night.'

As she watched the door close behind Kent, she sighed and muttered, 'Yeah, this was a great idea.'

Reilly was standing in front of her mirror, criticizing the outfit she'd bought in Macy's at the Westfield Mall the day before. She'd needed something appropriate for a memorial service, but had never been good at dressing for somber occasions. She sighed. It would have to do.

'Reilly.' Daniel's voice accompanied his knock at the bedroom door. 'It's time to go.'

'Coming.' Giving herself one final glance in the mirror, Reilly picked up her purse and went out to join Daniel.

The ride to the church took place in silence. Reilly supposed she should have been used to it by now. The last couple of days had been filled with the most silence she'd experienced in a long time. At least this one wasn't filled with the awkward memories of a night that probably should've never happened.

Speaking of which . . .

Todd and Emilie stood on the sidewalk in front of the church, talking to the computer expert Peni and, based on what Todd had told her, a woman Reilly could only assume was Peni's partner. As short as Peni was tall, Ivy looked very much like a poet who would be dating someone like Peni Westmore. Long corn-silk-blond hair with dark purple streaks. A flower-printed skirt that swished around her hemp sandals. A peasant top and dozens of sparkly bracelets.

Reilly suddenly felt very plain in her dark gray dress and simple gold locket.

As she and Daniel approached, her eyes flicked to Todd and she thought she saw a flash of something, but when she looked closer, it was gone, leaving her to wonder if it had really been there at all. She felt a stab of sadness before chastising herself. This was his close friend's memorial service. Fortunately, there was little time for anything other than quick introductions among the small group before they were herded inside.

Reilly barely heard any of the service, she was entirely too aware of Todd just an inch away. She'd tried to position herself further away from him, but couldn't without explaining to Daniel exactly why she didn't want to sit next to him. Instead, she just concentrated on not looking at him.

When the minister asked if anyone wished to share a memory, Todd stood.

His leg brushed against hers as he made his way out of the pew and Reilly's gaze flicked up to his face. He was staring straight ahead, expression stony.

'I first met Bradley when I was still at Quantico,' he began, his throat working. 'He'd just been made a junior investigator at CSI and was well on his way to being senior investigator. I'd needed to visit for a paper I had to write. I'm not sure what I'd expected, but Bradley definitely wasn't it. He showed me a side of forensic investigation that I hadn't considered before. He took me under his wing and showed me the ropes. After I graduated from the Academy, I came back to Tampa because I wanted to work with Bradley Ford. Even though he hadn't seen me for years, he remembered me. Bradley was like that. He cared about people, cared about helping them.' Todd paused, his voice catching. He cleared his throat and continued. 'He was my mentor, my big brother, my best friend. And I am going to find the person responsible for taking him from us. I'm going to get justice for my friend.'

On his way back to his seat, Todd's jaw was set, his eyes flashing with the anger he'd bottled up. He didn't look at anyone, didn't acknowledge his colleagues, as he settled back into his seat, his eyes on his hands as the next person got up to speak.

Reilly let out a breath she hadn't realized that she'd been holding. So that was it, then. If there had ever been a moment where he would've looked to her for some form of encouragement or support, it would have been then. Instead, he hadn't even glanced in her direction. Apparently, he thought their night together had been a mistake.

Well, Reilly decided; if she'd had any misgivings about continuing in Dublin at least that made her decision easy.

After the service, Daniel excused himself to make a call, leaving Reilly standing with the rest of the team and Ivy. As the others discussed the impending FBI takeover, Reilly gave Ivy an awkward smile. Daniel had told her to wait until he received official confirmation today that everything he'd talked about with Agent Kent the evening before would be authorized.

'Peni says you're from Ireland?' Ivy asked with a smile.

'Originally from California, actually,' Reilly clarified. 'I moved to Dublin a couple of years or so ago for a job.'

'So you're just back to visit, or to stay for good?'

Reilly sensed Todd's body tense, but ignored him. 'Just to visit. It's been great seeing Daniel and everyone again, but I have a good job in Dublin, and friends too.'

'And a boyfriend, I presume?' Ivy inquired with a smile.

Reilly shook her head, suddenly uncomfortable with where the questions were heading. She didn't like having these types of discussions at any time, much less in the presence of the man she'd slept with just a few days before.

Talk about awkward.

Fortunately, at that moment, Daniel returned. 'I just spoke to Cam at the Bureau.'

'What'd she say?' Todd was immediately alert and his tone was curt.

'She had to pull some strings, but she was able to convince her boss to let your crew stay on the case.' Daniel paused, glancing at Reilly. Her expression must've told him that she wanted him to share the news because he did just that. 'The only condition is that Reilly run point on the investigation from now on.'

'Figures,' Todd muttered darkly.

'What figures?' Reilly hadn't been happy about the decision, but she'd reasoned it was better than losing everything to the Feds. She'd known Todd wouldn't be happy about it, but she thought he'd at least keep quiet about it for the moment, rather than complain in front of the team.

'Come on, Reilly.' He finally turned toward her but didn't meet her gaze. 'You don't think it's a little strange that the FBI would rather have a consultant who's spent the last three years in Dublin running a case rather than the person with the next highest ranking within the department? I wonder who put *that* idea in their heads?' He gave his father a pointed look.

Daniel crossed his arms over his chest. 'Yes, I suggested Reilly be in charge, but only after Cam said she couldn't consider the idea without someone with a less personal connection heading it.'

'Whatever.' Todd raised a hand and shook his head. 'We've got to get back. We have a case to solve.' He glared at Reilly. 'If that's OK with you, boss?'

Reilly resisted the urge to tell Todd exactly what he could spend the next few hours doing and instead just raised an eyebrow. 'I didn't ask for this, Todd, but you might want to try being grateful that your father actually got us a way to keep the case.'

'Sure,' Todd sneered. 'Thanks, Dad. I'll try to make sure I don't let your protégé down.'

Reilly scowled as Todd stalked away. After an awkward moment, Emilie excused herself to follow. Peni and Ivy said their goodbyes as well, leaving Daniel and Reilly alone.

'It really was the only way, you know.' Daniel broke the silence.

'I believe you,' she said. Whatever vestige of hope she'd maintained that she and Todd would be able to work out this weird thing between them had vanished.

Not that it mattered, since once this was done, she was going back to where she belonged. Reilly couldn't, however, silence the small voice that countered that maybe she didn't quite belong anywhere.

Chapter 34

'I know your team has just gotten back to work after the terrible passing of Bradley Ford.' Captain Harvell's usual gruffness was tempered by his sympathy. 'I was so sorry to hear about it. Bradley was a good man, a valued member of the department.'

Todd gave a stoic nod.

'Agent Kent spoke with me yesterday and told me that you were taking point for the duration of the murder case, Ms Steel,' the captain said, turning to Reilly. Once again the chief was all business. 'He showed me a report of suspicious activity by actor Bruce Reynolds?'

'Yes, sir, a media interview.' Reilly had a vague recollection of Todd saying something about that, something Peni had unearthed apparently. She hadn't read through all of the reports she'd delivered to the FBI agent thus far, trusting the investigative team's notes to be up-to-date.

'We're bringing him in for questioning.' Captain Harvell's voice tightened. 'Agent Kent, actually, is bringing Reynolds in for questioning, and I'd appreciate your perspective.'

By the time Reilly arrived upstairs at the station, Reynolds was already in the interview room with Agent Kent. The actor looked completely different than he had when Reilly had last spoken with him. Gone was the arrogance, the snarky attitude. Reynolds was nervous, biting his nails, eyes darting around the room.

Agent Kent relied on intimidation as he interrogated the suspect. Rapid-fire questions designed to trip up inconsistencies. Lots of looming. Walking behind the suspect. Reilly felt like she was learning as much about the FBI agent as she was about Reynolds.

'What do you think?' Captain Harvell asked, after nearly thirty minutes.

Reilly shook her head. Her previous belief that the actor wasn't the kidnapper or the killer had been solidified after just the first few questions. 'Reynolds may come across as arrogant, but he doesn't have the ego or the courage to be our perp.'

'You don't think he's acting?'

'The way Agent Kent is delivering the questions, Reynolds barely has time to answer, let alone think. I've seen his movies. He's not that good an actor. He's got far too many nervous habits to be as cold and calculating as he would need to be to set up some of these scenes. Also, he's chewing his nails. No nail or skin fragments have been found at any of the scenes. Someone with that much anxiety wouldn't be able to stop himself.' Reilly was inter-rupted when the door to the room opened and a fresh-faced rookie entered. He spoke the words none of them wanted to hear.

'There's been another murder.'

It was one of the oddest things she had ever come across, Reilly thought a little later as she followed Todd across the sand.

Well, apart from the whole Wicked Witch thing, that was. She didn't think that one would ever be beaten for most bizarre murder. She was just glad she'd never been a fan of *The Wizard of Oz*. A friend had made her watch it once. Stupid bloody winged monkeys had freaked her out.

'Do you ever wonder how writers come up with these ideas in the first place?' Todd asked as they walked.

Reilly shrugged. 'I try not to think about it. Anyway, sometimes it's not the big picture that's revealing. Very often it's the little details that are the most telling.'

'You sound just like my dad.' For once, his words held amusement rather than anger and Reilly took note that this was the first actual conversation she and Todd had had since spending the night together. At least it proved they could still work together. Their common goal outweighed their personal issues.

For now anyway.

She suspected that when they went back to the lab later and she placed the call to Agent Kent to give him the required daily update, things would get messy again.

She'd always hated being caught in a pissing match between local and federal agents, but on this case everything was magnified.

Detective Mark Reed was waiting for them at the caution tape. 'How does someone go from something as gruesome as the beheadings to something as, well . . . weird as this?'

Reilly pulled on her gloves as she surveyed the scene. 'The killer's always been dramatic. He thrives on artistic value or cinematic flair. For him, it's not about shock for the sake of shock value. It's about making something that people will never forget.'

'Well, he's definitely on the right track here.' Reed crossed his arms and watched the crime-scene investigators approach the body.

The killer had this time chosen a man in what appeared to be his early twenties, average weight and height. He wore only a pair of dark shorts. The rest of his clothes didn't seem to be anywhere nearby.

'The lifeguard who found him said that he'd pulled a double shift yesterday so he was the last one to leave last night,' Detective Reed said. 'He said the beach was empty when he left at ten. Our victim was here by the time the lifeguard returned this morning at five.'

'Meaning he could've been here when the tide came in.'

Reilly knelt in the scorching sand, not sure which scenario was better. 'What time was high tide?'

Detective Reed answered the question. 'I checked that with the Coast Guard. One fifty-five in the morning.'

'Is he close enough to the waterline that he could've drowned?' she wondered.

Todd straightened from his crouching position and eyed up the distance. 'Definitely. Dr Kase will have to tell us for sure, though.'

'We figure the rest of his clothes, anything else he might've had on him as evidence is probably long gone. It might wash back up again, but the chances are slim.' Reed circled to the front of the victim. 'He didn't have ID on him.'

Reilly didn't say anything as she examined the tent pegs driven into the sand on either side of the victim's legs. The ropes around his ankles matched the ones around his forearms attached to similar pegs. Based on the raw and bleeding flesh beneath the ropes, it hadn't been a quick death. The poor kid had had the strength and time to fight back, this time at least.

It was a first.

'Let me know what you find,' Detective Reed said abruptly. He turned and walked back up the beach, and Reilly wondered why he seemed so shaken at this one in particular given the horror shows he'd been experiencing all throughout the entire investigation.

'The victim looks about the same age as Mark's son,' Todd explained, picking up on her thoughts. 'Lives in Wisconsin with Mark's ex.'

Reilly didn't have anything to say regarding this revelation. She couldn't imagine how hard it must be for a parent to see a victim the same age as their child. She knew how difficult it was when she came across a victim who reminded her of her sister. A son or daughter would've been nearly unbearable.

The realization hit her as she set aside her camera, and the link between the film festival and the murders finally became clear.

'He's threatening Sheldon's daughter . . .'

'What?' Todd looked at her, puzzled.

'The killer and the kidnapper are the same man.'

'But how—'

'I think the killer has been forcing Sheldon into writing death scenes, brand-new scenes for him to act out.' Reilly was sure this was what had happened now. The *Indiana Jones* angle for Bradley's murder hadn't panned out, and coupled with the setup for this one which also didn't ring any immediate bells with regard to any well-known movies, it was almost a certainty. That was assuming the killer and Sheldon weren't in cahoots, which given the screenwriter's reputation was unlikely.

She continued outlining her theory to Todd. 'This death and Bradley's are new scenes, unrelated to any movies we know about so far. Whether or not Sheldon knows what his kidnapper is doing with what's being written is another story.' She scooped up some of the sand in a vial. 'But I think he's threatening Kai Sheldon, and holding that threat over her father to get what he wants.'

'The hotel said they put extra security on her.' Todd put the evidence bag into a marked box. 'So if our murderer does have Sheldon, don't you think it's more likely that the guy's just trying to save himself?'

'Do you really think he's foolish enough to believe that he's going to be let go after writing scenes that caused the deaths of two people?' Reilly replied, shaking her head, full sure now that she was on the right track. 'And I also think Sheldon knows his captor well enough to know that he could access Kai. Otherwise, why would he go along with it?'

Todd stared down at the corpse in front of him without answering.

Reilly didn't say anything more, letting him think it through. She knew that Todd was likely pondering the same horrific thought that had been going through her mind the moment she'd suspected what had happened here.

Had Drew Sheldon really dreamed up the death scene they were looking at now?

And had the victim died before or after the killer had filled in the hole where the young man had been forced to stick his head? Had he suffocated, sand filling his nose and mouth as his body struggled for breath?

Or had it been done close enough to the tide that he'd technically drowned, water mingling with the grains of sand?

Chapter 35

The Maestro strolled across the container and sat in his usual seat.

Drew Sheldon looked decidedly the worse for wear. He'd still refused to change into the clean clothes that the Maestro had brought and hadn't washed since he'd been abducted. That couldn't be sanitary. He had a momentary desire to film the writer's descent into filth and broadcast it for all of the big-wig's Hollywood friends to see. Then again, that would be counter-productive and a waste of time. He had better things to do.

'First, let me congratulate you on the best screenplay you've ever written. The forensic investigator's death was good, but this one was so much better. The guy did exactly as you said.' The Maestro chuckled as he remembered the expressions of terror on his victim's face.

No actor could replicate something so pure, no matter how many Academy Awards they'd won. And forget a halfwit like Bruce Reynolds trying to do it. Although, now that he thought about it, it might've been fun to cast Bruce in one of these new scenes. 'When am I going to get out of here?' Sheldon's voice was hoarse. That tended to happen when a good part of the day was spent screaming for help. Apparently, he still hadn't learned that no one could hear him. Or he just liked the sound of his voice. Also a possibility.

'I told you,' the Maestro said, leaning forward. 'When I have my script. You've only done the first part. Now we're going to talk about the big finale.'

'Finale?' Sheldon's trepidation was written on his face.

'Oh, yeah.' A slow smile spread across the Maestro's face. 'And I don't want something that we've seen a million times. No machetes or chainsaws, villains with claws. Beheading, evisceration, all of that's been done, pardon the pun, to death. I want something creative, something so big that audiences will never forget it.'

Much later, Todd sat at home at his kitchen table, staring at the closed laptop. He hadn't told anyone he was taking Bradley's work computer home with him.

Technically, since Reilly was running the investigation, she should've been told, but, Todd argued with himself, it wasn't like she'd claimed the laptop for herself.

In fact, it seemed that everyone had forgotten about it. He certainly had until he'd gone into Bradley's office after coming back from the beach crime scene earlier. While rummaging through the desk drawers for energy drinks or coffee, he stumbled on the familiar black case.

Now, the machine sat in front of him, silent and accusing. He knew he could get in serious trouble if anyone found out that he'd taken it. But he wanted to know what Bradley had been doing, and the lead Reilly mentioned he'd been chasing down in the run-up to his capture. That meant something, Todd was sure of it.

'All right,' he said. 'Let's see if there's anything good on here.' He pressed the button and waited for it to boot up, sipping at his beer. It was three in the morning and, as always recently, sleep was being elusive.

In fact, the only night he'd gotten more than a few hours was the night that Reilly . . .

Todd scowled. He didn't want to think about that anymore. Pity sex. That's all it had been. He needed to stop thinking about it. No matter how great it was.

'First stop . . .' He barely noticed that he was talking to himself. 'Internet history.'

He pulled up the program and opened the history tab, hoping Bradley hadn't cleared the cache recently. The first two sites weren't any help as they were both password-protected. The third, however, took him to an online article from a movie industry website.

Todd's eyes widened as he read:

Up-and-coming director Wesley Fisher sat down to discuss his second film, the much-lauded *An Age of Dawn and Ice*, with Gwendolyn Kim. While his first film, *The Children of Desire*, had been one of the most highly anticipated films of last year, it drastically fell short of both critic and fan expectations. Fisher's second movie has received initial positive reviews but fans are still wondering if they should expect to be disappointed once more. When questioned, Fisher defended his movie adamantly, saying that the deeper meaning was lost by most and that those who bashed his film should stick to their intellectual equals – specifically citing *River of Blood*, the current box office hit penned by Drew Sheldon. *River of Blood* is a crowd-pleasing slasher flick that fulfills its promise to be as graphic as it can while staying just this side of an R rating. Fisher claims that he's so proud of his first film that he kept the prop ring that played a key part in the plot. According to Fisher, the ring is made of a rare form of amber, making its worth almost as high as the film's gross. Citing the eighteen-second 1895 film *The Execution of Mary, Queen of Scots* as an inspiration for cutting-edge work, Fisher stated that he hoped to make a memorable contribution to society through the medium of film. As he left, this reporter couldn't help but wonder if, in just a few short years, the only memory of Fisher will be a cautionary tale for young directors starting out in the business.

Todd swore. Amber . . . *The Execution of Mary, Queen of Scots* . . . Someone with an encyclopedic knowledge of film and, more importantly, a motive for revenge.

According to Daniel and Reilly's account of their interview with him at the hotel, Fisher had seemed intrigued by the notion of intercutting real life with films, but not overly interested. Given Todd's father's lack of interest in him as a potential suspect, he'd apparently handled himself without any notable signs of anxiety, which meant either he was a sociopath or just plain lucky. Todd was hoping for the latter, but afraid that they were dealing with the former.

Bradley must have realized the same thing and either gone to find out more about Fisher or talk to him directly. Either way, it hadn't ended well.

Todd's hand was halfway to his phone when he stopped. If he called Reilly, she'd just call the field office. The Feds would go in and either botch the job, or confiscate Bradley's laptop and suspend Todd. He couldn't take the chance of letting Holly and Bradley's murderer go free.

He stood and glanced at his watch. It was still early enough that the night manager at the Millennium Hotel would be there. Based on Daniel's observations of Fisher's behavior, Todd was willing to bet that the director wasn't on the best of terms with any of the hotel staff.

Getting a room number should be easy. After that, all Todd had to do was provoke some sort of response from Fisher. A confession. An aggressive move. Anything that would give him the opportunity to act.

And by act, of course, he meant take him in. There was certainly no need for anything violent to occur, though Todd wasn't sure if he'd be able to resist.

He hesitated, his hand hovering over his car keys. Rushing in unprotected and without calling the detectives for backup probably wasn't the best idea either. The guy had managed to take out Bradley, and the other male victims hadn't exactly been small.

He went into the bedroom and retrieved a box from the top of his closet. He'd purchased the Smith & Wesson M645 a few years ago when he and Bradley had decided they should spend more time at the range.

It had been a while since he'd fired it, but he'd been meticulous about keeping it in good condition. He loaded it, just as a precaution, and double-checked the safety. As he slipped it into his waistband and pulled the back of his T-shirt over it, he spoke out loud. 'Just in case. That's all.'

As Todd hurried back into the kitchen to pick up his keys, he couldn't help but mentally add that if the sick fuck gave him an excuse, he wouldn't hesitate to put him down.

Chapter 36

Reilly stepped into the cool silence of the lab and felt a rush of relief that it was empty. Granted, it was five o'clock in the morning and they'd all been working late the night before, but she doubted she was the only one having problems sleeping.

She'd hoped that she'd be the only one coming in early though. She needed some time to gather her thoughts without constantly worrying about Todd or Daniel. With Daniel's part in the current interference from the Feds, the tension between father and son had really ramped up lately.

She set down her bag and pulled up her email program. She was still waiting to hear back from the costume designer about the dress from the Mary, Queen of Scots, murder. She'd passed on the information to Bradley at the time but of course the poor guy hadn't been able to chase it up, and the others had been inundated ever since. So Reilly had followed it up herself.

A familiar ding indicated that her mail was done loading and she perched on the edge of her stool as she sorted through it. Usually, back in Dublin, the GFU wouldn't double-document every exchange, but with the team's personal stake in the investigation now, she needed to make sure everything they did was above board. Reilly didn't want the killer getting off because the defense hinted at impropriety. She needed to have facts to back up everything the lab did, every piece of evidence, every finding, every conclusion.

The next email was the one she'd been waiting for and she printed it out even as she read it:

I apologize for taking so long getting back to you. I had some trouble finding the order you'd requested as it appears to have been processed over a year ago. The dress in question was one of six I sold to a production company for a film they were making. The garments were shipped to Stars and Moon Productions in Los Angeles. Someone from the production company actually called me back a few months later to ask about a return and refund because funding had been cut. However, I only received back five of the dresses. When I contacted the company, the director stated that he wanted to keep one as a souvenir and agreed to pay for it. I believe the director's name was Wesley. I hope this helps with whatever you're investigating. Please let me know if there is anything else I can do for you. Sincerely, Magda Evanwood.

Reilly stared at the screen, her heart racing as she realized just what it all meant.

Wesley Fisher; the up and coming director who'd wanted Drew Sheldon to write him a screenplay. She reached for the phone. Surprisingly, given the hour, it only rang a few times.

'Agent Kent,' she said. 'We have a suspect name.' Her first instinct had been to talk to Todd, but given the level of rage and thirst for vengeance simmering inside him at the moment, she figured better to play things by the book.

'A name?' The Fed sounded surprised. 'How'd you get that?'

Because it's my job, you idiot. Reilly bit back the retort before it crossed her lips. 'A costume designer just emailed me. Short version is, she sold a dress worn by one of the victims to movie director Wesley Fisher.'

'And?'

Reilly closed her eyes, fighting the urge to ask the agent if he was being deliberately obtuse. 'Fisher is here in Tampa at the film festival. Daniel Forrest and I talked to him before.'

'You talked to a potential suspect?'

'That's not really the point.' Reilly spoke through gritted teeth. She didn't remember the other Feds she'd worked with being this thick-headed. 'Fisher had issues with Sheldon because Sheldon wouldn't write a screen-play for him.'

'So you're sticking with this theory that the screen-writer kidnapping and the murders are being carried out by the same person?'

Reilly wanted to scream. 'Yes. The profile fits. And now the evidence fits.'

'But you don't have anything physical to connect the two.' The agent sounded uninterested. 'Without forensic evidence, all you have is circumstantial at best.'

'Look, I don't care if you believe my theory or not.' Reilly's temper flared.

While she was still admired in her field for her exper-tise, a lot of the cops and prosecutors she'd worked with before she'd left considered her decision to move out of the country as a slap in the face. Then again, based on the way Agent Kent had been talking to her from moment one, she wondered if anything like that even came into play. 'It doesn't matter. Fisher needs to be questioned about the dress in any case. The designer confirmed she sold it to him. So either he's the killer and placed it on the victim or he's some way connected to whoever did.'

'All right,' Agent Kent said. 'I'll send someone over to the hotel to look into it. I don't suppose you have a receipt with Fisher's name on it?'

'No.' Reilly clicked the mouse. 'But I'm forwarding you the email now.'

'Fine. We'll take it from here.'

Before Reilly could say anything else, the line went dead. This whole hanging up before saying goodbye the Feds always did was really getting on her nerves.

'Asshole,' she muttered as she slammed down the receiver.

Now all she could do was wait.

Seven a.m. and Todd still hadn't made it in. Reilly frowned.

She knew he'd been pissed about how things had gone with the FBI, and with his dad. Knew that he'd been weirded out by what had happened between them, too.

But she'd thought they'd moved past that. And she'd never thought he'd blow off work. A harried-sounding Emilie had called to say that she was running late, but that hadn't really surprised Reilly. The youngest member of the team had never worked one of these types of cases before, certainly not one where she knew a victim. It took a lot out of veteran agents. For a newbie, Emilie was doing very well.

Against her better judgment, Reilly picked up her phone. It was possible that Todd would be more likely to answer if she called from the lab rather than her cell. As she sat and listened to it ring she questioned her reasoning. If he was late and saw that work was calling, he'd most likely assume it was her on the other end of the line. When it went to voicemail, she left a brief message and hung up. Where was he?

A beep at her computer distracted her and she crossed to it. When she hadn't heard back from the field office by six-thirty, she'd decided to run her own data-mining search on Fisher looking for anything related to his visit to Florida on anything other than the film festival.

She knew Agent Kent wouldn't approve, but she really didn't care at this point.

Wesley Fisher. Rented, one full-sized storage unit. Gatlin Boulevard.

Why would a director visiting from California need a storage unit here in Florida? Reilly mused as she reached for her phone again. What could he possibly be storing? Or more to the point . . . who?

She tapped impatiently on the desk as she waited for Agent Kent to answer. After a minute, she heard the usual clicks and buzz as she was transferred. The voice that answered was female and not one Reilly recognized.

'Hi, this is Reilly Steel from the Tampa CSI department. I'm the liaison on the movie-maker murders, and also the Drew Sheldon kidnapping.' She kept her tone professional, without a hint of the frustration and annoyance just below the surface. For all his talk of taking the information she'd provided and making logical conclusions, Kent had yet to acknowledge the connection between the kidnapping and the murders.

'And how can I help you?' The woman sounded vaguely bored.

'I called in earlier this morning with the name of a potential suspect. Agent Kent was supposed to check it out but I haven't heard back yet. I just—'

The woman interrupted in the same flat tone. 'Federal agents do not always have the luxury of keeping local law enforcement updated during the course of an investigation, especially lab technicians. If you're that concerned, I suggest you contact your local precinct to see if they've received any new information. Other than that, I can only recommend that you wait until Agent Kent is able to contact you. He will do so at his earliest convenience, I'm sure.'

'But I—' The line disconnected before Reilly could explain any further. She stared at the phone. 'You've got to be kidding me.' After a moment, she dialed again. 'Fine, you want me to contact the locals, don't get pissed if my information gets them the arrest.'

'Tampa Police Department.' This woman sounded a bit more polite.

'Hi, this is Reilly Steel from the CSI department. I'm looking for either Detective Reed or Detective Sampson.'

'I'm sorry, Ms Steel,' the woman apologized. 'Detectives Reed and Sampson are out engaged in something for the FBI.' Interviewing Wesley Fisher? Reilly hoped so, but she didn't have a cellphone contact for either of the detectives to hand. She was sure it was in the files somewhere but . . .

'Captain Harvell?' Reilly hadn't wanted to go to the captain because it wouldn't improve her relations with the detectives, but time was of the essence. She just hoped the detectives saw it that way and not that she was going over their heads.

'I'm sorry,' the woman apologized again. 'I'm afraid Captain Harvell called in sick today. Some sort of stomach bug that's been going around. Can I take a message?'

'No.' Reilly shook her head, trying not to let her emotions bleed through to her voice. 'I'll talk to them later.'

'Very well. Have a nice day.'

'Thank you. You too.' She said the words automatically, her brain already racing through her next options. It was possible, she supposed, that the detectives or Agent Kent would arrest Fisher, but doubtful. If Fisher was spooked and ran, he might kill Sheldon as a loose end. Someone needed to check out that storage unit before Fisher knew they were on to him, and if the cops and the FBI were both too busy, it didn't really leave a whole lot of other people to step in.

'This is a bad idea,' Reilly murmured as she reached for her cell and dialed Todd's number. 'A very bad idea.'

Chapter 37

The Maestro paced in front of his newest acquisition. He'd considered cleaning the dried blood off of the young man's face, but had ultimately decided against it. He just hoped it would show on film as blood and not dirt. 'You know, if you were really this eager to break into the movie industry, all you had to do was ask. You're a good-looking guy, very much leading man material. I'm sure we could've found something for you without all of this drama.'

'You can kiss my ass,' the dark-haired man spit out, glaring up at his captor.

'If you insist.' He was vaguely amused by the investigator's anger.

'Not something you're used to yourself though, is it?' The reply was snarky, pale eyes flashing with anger.

The Maestro laughed, amused by the young man's fire. That would make for an excellent performance. 'I guess you could say that. Though my recent foray into a new genre of movies has contributed to a change in the way I'm viewed these days.'

'You really like to hear yourself talk, don't you?' The man squirmed in his chair, apparently thinking he looked as if he were simply trying to get comfortable.

The Maestro wasn't fooled. He knew the younger man was testing his bonds. Not that it would do any good. He had purchased high-quality handcuffs a few days ago. After all, one never knew when extra restraints would come in handy. Anyway, the other man wasn't entirely wrong. He did love to hear himself talk. He was the only one with whom he could carry on an intelligent conversation.

Others always fell so short.

'I'm The Maestro now, a film-maker like no other.' He spread his arms wide in a grand gesture. 'Wesley Fisher is a failure who tried to raise the consciousness of his audience by creating meaningful pieces. Four movies, each grossing less than the one before. No one wanted to watch something uplifting and thought-provoking. No, they were too busy spending their money to see bad actors pretend to die in inexplicable ways.'

'Will you please just shut the hell up?' The man interrupted with a groan. 'Or kill me already. Just don't make me listen to you talk anymore.'

The Maestro scowled. Wasn't that just like an actor? This arrogant little twerp was totally unappreciative of what was about to be done for him. Before, he hadn't cared much about what the finale entailed, as long as it was epic. Now he was hoping that Sheldon's denouement included something pretty painful. He turned to the writer. 'How much longer until the finale's complete? My star appears to be getting anxious.'

'A day? Maybe two?' Drew's eyes darted between his fellow prisoner and their captor.

The Maestro wasn't stupid. He knew that the writer was trying to figure out how much time he could buy for the other guy to get them out. He rolled his eyes. It wasn't like he'd kidnapped a cop, just a scientist. And, based on the evidence at hand, not a very smart one.

'You have twenty-four hours, no more.' The Maestro walked over to the door where he'd set down his bag. 'Now, Todd, just in case you're thinking that your pretty blond sidekick is going to rescue you . . .' He drew two items from the bag and held them up. 'I'm going to take you to a more secure location so my writer here can work. It's your choice how you want to go.' He waved the cattle prod in one hand and a bottle of chloroform in the other. 'Hard or easy?'

'All right, Todd, where the hell are you?' Reilly scowled at her phone. She'd been calling his cell and landline for the last forty minutes, using both her own cell and the office line, but no luck. If she wasn't so pissed at him, she might have been a little worried.

'Sorry I'm late.' Emilie entered the lab, breathless and flushed. 'I slept in a little later than I'd planned.'

'No problem,' Reilly said absently. 'For all of the stuff we have left to pick apart, it'll be a challenge for us to actually find anything.' At least, anything more promising than the lead on Wesley Fisher.

'Not wanting to overstep or anything . . .' Emilie's concern was written on her youthful face. 'But are you OK?'

'Fine.' Reilly smiled tightly, realizing she was pacing. She couldn't do this anymore. She had a lead, a real lead, and no one would follow it.

Todd was MIA, the detectives were unreachable and Daniel wasn't allowed to touch the case any longer. Well, she was tired of waiting and tired of everyone acting like they had all the time in the world. She was tired of being scared that she'd screw things up. Now it was time to act.

'There's something I need to check out,' she told Emilie distractedly. 'Keep going over the latest victims' personal effects and run whatever analysis you need.'

'And if I do find something?' Emilie immediately switched to professional mode. Unlike Todd, she'd had no problem whatsoever accepting Reilly as the senior investigator.

'Call me.' She pocketed her phone as she headed for the doors.

The morning was already sweltering and Reilly turned on the air conditioning of the CSI van with a sigh of relief. The cool air flowed over her as she input the address she'd found into the GPS. By the time she pulled out of the parking lot, she was able to breathe again.

She pulled into the storage company's yard and took a moment to gather her thoughts. She had no warrant, no department credentials.

Not only would the owner have every right to refuse her access, she could conceivably get into trouble, even be thrown off of the investigation if the matter was pressed. However, she'd found one thing to be true in both Dublin and the US when it came to working a case. Confidence can usually sell a plausible lie.

Reilly checked her hair and make-up in the rearview mirror and smoothed down her skirt, thankful that she'd run out of clean versions of the new business clothes she'd purchased. While still conservative, the sundress she was wearing today was definitely conducive to her plan.

A little flirting was never a bad backup either.

The office was dark after the bright morning sunlight and Reilly paused in the doorway, blinking as her eyes adjusted. The young man at the counter was still staring as she walked forward. Maybe this wasn't going to be as difficult as she first thought.

'Hi, I'm Reilly Steel. I'm with Tampa CSI and I really could use your help.' Reilly gave the clerk a wide smile.

'You don't look like a cop,' he blurted out. His face turned red. 'I mean, you need my help?'

'Yes . . .' her eyes flicked down to his name tag. 'Brandon, I need to know about a storage unit rented by a man named Fisher.'

'Oh, I don't know.' Brandon rubbed the back of his neck and tried not to look like he was hoping for a better view. 'Anything like that, I'm supposed to get my boss 'cos he'll want to look over the warrant.'

'Brandon,' Reilly whispered as she leaned forward, a little bit ashamed that she'd had to resort to these tactics. When she was done here, she was going to have it out with Agent Kent. 'Here's the thing. This man I'm looking for, he's a really bad guy and I need to get into that unit right away. I'm sure your boss will understand. In fact . . .' She winked, hating herself for doing it, '. . . there's even a chance that this could help lead to his arrest and I'd be more than happy to tell your boss and everyone what a vital role you played in capturing such a bad guy.'

'Well . . .'

Reilly could see Brandon's resolve weakening and resisted the urge to reach across the counter and tell him to hurry the hell up. She could feel the time slipping away and she didn't know how long she had before the Feds descended on this place.

Even if Fisher didn't cave when he was interrogated, she was sure either the detectives or the field office would at least run his name and find the same things she did. If she was caught trying to get in, she probably could forget getting her US credentials back if she ever decided to work in the States again. If she found Sheldon, however, her renegade actions would most likely be overlooked. Hell knew it wasn't the first time she'd gone rogue.

'All right.' Brandon grinned at her, and she felt a wave of relief.

'I need to know what unit Mr Fisher rented and if you

have the keys.' Reilly barely managed to keep her words from coming out harsh and clipped. She'd gotten what she wanted but there was no need to scare Brandon away simply because she was impatient.

He tapped away on his computer, using the classic hunt-and-peck method of so many who'd 'learned' to 'type' by texting. Reilly was mildly surprised that he wasn't mouthing each letter as he searched.

'Mr Fisher rented one of our full-sized storage spaces at the far end of the lot. The notes say that he specifically requested the most isolated unit we had available.' Brandon beamed at Reilly. 'Number 314.'

'Keys?' Reilly prompted.

'Oh, we don't have any. All locks are provided by the customer.'

Damn it. Reilly tried not to show her frustration. It seemed she was going to have to do things the hard way. 'Do you have a bolt cutter?'

Brandon looked doubtful once more. This was why she'd kept her 'nice guy' face on. Never burn bridges, even if you are in a hurry.

'You don't even have to give it to me,' Reilly said in her best soothing tone. 'Just tell me where it is and I'll get it myself. Plausible deniability.'

'Plausi-what?'

Reilly smiled while mentally berating the public education system. 'You can say that you didn't give it to me, I took it. That way, you don't have to worry about getting into any trouble.'

'Oh, OK.' Brandon's doubts vanished. 'It's around back.'

'Perfect.' Reilly straightened. 'And which way is unit 314?'

Chapter 38

Todd was still trying to figure out how he'd gotten himself into this mess when the vehicle he was in came to a stop.

This was not good. So very not good.

He closed his eyes even though the trunk was dark and took slow, even breaths in an attempt to calm his racing heart and to push back the panic that threatened to overtake him.

When he'd first arrived at the hotel, flashed his badge and asked for Wesley Fisher's room number, the night manager had complied.

Todd had gotten into the elevator with his usual swagger, completely confident in his ability to handle Fisher. What he hadn't counted on was someone following him into the lift, nor what was hidden beneath the guy's jacket. He had a vague recollection of pain shooting through his body as he hit the floor.

The next thing he knew, he was trussed up like some Thanksgiving Day turkey in the trunk of a car and his head was throbbing. The side of his face itched and he had a feeling it was from dried blood. The scratchy blanket rubbing against his cheek immediately brought to mind the fibers Emilie had matched from two of the crime scenes.

That was Todd's first indication that he was screwed.

When Fisher had pulled him out of the trunk, he'd barely had time to register that they were at a storage unit before the brandished cattle prod had poked him in the back. No electricity that time, but the threat had been enough to get Todd moving. His first encounter with the prod had been enough.

He'd focused on trying to pick up as much surrounding information as possible as he stumbled through the doorway – and then the smell had hit him. One look at the dirty, angry man on the cot had explained it all.

Fisher – or The Maestro as he called himself now – had spent the next twenty minutes or so pontificating until Todd had been ready to 'volunteer' for whatever scene was being scripted.

Anything just to stop the lunatic from talking.

When Fisher had told him to choose between chloroform and the cattle prod, Todd's heart had sunk. Fisher was smarter than Todd had originally thought. Leaving Todd and Drew Sheldon together would raise the odds of escape or of them being found.

Todd had considered his options before gritting his teeth and choosing the cattle prod.

It had hurt like hell and scrambled his brains for a bit, but he'd still been more aware of his surroundings than he would have been if he'd been drugged. As it was, he was fairly certain he knew the general area where he'd been taken. He flexed his wrists and legs, testing his muscles. If he surprised Fisher the moment the man opened the trunk, Todd was sure he could gain the upper hand.

A sliver of light shone into the black interior and Todd tensed, coiled to spring. He'd incapacitate Fisher first, then search for a cellphone. He could make the call that would bring reinforcements and label him as the one who'd brought down Holly and Bradley's killer.

He felt the first jolt of electricity before he saw the prod and swore even as his teeth slammed together. His chance at escape and glory was lost.

He'd be lucky if he could stay conscious long enough to confirm his surroundings. As a different kind of darkness claimed him, Todd realized that even that little bit wasn't going to be possible.

Reilly was two units away from 314 when she realized that she hadn't brought a weapon. She paused, weighing her options. She could return to the main office and call the FBI or the detectives again, hoping they picked up. She could go sit in the van and keep calling from her cell until they finally answered, all the while hoping Fisher didn't either show up or, if he was already there, leave.

Or, she could just keep going and, if necessary, use the bolt cutters she'd borrowed.

Bolt cutters versus a serial killer. Yeah, that would end well.

'Don't be such a wuss,' Reilly muttered to herself. She raised the bolt cutters and tightened her grip. 'You chose to come out here alone. Pull it together and do something.'

Jaw set, she started to walk again, taking more care with each step that took her closer to her goal. When she reached the door, she crouched and slipped on a pair of gloves before sliding the cutters into place. The snap was louder than she'd anticipated and she froze, straining for any sound of discovery. After several seconds had passed, she grabbed the handle and lifted the door.

Heart pounding, she took a step inside. The stink rolled over her, making her gag even as her eyes adjusted to the change in light.

'Hello?' A tentative croak from the depths of the dark made Reilly jump.

Silently berating herself for her nerves, she paused, waiting for the call to come again.

'Hello? Is someone there?'

Definitely male. Sounded like someone who'd spent the last few days screaming loud enough to harm his vocal cords.

Probably not the killer then. Otherwise, they were dealing with someone even crazier than they'd thought.

'CSI.' Reilly surprised herself with a steady voice. 'Identify yourself.'

'I'm Drew Sheldon.' The relief in the man's voice was nearly palpable.

'Are you alone, Mr Sheldon?' Reilly held back the excitement that surged forward. She was right! She dampened down her rising adrenaline, aware that she still had to be smart about this.

'Yes, yes, they're gone.'

As she made her way further into the unit, the vague shapes at the back began to take on more solid shapes, including the figure of a man who stood next to a cot stained with things that Reilly didn't want to think about. Despite his matted hair and filthy attire, she recognized the picture that had been flashed everywhere around the city since he'd been reported missing.

'Mr Sheldon.' Reilly hurried over to the screenwriter's side, ignoring the smell that grew stronger the closer she got. She tried not to gag with each breath and it slowly became easier.

'Wesley Fisher . . .' he gasped, struggling to talk.

'Kidnapped you, I know.' Reilly looked down at the chain connecting the man to the cot. She raised her bolt cutters, looking at them dubiously. She wasn't entirely sure they'd get the job done. That was a huge chain. The padlock on the door was tiny by comparison.

'No. I think he's in danger.'

'What?' Reilly stared at Sheldon, baffled.

'That psycho who took me . . . he's Paul Lennox. Wesley Fisher's number two.' The writer could barely get the words out.

'Number two . . . I don't—'

'Co-producer. They collaborated on a couple of movies but the relationship recently went sour. Wesley's next on his list, possibly his main target. Lennox blames him for their box office failures. Decided to go solo . . .'

Reilly's eyes darted back to the man's face, her voice terse. 'You mean it's not Wesley Fisher who's been killing all these innocent people?' Her mind raced. Co-producer. . . Which meant that Lennox would have had access to props from Fisher's movies, like the Queen Mary costume. Or access to this lockup. He may even have rented it himself but under the guise of being Fisher so as to head off any suspicion . . .

'No.' Sheldon shook his head. 'It's Lennox. He's after Fisher. And now he's taken someone else.'

'Someone else?' Her stomach sank. There was no one else in the unit. If the Maestro – Lennox – had another victim, it wasn't here.

Not good.

'Brought him in this morning,' Sheldon continued. 'Good-looking guy, dark hair, a bit on the sarcastic side.' Sheldon paused and gave Reilly an appraising look. 'You're a pretty blond.'

'Um, thank you?' Reilly wasn't entirely sure how to take the compliment or where it had come from. Jeez, was the whole of Hollywood the same about women? Then she considered that it might be that Sheldon's mental status may have been compromised by his incarceration.

'No,' the screenwriter protested quickly. 'I mean Lennox said something to the other guy about his pretty blond sidekick coming to rescue him.'

Reilly felt the color drain out of her face.

Suddenly she knew.

Chapter 39

The Maestro sat at the rickety kitchen table, his laptop open as he waited for Sheldon to deliver the final scene. His fingers tapped against the tabletop, his foot against the floor. He liked to think of himself as a patient man, but the anticipation was nearly unbearable.

Maybe he should write his final letter now rather than waiting until after filming was wrapped. It would allow him to send it out on a delay so the news would get it around the same time the finale was being reported. The Feds and the cops would both think that he was still hanging around when he'd already tied up all of his loose ends and was on his merry way.

Sheldon would die, of course, but if the final scene pleased enough, he would make it quick and painless. Even if the writer was found fairly quickly, it would be too late.

But the Maestro doubted the body would be discovered until his lease on the unit ran out and the company went down to clean it out.

He didn't envy whoever opened that door.

He checked his laptop again but there was nothing new yet. That was all right, he supposed. He didn't want a rush job. There was a deadline – no pun intended – but that didn't mean he had to settle for poor quality.

'Now, my final letter to the people,' the Maestro muttered. 'I need to include how pleased I've been with their reactions and what a great place it's been. Mention that I'm moving on but without enough detail to reveal my next location. Don't want to give the people of Cleveland a chance to prepare.'

After a moment, he began to type, reading out loud as he worked. 'The time has come to say our final farewell. I have grown quite fond of the Tampa Bay area and am grateful to have had such a receptive place for my debut. I can only hope to receive a welcome just as warm from my next location. As true art always shifts and changes, I look forward to evolving as an artist while maintaining the integrity of my work. I hope that you have enjoyed our time together as much as I have and I ask you to keep your eyes open because I'm not done yet.'

Todd had no idea how much time had passed while he'd been unconscious again.

He was thirsty and his tongue felt like cotton in his dry mouth. That could've meant anything from a couple of minutes to a few hours. He did, however, feel the overwhelming need to pee, which probably meant his time under was actually a few hours.

He blinked a few times, his eyes adjusting to the dim light and his head throbbing as he took stock of his situation.

If his years playing football in high school was any indication, he had a concussion from his fall, compounded by the jolts of electricity to which he'd been subjected. His wrists were sore, chafed nearly raw, but the handcuffs were gone.

He moved his feet. They too were unencumbered. He was lying on a cot bed similar to the one he'd seen Drew Sheldon on earlier, though this one appeared to be much cleaner. He sat up, groaning as the pain in his head spiked. Yup, definitely a concussion.

Todd swung his feet over the side of the cot, took a deep breath and stood. His stomach roiled but didn't completely rebel, so he considered it a win.

A string brushed against his head and he instinctively grabbed at it and pulled. A click later and a pale light flooded the room. And it was an actual room, Todd saw, not some sort of warehouse.

Judging by the rough bedrock walls and bare plank ceiling, he was in a basement.

The cot sat against one wall, a chair against the other. In the far corner was a bucket that Todd was fairly sure was supposed to be his toilet. A set of stairs led up to a wooden door. No windows, no other ways in or out.

He needed to check the door, find out if he could hear anything, determine just how thick the door was. He needed to know if Fisher was gone, if there was a way out or a way to alert someone to his presence. But first, there was something else he needed to do.

Todd crossed to the bucket in the corner.

'I'll get you out of here and then I'll wait to catch Lennox when he comes back for the script.' Reilly tried a different link in the chain. She knew she should call the FBI or cops, but she also knew they'd be pissed enough that they'd either detain her here when they arrived or send her away altogether.

If she just delivered Sheldon to the hospital, she could get back before anyone else knew about her involvement. She didn't care about the rules or protocol anymore; she wanted to find Todd and she wasn't going to let the people who'd brushed her off before now swoop in and take her off the case.

'He's not coming back for it.' Sheldon's statement drew Reilly's attention.

'What do you mean, he's not coming back?' Reilly tried to quell the fear that rose inside her. Lennox had to come back. She needed him to so she could catch him and make him tell her where he'd taken Todd.

Daniel was not going to go through what her own father had when he'd lost Jess. And she was not going to lose anyone else she cared about. Even if her feelings for Todd were a bit perplexing at the moment.

'He set up this shared document account.' Sheldon gestured to a laptop. 'I just type and he can see it.'

Reilly stood. 'So he doesn't need to come here until he's done with you, which means his next movie scene will be completed and Todd will be dead.'

Her mind raced as she tried to come up with a plan that didn't involve her friend's death. 'Wait a minute,' she said, turning toward Sheldon. 'Since Lennox set up each of the scenes himself and has been acting in some of them as the killer, once you write the finale, we'll know where he's going to be.'

'One little flaw in that plan.' Sheldon rattled his chain as he absent-mindedly scratched his ankle. 'For that to work, I have to write the finale. Which I can't very well be doing while being questioned by the police or examined at the hospital.'

'Right.' Reilly scrambled for another idea, grateful that the writer seemed to be working with her on this. 'We'll get you set up in a nice safe house and . . .'

Sheldon was already shaking his head. 'Lennox set up the account to only be accessed from this computer and the laptop he has with him. And before you suggest that we just take it with us, that won't work either. He set up location services so every time I log in, the document's tagged with the IP location. He was worried I'd try to escape, since I knew he'd kill me when the script was done.'

'Damn it,' Reilly said.

'But couldn't the Feds or somebody . . . I don't know, hack the system or something? Make the GPS report that the laptop's here when it's really someplace else?' Sheldon suggested.

Reilly hesitated. The writer had a point. The Feds most likely had a tech who could do it. Hell, Peni probably could hack the system. But since she hadn't put Peni's phone number into her cellphone and her only copy of the cyber specialist's number was back at the lab, it would mean involving people who would potentially take her off this.

Now, with Todd missing, it was more important than ever that she stay. Reilly understood the way Lennox thought, his motivation and desires.

'But there's something about that scenario that doesn't quite sit well with you, isn't there?'

She looked up in surprise. For someone who'd spent so much time locked in a storage unit, Sheldon was surprisingly observant and level-headed.

He gave Reilly an appraising look. 'You're here by yourself and haven't called for backup yet. You're not actually supposed to be here, are you?'

'Not exactly.' She sat on the edge of the chair facing Sheldon. She was out of options and running out of time. The screenwriter had told her that he only had twenty hours left to complete his script. If she didn't find Todd before then, he was a dead man. 'I'm not a cop. I'm a forensic investigator. Short version, Lennox killed the senior investigator on the CSI team, but the FBI agreed to let them stay on the case if I took over because I don't have a personal stake in this.'

'You mean you *didn't* have one.' Sheldon gave her a knowing look.

'Right,' Reilly admitted. She didn't add that she wasn't entirely sure what that personal stake meant, but this wasn't the time or place for introspection. 'Anyway, I thought I'd figured out that Fisher was the killer, and that he'd also kidnapped you. I asked the FBI to check out the hotel where Fisher was staying before I found out that he'd rented this storage unit.' She guessed they'd been unreachable because they were in the process of questioning Wesley Fisher, so at least the director was safe. Reilly wondered if Fisher's former partner knew this, which was likely, and if so was Lennox planning to switch out his final intended victim?

'You've lived away from the States for a while too, haven't you?' Sheldon ventured.

Reilly blinked. Not the question she'd been expecting. 'Yes, almost three years. How'd you know?'

'I'm in the movie business.' Sheldon gave her a self-satisfied smirk. 'A lot of Americans who live abroad pick up little bits of accent, faint enough that most people wouldn't notice. The reason I asked is, that means you're not technically part of the Tampa law enforcement, doesn't it?'

Reilly nodded. 'I have credentials, but if my superiors find out that I came in here alone, they'll pull me off the case.' She took a deep breath and laid the last of her cards on the table. 'If they do that, and by the time I've finished explaining everything to them, I don't think anyone will get to Todd in time.'

Sheldon's eyes narrowed as he studied her and she found herself wanting to squirm. It was one of those looks Daniel got when he was sizing up someone to decide whether or not he believed them.

'I have an idea,' the writer said then. 'It's a little crazy, but it just might work.'

Chapter 40

Paul Lennox pulled his car up to the curb several yards from the hotel.

He'd just dropped off his letter at the news station, deciding that his final act in Florida deserved a personal touch. He'd intended to return to the hotel and seek out Fisher, but quickly recognized that he had company.

The FBI people in their ever-conspicuous suits were lingering outside; the younger ones were throwing longing looks toward the air-conditioned lobby. It appeared that they'd figured something out after all. Or it might have been the blond. There was no way either the Feds or the locals had figured everything out on their own. Either way, Wesley was out of his reach. For the moment at least.

Which meant a casting change was necessary.

Lennox opened up his laptop and checked the GPS of Sheldon's PC.

Good. The screenwriter mustn't have been discovered yet, otherwise the location would've moved. No agent would leave something so potentially incriminating just sitting around. That supported the Maestro's theory that they didn't know as much about him as he'd originally feared.

Also, it meant he was still on track to finish his project. But he'd have to do it soon. He'd come so far with Sheldon that it would have been a huge waste of time and energy to have to find another writer, go through all the hassle of explaining his mission, all while trying to stay under the radar long enough to finish the film. Not to mention the headache of the continuity issues that arose when changing screenwriters mid-movie.

At least he had all of his important things with him. Laptop, camera equipment, cattle prod and chloroform. And his leading man of course. He smiled. All the basic essentials required when filming a blockbuster.

He just needed to head back to the safe house where he'd stashed his understudy, and wait for Sheldon to finish the finale. Part of him was tempted to go back to the storage unit and tell the writer to hurry the hell along, but he'd worked with enough creative types over the years to know that rushing was never a good idea.

That's how mistakes were made. He could afford to wait.

He would need to get rid of his rental car though. Wouldn't do for the Feds to put out an APB on the plates, and then have someone spot it at the safe house. That would ruin everything.

No, better safe than sorry.

He needed to park the rental somewhere obscure and commandeer another vehicle. Unfortunately, it looked like he'd need to either buy a piece of junk with the little cash he had on him or steal one. While the latter would certainly be cheaper, he was loath to do anything to draw possible attention to himself. Oh, well, a man was more than the car he drove. Besides, when this movie hit the box office, he could buy himself a whole fleet of fancy cars.

He had every confidence in the world that even without Wesley Fisher as its star, his big finale was going to be the biggest thing anyone in Hollywood had seen. Since the *Ben-Hur* chariot race, even. And, despite the urban legends surrounding the classic movie, his would certainly be more deadly.

The Maestro felt like a child waiting for Christmas morning.

Reilly stared at the bedraggled writer, a mixture of admiration and disbelief on her face. There was no way he could be serious, was there? 'You're joking.'

'I'm not,' Sheldon said, his expression somber. 'I'm not risking this son of a bitch getting away just because we don't know where to find him. The bastard threatened to kill my daughter. He's not just going to walk away from this.' The writer shook the chain on his ankle. 'Though I wouldn't mind having my leg free while I work.'

'We're going to need bigger bolt cutters then.' Reilly realized that the conversation had quickly transitioned from the theoretical into working out the logistics.

'And you might want a better choice of weapon just in case Lennox does suddenly show up.' Sheldon opened the laptop. 'Is there anyone you can call for backup? Because, no offense, but I hate to think of you going up against this psycho alone. I've already seen him take out men twice your size.'

Reilly stood and took her phone from her pocket. She gave Sheldon a half-smile. 'I'll have you know that I'm actually a black belt. Or, at least, I was when I was twelve.' She frowned at the lack of signal on her phone. 'But there is one person I need to call. He can bring me a weapon and anything we need to get that chain off. You get started on your finale and I'll take care of the weapons.'

'Sounds like a plan.' Sheldon turned toward the laptop and Reilly headed for the door. Before she got there, she heard the writer add in a soft voice. 'I'll try my best to make sure we get your friend back.'

'I certainly hope so.' Reilly could barely speak around the lump in her throat. It took a moment, but she managed to squash down her anxiety. She couldn't afford to fall apart. She was stronger than this.

She stepped out into the blinding late-morning sun. The heat rolled over her, leaving her sweating and struggling for air in seconds. She wasn't sure which was worse, outside with clean, muggy air or inside where the climate-controlled atmosphere was fetid and foul.

She shook her head. She had more things to worry about than the air quality. It was time to make the call she'd been dreading. She didn't want to do it, but she was running out of time.

She hit her speed dial and waited. Two rings and a familiar voice greeted her.

Reilly took a deep breath. 'Daniel, I need your help.'

Todd punched the door again without expecting any results.

For, as substandard as it had appeared, the door was as solid as any Todd had ever seen. Pain flared, hot and bright, through his knuckles, but he welcomed it. It sharpened him, made him focus. Besides, if Fisher succeeded, bruised and possibly cracked knuckles were going to be the least of Todd's concerns.

He'd examined every inch of his prison. No cracks in the floor or walls. While the ceiling seemed to only consist of flooring from above, it was too solid to break through, same as the door. He'd yelled enough to know that either the house was empty or there was a layer of soundproofing he'd missed. He was willing to bet it was the former rather than the latter.

Todd plopped down on the cot. No windows to see where he was, to gauge the passage of time or try to use as a means of escape. Unless he could pull a *Shawshank* and dig his way out with a spoon, he was screwed. He was also pretty sure Andy Dufresne hadn't actually used a spoon, but the general idea remained the same. He was stuck.

That left him only one option. Wait. Wait until Fisher came back down to get him. Overpower the director and take him down. If only he could get rid of the damn cattle prod. Todd didn't want to mess with that again. He could still smell the singe of burned hair, taste the copper on his tongue from where he'd bitten it. He had a new-found sympathy for cows.

This time, he'd ask for the chloroform. Fisher would have to come close to administer it, and when he did, Todd would be ready. It was time to put those self-defense lessons to work.

Granted, the stuff they'd made them do at the Academy had been over a decade ago, but it was either that or figure out a way to make a weapon from a couple of dead bugs and a threadbare pillow.

He was fairly sure that even John McClane in his best *Die Hard* days couldn't have worked with so little. But it didn't matter what he used. He had to try. For Bradley. For Holly. He had to bring Wesley Fisher to justice, make him pay for what he'd done.

Todd just wasn't sure how he was going to do that while locked in a basement.

Chapter 41

Anxiety etched Daniel's face as he moved across the parking lot.

Reilly hadn't told him much, only that she needed help with a lead she was chasing, that Todd was in trouble and that she couldn't use the Feds or local cops. Telling someone that their only son had been kidnapped wasn't exactly the type of news that engendered lengthy discussion. Daniel had simply gathered the things Reilly had asked for, then got in the car and drove.

If Todd had been taken by the same man they'd been investigating, he knew there wasn't any time to waste. Daniel already knew more than he cared for about the same man's dark, twisted mind.

He reached Reilly, his face full of questions, and he could immediately see how stressed she was and that her nerves were stretched to the point of snapping. 'There's no easy way to say this, so I'll just come out with it. He has Todd.'

Daniel's face paled and he took a step toward her. 'How do you know?'

'It's that guy we met at the hotel – Fisher's co-producer; he told us where to find him.' Reilly back-tracked the explanation, realizing that they'd very briefly encountered Lennox at the time but had no reason to believe him a suspect in either Sheldon's kidnapping or the murders. 'He's our killer and our kidnapper.'

Reilly watched her old friend attempt to gather himself; to muster his usual calm, calculated state of mind when dealing with a psychotic criminal.

'But how do you know he has Todd? And where are the Feds . . . the detectives?' He looked around, baffled by the absence of law enforcement.

'The reason I called you here is because, like we suspected, the murderer, Lennox, kidnapped the screen-writer.' As Daniel struggled to come to terms with what was going on, Reilly motioned for him to follow her into the storage unit. 'Mr Sheldon?'

'Ah, the backup.' The writer squinted up at Reilly before turning to Daniel. 'Drew Sheldon, nice to meet you. Please excuse the mess. The maid hasn't been in for a while.'

'Is he for real?' Daniel's voice held an understandable edge.

'Your backup doesn't have much of a sense of humor.' Sheldon turned back to his laptop.

'That monster has my son, so unless—'

'And that monster threatened my daughter!' Sheldon snapped. 'You're not the only parent here.'

'Reilly—'

'Did he at least bring something to get this damn chain off my ankle?' Sheldon directed his question to Reilly.

'Will someone please tell me what the hell is going on?' Daniel turned to Reilly. 'You call me, ask me to bring a gun and a chain cutter, tell me that madman has kidnapped my son and then show me some writer chained to a cot in a storage unit—'

'Daniel,' Reilly interrupted, the last of her patience having evaporated with the heated exchange between the two men. 'Lennox, a failed producer, took Sheldon to make him write a script for his movie. This morning, he brought Todd here and because he can't get to his ultimate target, Wesley Fisher, we think that he's going to use Todd in the finale of his film. Drew is supposed to complete the script as soon as possible or Lennox is going to go after his daughter.'

'But how did Lennox get Todd?' Daniel started to speak.

'Do you mind?' Sheldon spoke up. 'If you're going to do the whole lengthy explanation thing, could you at least give me some peace and quiet to work? I've got a lot to do and not a lot of time in which to do it.'

Reilly motioned for Daniel to follow her. They stood in the doorway, allowing them to be in the shade and further away from the stench surrounding the writer.

'I know you're worried and you're right.' For Daniel's sake, Reilly tried to dampen down her own panic and keep her voice firm, professional, the way he had done back when he'd come to Dublin to help her deal with her own family crisis.

She knew that bogging themselves down in the how's and why's of Lennox capturing Todd would only complicate things and delay them further. 'Sheldon's right, we don't have a lot of time. Lennox took Todd somewhere, we don't know where and we don't have any way to track him. With all the police and Feds around, I don't think the guy would be stupid enough to head back to the hotel any time soon and certainly not with a captive. I suggested to Sheldon that we could wait for him to come back here for the script but, long story short, Lennox has some sort of share program set up so he doesn't have to come back, not until he's ready to get rid of Sheldon. There's a GPS on the laptop so we can't take Sheldon out of here to write. He volunteered to stay here a bit longer and finish the script because he doesn't trust Lennox and is worried about his daughter. Once he's uploaded it, he'll give us the location of where he's setting the scene and we can pick Todd and Lennox up there.'

'So we're just supposed to sit here and wait for this guy to finish writing some death scene so Lennox can put Todd in it like he did with his other victims?' Daniel glared down at her. 'For God's sake, Reilly . . .'

'It's the only option we have.' Reilly's tone softened at the anguish on her friend's face. 'There's just no way the

Feds will be able to find Todd before Lennox figures out Sheldon isn't doing as he was told.' She paused, then said, 'And you know they'll make you sit on the sidelines while they look. Could you really do that? I know I can't.'

Daniel swore, his expression resigned as he realized she was right. 'So how do we do this?'

'Once Sheldon's done with the script, we call Kent and tell the Feds that we've found our missing screenwriter. Sheldon's agreed to say that I found him after he'd already finished his finale. We might get a slap on the wrist, but it's not going to be their main concern. Once Kent and the department know the location of the perp, they'll go after him and since we're here . . .'

'They'll let us tag along,' Daniel finished, nodding, understanding that at times like this nobody would be worrying too much about loose ends. That would happen afterward, once the killer was brought down.

Reilly nodded. 'It'll be crazy, lots of stuff going down during all of the chaos.'

'All right. What's the writer's great idea? Have some kind of massive showdown at the police station?'

'While the irony of that would be entertaining,' Sheldon's voice commented from the dark depths behind them, 'I doubt Lennox would be quite that adventurous or stupid.'

'All right then, Shakespeare!' Daniel snapped. 'What's your big finale?'

* * *

The Maestro laughed out loud as he read what his pet writer had created. 'Classic motif with a twist. Just a touch of irony. I like it.'

He'd been concerned that Sheldon wouldn't be at his best at this point; that he'd be too worried about what would happen when it was all done. It wasn't like the writer was entirely unintelligent. He knew that his life wasn't going to be worth much when he was no longer needed.

He had always intended to kill Sheldon, of course. It wasn't anything personal, but he had been truthful about making it as painless as possible as long as Sheldon had done his job. It now looked like it was going to be a syringe of morphine or a chloroform-laced pillow over the face rather than the other option. He was glad it was going this way. Aside from being painless for a man who'd helped him so much, it was so much less messy than a meat cleaver and bucket of toilet-bowl cleaner à la *Misery*.

He stood and crossed to the basement door, then reached for the doorknob and hesitated. The investigator had proven himself to be arrogant and cocky, a dangerous combination.

In hindsight, he probably should've left him in the handcuffs, but he'd seen way too many movies where guards or villains were strangled by a pair of cuffed hands. The Maestro reached for his weapon, considered it, then added a can of pepper spray for good measure.

He was nothing if not thorough.

He opened the door quickly, hoping to catch his prisoner off guard. It worked. Todd stood halfway down the stairs, a surprised look on his face. It didn't last long, but the half-second was enough for him to get the cattle prod in place and kick the door shut.

The electricity crackled as he made his way slowly down the stairs, infinitely pleased with himself as pretty boy backed up.

'Why don't you have a seat?' The Maestro gestured with the prod.

Todd scowled but did as he was told. That was good. The last thing he needed when composing the scene that would make him famous was a temperamental star. He'd had his fill of that with Bruce 'Nut-job' Reynolds.

'Just give it up, Fisher,' the investigator glared. 'You're never going to get away with this.'

The Maestro shook his head and smiled, amused. 'You don't have a clue, do you? I'm disappointed. And is that really the best line you can come up with? I'm glad I had someone write for you. Because, to be honest, you suck at improvisation. Good thing you didn't decide to pursue a career in acting, though you certainly have the face for it.' After a moment's consideration, he decided against sitting too. This one was a bit more volatile than Sheldon.

'Come on, you've seen all the movies.' Todd's voice changed tone. 'You know how this ends. The bad guy makes a mistake, and either gets captured or dies. No matter what, he loses.'

The Maestro laughed. 'I don't know what movies you've been watching lately, but the best thing about horror films is that the antagonist never really disappears. Ever seen *Friday the 13th*? How many *Nightmare on Elm Street* and *Halloween* sequels are there? And they just keep on coming . . .'

'But the killer did die in the first *Friday the 13th*,' Todd countered. 'Remember, it wasn't actually Jason, but his mom. And the last woman standing chopped Mrs Voorhees' head off with a machete.'

The Maestro smiled and shook his head. OK, so Todd knew movies. 'But that wasn't the end,' he countered. 'Jason's mom may have died, but Jason got his revenge and he kept coming back for more.'

'All right then, what about *Scream*?' Todd asked.

'Faulty comparison.' The Maestro was beginning to enjoy the discussion. '*Scream* was originally written by Williamson as a trilogy satire to provide commentary on the horror genre. Though the fourth did end up proving my point that there's always someone willing to come forward to fill an empty space. Nature does abhor a vacuum.'

'True.' Todd nodded. 'There are copycats, but that just means the original killers were still captured or killed. The movies you mentioned before where the original killer – with the exception of Jason's mother – either survives or returns, the killers are supernatural, which is how they keep coming back. You are not.'

The Maestro scowled. This wasn't fun anymore. 'You are forgetting something vitally important though, about all of those films. It's never the cocky male hero who survives. Only the virginal heroine. And you are neither.'

'Come on,' Todd said, grinning maniacally. 'I could play the virginal heroine just as well as . . . oh, who am I kidding? I couldn't pretend to be a virgin any more than you could pretend to be talented.'

He'd had enough; the barb hit his ego harder than it should have. 'I didn't come down here to argue plotlines with you. I just came to let you know that we're going to be leaving shortly. Sheldon came through. Looks like you'll be getting your big break soon enough.'

'Oh, goody,' Todd deadpanned, not looking nearly as terrified as the Maestro wanted him to be. 'Like they say on TV, I've been dreaming of something like this all my life.'

'It's a classic that even a plebeian such as yourself should be able to appreciate,' he went on, without acknowledging Todd's quip. He needed to get back in the right mind-set to direct. 'Combined with enough bang for any dumb blockbuster audience.' His eyes narrowed as he watched Todd's muscles tense. 'I was going to ask for your preferred method of being knocked out for our little trip to the train yard, but I think I'm going to play it safe.'

He darted forward before Todd could react and triggered enough voltage to make Todd's body jerk and spasm. The investigator's eyes rolled back in his head and he slumped onto the cot. The Maestro considered the unconscious body for a moment before heading upstairs to get his new bottle of chloroform.

Better safe than sorry.

Chapter 42

Reilly watched Sheldon pace back and forth, and fought back the urge to join him.

The screenwriter's nerves had been showing from the moment he'd announced that the scene was finished. She had purposefully asked that he not share the location until the authorities arrived. She didn't trust Daniel, or herself for that matter, not to act on it.

Reilly knew that the moment either of them heard where Todd would be, they wouldn't be able to stop themselves from going straight there, and while that was what she wanted, she knew it wasn't the smartest thing to do. And now they had to put personal involvement aside, try and forget it was Todd they were looking for, and start thinking smart. It was the only way to save him.

'I thought you said they'd be here by now.' Sheldon glanced back at the storage unit. Once Daniel had managed to get through the chain, the writer had asked if they could all move outside. Reilly couldn't blame him. Given the length of the writer's incarceration, the interior of that unit was pretty ripe. She didn't envy the people who would have to clean it.

'Yeah, well, Agent Kent said they were on their way,' she replied, irritated too, 'but he's not exactly the fastest responder.'

'Here's the thing . . .' Sheldon wiped his hand across his sweaty forehead, leaving streaks of dirt and other things Reilly wasn't sure she wanted to identify. 'The final scene's a little time sensitive.'

'What do you mean?' Her stomach clenched. That didn't sound good.

'I know you said you didn't want to know before the Feds got here,' Sheldon said, 'but I don't think it can wait.'

'Just spill it already.' Reilly glanced at Daniel. He looked as tense as she felt.

'The scene takes place just outside of Orton train station, right where the tracks split. I've always liked steam trains and I'd planned on taking Kai this week to see one of the few that still come through there. We were going to go today . . .'

'What happens in the scene, Mr Sheldon?' Daniel urged, and Reilly closed her eyes, now almost entirely certain she didn't actually want to know the answer.

'I had to appeal to Lennox's love of twists on the classics. In the scene, the killer ties the hero to the northbound track and then, just around the bend – hidden by a clump of trees – parks a truck full of gas. After the train kills the hero, it'll plow into the gas truck and . . .'

Daniel and Reilly both swore.

'Wait.' Sheldon held up his hands. 'One of the reasons I wrote it that way is because it meant Lennox would have to stay on location to get the second shot. The ground drops off to a slant there so he can't put up a second camera to capture the explosion remotely. He's going to have to manually move the camera from the westbound track to get the angle right. It's the only way it works.'

Reilly glanced at her watch. 'How far is it from here?'

'Ten minutes or so.' Daniel handed his phone to Sheldon. 'When Agent Kent gets here, tell him everything. If you think of anything else we need to know, call this number.' He indicated Reilly's number in the contacts list.

Sheldon nodded. 'Go.'

Reilly and Daniel jogged to his car, a grimace of pain on Daniel's face with every step. She looked at him strangely and then remembered. Beach volleyball . . .

She'd barely pulled her door shut before Daniel was peeling out of the parking lot, sending a spray of gravel out behind them. As they raced away, Reilly glanced out the back window. The familiar blue and white of the City of Tampa police cars could be seen speeding toward the rental office. She estimated they were about five minutes away. Even if they went straight to Sheldon and instantly believed him, chances were slim they'd make it to the train station in time.

It was up to her and Daniel.

'The case on the floor.' Daniel broke the tense silence. His eyes never left the road in front of him. 'The gun you asked for is in there, and there's one for me too. They both need loading.'

Reilly nodded and pulled the case onto her lap. Daniel rattled off the combination and she lifted the lid. He'd been the one to teach her how to shoot, and she'd maintained her monthly trips to the range up until the week before she'd left for Dublin. Just how rusty would she be?

Inside the case, was a matte-black Beretta nestled next to his silver Desert Eagle. She hadn't gone shooting while in Dublin, and she just hoped it all came back.

'I've kept them both in working condition.' Daniel's voice was tense. 'Fired at the range just a few weeks ago.'

'Good to know,' said Reilly as she set the weapons on the console and pushed the case back down to the floor. Her fingers tapped a staccato on the armrest, the only sound other than the hiss of the air conditioning and the gentle rumble of the Chrysler's engine.

She spoke up. 'You do know you and I are going to get in a shitload of trouble for this, don't you? The worst I'll get is a slap on the wrist for sticking my nose in where it doesn't belong. You could end up not being able to work again if the Feds are pissed enough. I doubt they'd arrest you, but Agent Kent isn't one to let something like this slide.'

Daniel set his jaw. 'If it saves my son's life, I'll consider it well worth the price.'

'You and me both.' Reilly's expression was grim. 'All right then, let's get this bastard.'

The Maestro surveyed the location with a critical eye. Sheldon really knew this spot well. His information was perfect. The northbound track curved along a culvert, disappearing behind a small group of trees.

With his car positioned exactly as Sheldon had written it, there was no way the train operator could see it before it was too late. Any other place along the track would give anyone enough time to stop well before collision, maybe even before hitting the hero, spoiling the entire scene.

However, with the vehicle basically hidden, there was no way to include it in the same shot as Todd without moving the camera. The culvert made setting up a second camera impractical and the rush of air from the train would knock any tripod over into the ditch.

No, he would need to stay through the whole thing so he could physically pan the shot. The best angle for what he needed was from the westbound track.

He swore as he struggled with the tripod. It wouldn't stay in position evenly, causing the picture to be filmed at a tilt. He swore again, more vilely than before. It looked like he was going to have to hold the camera himself.

Oh, well, hand-held did have its perks. Generally, the style was used to convey a sense of unease or fear. Maybe it would end up fitting nicely with the theme of the film. One never could tell. And there was no way it would be worse than that 90s film about those idiots lost in the woods. Amateurs.

The Maestro glanced at his watch. It was nearly time. Just as he thought it, a train whistle sounded in the distance. He grinned, barely able to contain his excitement. This was it, the moment he'd been waiting for. Forget that loser, Wesley Fisher; after today, everyone would know *his* name. He'd be cited in every film school from Los Angeles to the Big Apple. His would be the movie to beat, the standard by which all other movies would be judged.

The Maestro turned the camera on his star and prepared to record.

It was finally time for Paul Lennox to make motion-picture history.

Chapter 43

His job came with certain risks, he'd accepted that from the moment he'd decided to work CSI. Dangerous neighborhoods, mob- and gang-related cases where death threats were as common as breathing. More than one case with dangerous toxins resulting in quarantines and the occasional hospitalization, one time for almost a full month.

At no time since deciding to pursue a career in forensic science, however, had Todd expected to be kidnapped by a psychotic movie director and tied to a set of train tracks. The Academy hadn't prepared him for this scenario. Not that anything really could have prepared him for this.

Todd turned his head, the heat from the metal tracks rising in waves to his cheek. He could almost feel his skin blistering but ignored the pain. It was as inconsequential as the throbbing ache from his concussion or the pain in his muscles from the cattle prod. He had to take in as much information as quickly as possible. The vibration from the oncoming train was faint, but present.

Even as he thought it, a shrill whistle pierced the air.

Fisher had put the handcuffs back on while Todd had been unconscious. After reaching the train yard, the director had wrapped the cuffs in rope, apparently following some directions from the script he had.

Todd's head had been so muddled from the combination of electricity and drugs when they'd arrived that he'd barely been able to think. Only now was his mind clear enough to take stock of the entirety of the situation.

It wasn't good.

The ropes had been wound around his limbs and under the metal, securing Todd's body by the legs and shoulders until all he could do was wiggle. He tested the bonds again, tensing his wrists to try for some give, anything that would give him some hope of maybe getting free. Nothing. His muscles had been weakened by the repeated shocks and, even as the chloroform wore off, he didn't have the strength he needed.

Todd cried out in frustration, coughing as he inhaled dust. It wasn't supposed to be like this. Sweat ran into his eyes, stinging, and he cursed, unable to wipe it away.

He wasn't supposed to die like this, helpless, eyes burning, skin blistering under the scorching sun, head pounding. Certainly not before he'd done so many things.

He wanted to travel. Ski in Aspen. Dive at the Great Barrier Reef.

And professionally. He wanted to run the CSI department. Distinguish himself from his father while at the same time making his dad proud. Finally make him proud.

And then there was the more personal stuff. For all his screwing around when it came to dating, Todd knew he wanted to get serious some day. Get married. Maybe even have a kid or two.

As he faced what he feared were his last minutes, Todd found himself wondering how much he'd actually be missed. He knew his family loved him and he did have friends, but there would be no grieving widow, no fiancée with dashed dreams. No child to carry on his name.

He supposed he should be grateful that he wouldn't be leaving some woman widowed or child devastated. A part of him, however, was saddened by the idea that eventually his memory would fade and, once his parents were gone, no one would care that he'd died a horrible death one hot Florida afternoon.

And then there was Reilly . . . Todd closed his eyes. He knew that their night together had been nothing more than comfort, but he'd be lying to himself if he said he hadn't wondered if perhaps there could've been more.

He'd been so angry at her, maybe irrationally so, since she'd been put in charge of the investigation, but now, as the rumble of the oncoming train vibrated through his body, he admitted that if he'd had to do things over, he'd have changed everything for a real shot with her.

Todd let the image of Reilly's face fill his mind as the blare of the train's whistle drowned out everything else. If he had to go like this, at least their time together would be his last thought.

Reilly's heart was pounding, blood rushing in her ears. She gripped the door handle so tightly that her knuckles turned white. The vehicle bounced over the rocks and dirt as Daniel bypassed the road. Her teeth clicked together, each rut a jolt to her entire body, but she was barely aware of any of them.

The train was early, or else Sheldon had made a mistake, and they were racing against it.

Then, she could see the bend in the track, the split. 'There!' She pointed.

On one track was a prone figure, body lying across the northbound track. A few yards away was someone standing on the other track, hands holding what looked like a black box.

Reilly didn't need to be told that it was Lennox holding a camera. Anger bubbled up, burning away some of her fear. She let the hotter emotion take control. She could use it. Anger gave her strength, kept her moving. The last thing she needed in this situation was to freeze.

As Daniel revved the car faster, Reilly clung to the heat inside her, fanning the flames. It was either that or admit that they were already too late and she wasn't ready to do that. If she admitted it, she'd have to accept that she was never going to see Todd again. And that was not acceptable. She would not be too late this time.

'Come on, Daniel,' she said through clenched teeth, not daring to look over at her friend, afraid of what she might see on his face. It would be awful to see his helplessness and frustration, but much worse to see resignation.

All she could do was pray they reached Todd in time and tighten her grip on the door. The familiar words repeated in her head as if she were trying to convince herself that she was caught in a nightmare: '... lay you down and take your rest; Forget in sleep the doubt and pain; And when you wake, to work again ...'

The excitement had knotted in his stomach, hard and hot.

The Maestro had to stop himself from dancing around as he panned his shot from the hidden truck, over his star ... He frowned. Todd had stopped struggling. In fact, he had his eyes closed, a peaceful expression on his sunburned face.

Well, that was no good. Where was the panic? The screams and pleas for mercy, everything needed to create an unforgettable death scene?

Unfortunately, as the train whistle reminded him, the Maestro didn't have the time to chastise the misbehaving investigator. No matter. He could use a wide shot rather than a close-up. It might have a better effect anyway.

He continued his camera pan, stopping as he focused on the train speeding toward the northbound track. Soon, they'd be in position to see Todd on the tracks. He wished he had a camera inside to get a shot of the driver's face at the moment of realization.

He almost felt bad for the passengers on the train. They had no idea that they were racing toward the biggest roles they'd ever have the opportunity to play.

Reilly was out of the car before it stopped moving. She heard Daniel behind her, his gait shuffling as he struggled to make his twisted knee obey.

She didn't wait for him as she ran, her dress whipping around her legs. Her sandals slipped on her feet as she ducked under the old barrier and she swore. She could hear the roar of the train as she pushed her body even faster. Hot pain flared up her ankle as it twisted underneath her, but she forced herself through it.

She could see Todd now; see his eyes closed and body still. But she could see the train now too and it was too close. They hadn't been fast enough. She hadn't been fast enough.

Again.

'Todd!' She screamed his name, knowing it would change nothing, knowing that he couldn't even hear her, not with the train so close. Somehow, his eyes opened, his gaze locking with hers. Reilly fell to her knees as she stumbled, the gravel cutting into her flesh. She watched, helpless, as the train reached the split.

She was still trying to drag in enough air to scream when, all of a sudden, the train's course shifted.

The director didn't even have time to react. The train's brakes were still screeching as Paul Lennox became the final victim in his own film.

Chapter 44

He hadn't been able to resist opening his eyes and his heart had nearly stopped when he'd seen Reilly running toward him. He'd kept his eyes on her, his whole body tensing as he waited for impact.

It hadn't come. Instead, there was a blast of air mingled with the screech of brakes. Todd turned his head even as he felt a warm shower of liquid rain down on him. The unmistakable scent of blood filled his nostrils and understanding crashed over him.

He was alive.

'Todd . . .' Reilly was suddenly beside him, filling his vision. Her hands were shaking as they reached for him.

'I'm OK,' he hurried to assure her. 'What happened?'

'The train.' Reilly glanced toward it, an inscrutable expression coming over her face. 'It went on the other track.'

'It killed him? Fisher's gone?'

'Todd – son.' Daniel appeared next to Reilly.

'I'm OK, Dad.' Todd squirmed. 'Any chance of getting me untied any time soon?'

Reilly and Daniel both immediately went to work, tugging at the ropes. Todd couldn't stop himself from watching Reilly as she worked. She pushed back a chunk of hair that had fallen in her face and left a streak of crimson on her pale skin. Todd grimaced, realizing that the blood had come from his face. He'd never wanted a shower more in his life.

Reilly struggled to keep her emotions in check as she worked at the knots holding Todd in place. Her bloody fingers slid over the ropes and she rubbed her hands on her skirt. Rust-colored smudges stained the fabric but she didn't care. The pain in her knees didn't even bother her. She was vaguely aware of Daniel cursing as he tugged on the knots around Todd's ankle.

'The guy . . . it wasn't Fisher,' Reilly told him haltingly. She'd forgotten Todd hadn't met Wesley Fisher, so couldn't have known that it wasn't Fisher who'd taken him. And clearly Lennox hadn't bothered to correct him.

'Reilly . . .' Todd's voice drew her attention from the ropes to his face. 'I'm fine. Just take a deep breath.'

She nodded. Her hands stilled and she followed his advice, inhaling deeply through her nose, wrinkling it at the scent of flesh and blood. As she exhaled, her nerves steadied and she found she was able to concentrate. There would be plenty of time for explanations later.

The first of the knots came loose as the wail of police sirens cut through the air. As one slipped free, the others followed more quickly until Todd was able to sit up. He rubbed at his raw wrists, flexing his fingers.

A wave of relief so intense it was nearly overpowering washed over her. Before she could think about what she was doing, or about the fact that Daniel was right there, Reilly leaned forward and kissed Todd. It was brief, barely more than chaste, but his eyes still brightened momentarily.

'Sorry,' she muttered, heat rising to her cheeks.

Todd opened his mouth to speak, but whatever he was going to say was lost as the noise of approaching agents reached them. As Reilly turned, she caught Daniel's eye. While most would assume the smile on his face was entirely down to finding his son, Reilly recognized something that looked like surprised delight directed her way.

'What the hell happened here?' Agent Kent panted as he skidded to a halt.

'Todd. Jesus, are you OK?' Detective Julie Sampson raced past Mark Reed to get to Todd.

'Paul Lennox, Wesley Fisher's number two,' Reilly announced, and stood, composing herself. She turned toward the trio. 'He was our killer and kidnapper.'

'Drew Sheldon told us as much,' Detective Reed replied. He appeared to be the least winded of the three. 'And Fisher had alibis.'

Reilly gestured toward the stopped train. She could hear people clambering off of the cars, shouting to each other. 'Lennox was on the westbound track filming Todd on the tracks. The train didn't stay on the north track like Sheldon said it would.' She struggled to piece together what had happened. She'd been so focused on Todd that she had to concentrate to get the rest. 'The switch must've been thrown somehow. Lennox didn't have time to get out of the way.'

'The blood?' Agent Kent gestured to Todd.

'Lennox's, for the most part,' Todd confirmed, surprisingly lucid, considering. His father helped him to his feet. He winced, though whether from injury or just stiff joints, Reilly couldn't tell. 'I thought he was Fisher. He knocked me out when I was on my way up to Fisher's room at the hotel. Aside from the concussion, sunburn and lingering effects of being tasered and drugged, I'm all good.'

'Pig-headed fool . . .' Daniel muttered affectionately.

'Get a CSI crew down here!' Detective Reed barked at one of the nearby officers, who immediately called it in. Then he looked back in panic at the crowd of train passengers gathered near Fisher's remains, most of whom Reilly noticed were taking pictures of or filming the dead director's body – no doubt ready to sell the footage to media or post it all on the internet. This time, Paul Lennox would be the one being watched.

Talk about irony.

'And a bus.'

'I don't want you two going anywhere just yet.' Agent Kent scowled at Reilly and Daniel. 'I'm going to want to know just how you ended up here before the rest of us.'

'Before you do that,' Todd couldn't resist adding, 'might I recommend getting those people on the train rounded up before they track pieces of our crime scene all over the place?'

Agent Kent's face paled. 'Oh, shit . . .'

Chapter 45

The spicy smell of Cuban food wafted through the air, mingling with the sounds of laughter. Reilly listened from the kitchen of Daniel's beach house as Todd and the trio of women – Emilie, Peni and Ivy – laughed outside on the deck beneath the lanai, snippets of conversation floating back to her.

'. . . so Ivy takes this bucket of lime green paint . . .'

'. . . of course, the professor's sitting right next to me . . .'

'. . . was the first and last time I ever drink purple nurples . . .'

'. . . should never be allowed in a karaoke bar . . .'

She scooped up a handful of peppers and dropped them into the pan. The chunks of red briefly turned her stomach, but she forced back the memory.

The last two nights, her regular nightmare had been replaced by a new one. She was back at the train yard, her feet tangling and tripping her as she ran toward Todd. She fell in the same spot and felt familiar helplessness wash over her. She tried telling herself that it was OK, that the train would take the other track, kill Paul Lennox and Todd would be fine.

Then came the flood of guilt that she wasn't more concerned about someone else dying. Before she could tell herself that Lennox was a murderer and not worth saving, the train was there. Only this time it wasn't turning. The screech and whistle overpowered her screams as Todd disintegrated into a mass of flesh and blood.

Each time, she'd woken in a cold sweat, gasping for air, hoping she hadn't screamed. After an hour of tossing and turning, murmuring the words into the darkness, she'd fallen back into a troubled sleep only to repeat the entire thing less than an hour later. Even her carefully applied make-up couldn't hide the bags under her eyes. The same mantra had been playing in her head nearly non-stop as she tried to fend off the demons. ". . . lay you down and take your rest; Forget in sleep the doubt and pain; And when you wake, to work again . . .'

Everyone assumed her exhaustion was from the long hours spent answering questions, first from the Feds, then from the TPD detectives. How had she figured out where Drew Sheldon was? Why had she thought Wesley Fisher was the killer and the kidnapper? When had she arrived at the storage unit? Had she waited to call in when she'd found Sheldon? Why had Daniel been with her?

Reilly had answered honestly for the most part, tweaking her answer only regarding the timeline. While she could cite the Feds' and detectives' brush-offs as her reason for heading into the field, she knew there was no way to justify not calling in the instant she'd found Sheldon and declared the area safe. She'd been worried that the writer wouldn't back her story in the end, but when, after five hours, she'd been allowed to leave with only a mild reprimand, she'd known he hadn't said anything.

It hadn't been until later that night, during one of her between-nightmare times, that Reilly started to think about what had really happened. She'd trusted Sheldon to write a scene where Todd wasn't in any danger, but yet the writer had waited to tell her where to go until it was almost too late.

It was then that she'd remembered a comment Sheldon had made about how he knew the train's schedule because he'd wanted to take his daughter to the tracks.

Before she'd gone into the lab, she'd swung by the hospital to check on the writer. While chatting, she'd casually slipped in a comment about the switch causing the train to go on the westbound track. Sheldon had just shrugged, but Reilly had seen the shadow flit across his eyes. She'd known then that he had only supported her timeline because it covered him too.

Evidently, he'd known that the train had been scheduled to go west when he'd put Todd on the northbound track.

Then, just before she'd left, he'd added, with no prompt-ing or context, 'The son of a bitch threatened my daughter.'

Reilly had nodded once and walked out. She hadn't told anyone about the exchange or about what it meant. She should have felt guilty, she knew, but she couldn't quite seem to get that far. She hadn't known at the time. Lennox's blood wasn't on her hands and if Sheldon could live with that, she could live with keeping quiet.

The only thing Reilly did feel guilty about was that a part of her was glad Paul Lennox was dead, that he wouldn't have the opportunity to try to take advantage of the justice system and claim insanity or use some fancy lawyer to get out of the charges.

Once and for all, Lennox had been stopped. He would never kill (or direct) again.

'If you don't pay attention, you're going to burn dinner.' Todd was so close to her elbow that Reilly jumped. He'd barely spoken to her since the train yard and even those conversations had been stilted. She wasn't sure if it was the kiss or the whole situation . . . no, she was pretty sure it was the kiss. She'd been kicking herself about her impulsive action for the past two days, but she was confident that it would get better. After all, it was just a kiss.

'Oh . . .' She blinked, and resumed her stirring.

'Anything you want to talk about?' Daniel had been asking her the same question since she'd gotten back from the police station later that night.

As she had to his father, she shook her head. The last thing she wanted was to tell Todd about her nightmares or about what she'd discovered. She was sure that given how close to death he'd come, he had enough demons of his own to contend with. 'Just haven't been sleeping well.'

Before he could probe further, a voice called from the doorway.

'Need any help in there?' Peni's voice carried easily.

'Almost done,' Reilly called back. She fixed a pleasant expression on her face and turned down the flame beneath the pan.

By the time she carried the last of the meal out onto the deck, the others had already found their seats around the wrought-iron table. Reilly set the bowl of food down in the middle of table and took the last free spot, giving everyone the same fake smile. Todd's eyes flicked toward her in concern again, but made no contact before darting away again.

'Everything looks amazing,' Emilie said politely.

'And smells divine,' Ivy gushed.

'Thank you.' Reilly slipped into the empty seat across from Todd. She'd taken quite a liking to Peni's girlfriend. The poet's carefree nature and sweet disposition was a refreshing change from all of the recent death and dismemberment.

With Todd on mandatory leave after the incident, it had been up to Emilie and Reilly to finish bagging the last of the evidence to hand over to the Feds in the aftermath.

They'd finished late the night before and Reilly had never been so glad to hand over a case. She wanted nothing more to do with this particular psycho.

She knew that Daniel had gone with Todd to tell Alice Young that her daughter's murderer was dead, though she hadn't asked how it had gone. She didn't need to. She'd been on the receiving end of that kind of conversation before.

As small talk went on around her, Reilly focused on eating, on finally relaxing a little. It was only early evening and, while she'd been tired before, even exhausted, this was only the second time in her life that she'd been bone-tired, the type of weariness that seemed to fill her very marrow.

When the doorbell rang partway through the meal, and Daniel was in the restroom, Reilly excused herself to answer it, smiling as she felt Todd's eyes on her. The awkwardness was already starting to dissipate.

'Steel,' Detective Reed addressed her from the doorway. Now that the case was closed, he'd been much more pleasant to talk to. Detective Sampson was a different story – still pissed at Reilly for what she considered insubordination.

'Detectives.' Reilly gave them the same strained smile she'd used with the others. She stepped back and motioned for them to enter.

'Thank you.' Mark Reed gave her a genuine smile. 'It's still hot as hell out there.'

'A group of us just sat down for dinner if you'd care to join us. Daniel and I made way too much,' she offered.

'That's very kind of you, but we can't stay long,' Reed said, shaking his head as he and Julie Sampson ventured out onto the deck. They waved hello to the others round the table, and seemed grateful for the slight breeze coming off the gulf.

'Sorry to interrupt your dinner. Just wanted to come by and let you all know that the Feds were already able to close two open homicide investigations in California, and it looks like they may be able to link Lennox to at least three others and a dozen assaults,' Reed told them.

After conversing among the others for a little longer, Sampson and Reed eventually went to take their leave, dampening down entreaties from Todd to stay for a drink.

As Reilly accompanied them back out front, Reed continued to chat. 'I heard Todd got offered Bradley's old job,' he said.

'Yes, he deserves it.' Reilly was pleased about this news, though she guessed Todd would never be able to get past the fact that the promotion had only come about because of his partner's demise. It was for this reason that he hadn't said much about it since confirmation had come down from Captain Harvell, and he had changed the subject a couple of times already this evening when the news had come up.

It was a pity, because she guessed that from Todd's point of view the default advancement would only make him doubt his abilities and strengthen the need to prove himself even further. And the fact was he really did deserve it. Granted, he'd gotten himself into trouble while trying to track down Wesley Fisher, but Reilly knew that the best investigators were almost always the ones who were willing to go out on a limb and take chances.

'I'd kind of wondered if they might have offered the position to you.' Detective Sampson gave Reilly the same knowing smile she used to get when women at Quantico found out she was friends with Daniel. She didn't trust that smile.

'Not likely, my involvement was purely temporary, an emergency stop-gap. Anyway, I already have a job,' she added, trying to keep her tone light.

'So, still planning on returning to Dublin then?' the female detective continued.

'Why wouldn't I be?'

Reilly wasn't going to admit that while here in Clearwater, her intentions had been wavering from time to time, and the emotional intensity of this particular case was making her start to wonder if she even wanted to continue in this line of work anymore.

The Florida climate and lifestyle, not to mention spending time with Todd, made the possibility of coming back to the US more appealing, but then the recent awkwardness between them made her think that she should just stay the course with the job in Dublin.

'Well, when you do head back, we'll be sad to see you go.' Detective Reed's eyes were filled with genuine warmth. 'And speaking of going, Detective Sampson and I really should head away. It'll be nice to finally have a weekend off.'

'Thanks for stopping by.' Reilly shut the door behind them. She stayed there for a couple of moments, gathering her composure again.

As she stepped back into the hallway, she met Daniel on her way to the kitchen. 'The detectives just stopped by to let us know that the FBI's been linking Lennox to several old cases,' she said, trying to sound cheerful, but the bright note rang hollow to her own ears. 'I'm going to go get dessert.'

She headed for the kitchen before he could respond. Once there, she opened the refrigerator door and reached for the applesauce, graham cracker and whipped-cream concoction that Ivy had brought with her.

She spooned it into another bowl, more for something to do than any real need.

'Everything all right?' Daniel's voice pulled Reilly from her reverie and back to the present.

'Fine.' She took out bowls and spoons.

'You don't look fine.' He leaned against the counter.

'Gee, thanks.' She scowled playfully at him.

'What is it? The case is over, we saved Todd, Lennox is dead . . .'

She sighed. 'I know that.'

'Then what? I heard what the detective said. *Are* you a little peeved that you weren't offered the job?'

Her eyes widened. 'Are you kidding me?'

'Well then, what about the other job?'

'What other— Daniel . . .' Reilly tried for a stern face, but only managed exasperated. She hated when he misdirected a conversation like that, in order to turn it round to what he really wanted to talk about. 'We've discussed this.'

'No,' he insisted. 'You haven't been willing to discuss it at all. And I was prepared to let it go if it seemed like you were truly happy in Dublin. But if you're having second thoughts – for any reason – I don't see what the problem is.' Daniel walked toward her, his dark eyes soft. 'You'd be an incredible asset anywhere you go.' He put a hand on her arm. 'You stepped in to help on a case and ended up solving it. You took what could have been a total disaster and saved it. I've never been more proud of anyone, ever.'

Reilly shook her head, reminding him of his son's contribution. 'Todd figured out Fisher's identity before I did.'

'Only because he found what Bradley was chasing up,' Daniel countered. 'And it was the costume you found and the movie you identified that led Bradley to Fisher and ultimately Lennox.'

Reilly held up a hand. 'Enough. I get it. I helped – a bit.'

'Then I shouldn't have to explain why I want to hire you.' Daniel took a step back. 'You're not just the best person for a job like this – you're the only person.'

Later, after everyone had gone home (Todd included) and Daniel had retired to his study to read, Reilly stood on the deck, watching as the sun disappeared into the gulf, the red-orange rays reflecting off of the darkening water.

The heat rolled over her, enveloping her in a comforting embrace, and she wondered if she would be able to do without it again, same as all the things she would have to do without when she went back to Dublin.

American coffee . . . corn bread . . . sunshine and blue skies . . . warm sand beneath her feet . . . morning runs on the beach . . . Pittsburgh medium steak . . . dazzling west-coast sunsets like this one.

But then there were many good things about Dublin too.

Challenging though it might be, she did love her job at the GFU; loved being part of major investigations, and spending time around her team, especially Lucy, who Reilly knew had come to view her as a surrogate big sister of sorts. Then there was Chris. Reilly didn't know if she'd ever be able to figure out Chris – or at least where their relationship *truly* stood. It had been so good to hear his voice when he'd called last week. But that was before her . . . involvement with Todd. And Reilly couldn't deny that on that one night, that connection they'd shared was so far beyond anything she'd broached with Chris. Yet still she had mixed feelings about both men; what they meant to her now, or what they might mean in the future.

If anything.

And then there was her dad. She wasn't sure how Mike would feel if she told him she was considering a move back to the US. She guessed he wouldn't be too upset – it was her home, after all. In any case, they both had their own lives and she knew that her father would go along with whatever made her happy.

Reilly sighed, feeling more confused than ever.

She wasn't sure if she was ready to make a decision, but it didn't matter if she was or not. She guessed that changes were coming, whether or not she felt prepared.

All Reilly could do was what she'd done all throughout her life. Try to meet head on any challenges that came her way . . .

Acknowledgements

Many thanks to Emma Lowth, Carla Josephson and Jo Dickinson for their terrific input, and to the brilliant S&S team, who are fantastic to work with. Also, to Simon, Helen and Declan, who look after us so well in Dublin.

Big thanks to Sheila Crowley, Rebecca Ritchie, Katie McGowan and all at Curtis Brown UK.

Thanks to booksellers, readers, reviewers and bloggers for being so supportive of the books – it is much appreciated. And thanks to those who've been in touch via Facebook and Twitter, to tell us what they think of Reilly's adventures. We hope you enjoyed *The Watched*.

SIMON &
SCHUSTER

Casey Hill
Taboo

Forensic investigator Reilly Steel, Quantico-trained and
California-born and bred, imagined Dublin to be a far
cry from bustling San Francisco, a sleepy backwater
where she can lay past ghosts to rest and start anew.
She's arrived in Ireland to drag the Irish crime lab into
the 21st century, plus keep tabs on her Irish-born father
who's increasingly seeking solace in the bottle after a
past family tragedy.

But a brutal serial killer soon puts paid to that.
When a young man and woman are found dead in
an apartment, the gunshot wounds on their naked
bodies suggest a suicide pact. But Reilly's instincts
are screaming that something's seriously amiss, and
as more bodies are discovered, the team soon realises
that a twisted murderer is at work, one who seeks
to upset society's norms in the most sickening way
imaginable . . .

Paperback ISBN 978-1-84983-372-1
eBook ISBN 978-1-84983-373-8

SIMON &
SCHUSTER

Casey Hill
Torn

Read the clues. Decode the science. Reveal the murderer.

That's Reilly Steel's mantra. Find the answers, solve the
crime. But the Quantico-trained forensic investigator
is finding her skills aren't enough when a ferociously
intelligent killer strikes Dublin. The modus operandi is
as perplexing as it is macabre. What connects the two
seemingly disparate, high-profile victims?

Their corpses refuse to give up their secrets and the
crime scenes prove a forensic investigator's worst
nightmare. The police are just as frustrated by the
crimes' impenetrable nature and it's only when a third
murder occurs – equally graphic and elaborate in its
execution – that they discover that this particular killer
is using a very specific blueprint for his crimes.

Who is the killer's next victim, the *real* target? And
what's his endgame?

Paperback ISBN 978-1-84983-379-0
ebook ISBN 978-1-84983-380-6

SIMON &
SCHUSTER

Casey Hill
Hidden

When a young girl is discovered dead on an isolated
country road, it seems at first glance to be a simple
hit and run. Then the cops see the tattoo on her back
– a pair of beautifully wrought angel wings that lend
the victim a sense of ethereal innocence. Forensic
investigator Reilly Steel is soon on the scene and her
highly tuned sixth sense tells her there is more to this
case than a straightforward murder.

But with almost zero evidence and no way to trace the
girl's origin, Reilly and the police are at a loss. Then the
angel tattoo is traced to other children – both dead and
alive – who are similarly marked, and Reilly starts to
suspect they have all been abducted by the same person.
But why? And will Reilly get to the bottom of the
mystery and uncover what links these children together
before tragedy strikes again?

Paperback ISBN 978-0-85720-985-6
ebook ISBN 978-0-85720-986-3

LIKE YOUR FICTION A LITTLE ON THE DARK SIDE?

Like to curl up in a darkened room all alone, with the doors bolted and the windows locked and slip into something cold and terrifying...half hoping something goes bump in the night?

Me too.

That's why you'll find me at The Dark Pages - the home of crooks and villains, mobsters and terrorists, spies and private eyes; where the plots are twistier than a knotted noose and the pacing tighter than Marlon Brando's braces.

Beneath the city's glitz, down a litter-strewn alley, behind venetian blinds where neon slices the smoke-filled gloom, reading the dark pages.

Join me: **WWW.THEDARKPAGES.CO.UK**

AGENT X

@dark_pages